The
Cane Mutiny

The Cane Mutiny

A Den of Antiquity Mystery

Tamar Myers

WHEELER
CHIVERS

This Large Print edition is published by Wheeler Publishing, Waterville, Maine USA and by BBC Audiobooks Ltd, Bath, England.

Published in 2006 in the U.S. by arrangement with Avon Books, an imprint of HarperCollins Publishers.

Published in 2006 in the U.K. by arrangement with Lowenstein-Yost Inc.

U.S. Hardcover   1-59722-312-3   (Cozy Mystery)
U.K. Hardcover 10: 1 4056 3904 0   (Chivers Large Print)
U.K. Hardcover 13: 978 1 405 63904 0
U.K. Softcover 10: 1 4056 3905 9   (Camden Large Print)
U.K. Softcover 13: 978 1 405 63905 7

The text of this Large Print edition is unabridged. Other aspects of the book may vary from the original edition.

Set in 16 pt. Plantin by Al Chase.

Printed in the United States on permanent paper.

British Library Cataloguing-in-Publication Data available

Library of Congress Cataloging-in-Publication Data

Myers, Tamar.
   The cane mutiny : a Den of Antiquity mystery / by Tamar Myers.
     p. cm. — (Wheeler Publishing large print cozy mystery)
   ISBN 1-59722-312-3 (lg. print : sc : alk. paper)
     1. Timberlake, Abigail (Fictitious character) — Fiction.
2. Antique dealers — Fiction.   3. Large type books.
I. Title.   II. Series: Wheeler large print cozy mystery.
PS3563.Y475C36 2006
813'.54—dc22   2006014639

For Rabbi Henry Okolica
of blessed memory

1

The city of Charleston, South Carolina, has more ghosts than natives. But it is not quite true, as one rude tourist recently put it, that our ghosts — or, Apparition Americans, as they prefer to be called nowadays — show more life than their flesh and blood counterparts. I was not particularly surprised, therefore, to see a pirate hobbling down the alley behind my antiques shop, the Den of Antiquity.

It happened one exceptionally foggy night in early April, when Mama and I were returning home from a musical recital at the College of Charleston. I'd decided to stop by my shop on King Street to retrieve a book on antique canes that I had recently purchased. My plans for the remainder of my evening were to snuggle up in bed next to my handsome husband, Greg, and peruse the book while he watched the end of a basketball game. Mama's plans were to curl up in front of her own TV and watch reruns of *Leave It to Beaver*.

At any rate, upon seeing the Apparition

American, I stomped on the brakes, and as soon as we'd jerked to a stop, I flipped on the high beams. Unfortunately the light reflected off the moisture in the air, and in the split second it took to put the low beams back on, the ghost had disappeared.

"Did you see that, Mama?"

"Abby, I'm old, not blind."

"That was a pirate, wasn't it?"

Mama sighed. "A very handsome pirate. If my arthritis wasn't acting up, I'd jump out and chase after him. Wherever it is he went."

My heart was still pounding, and my legs too weak to support my full weight, so I remained behind the wheel of my silver Mercedes. I did, however, drive the entire length of the alley, and finding no one about, either spectral or real, hightailed it back to my house on Squiggle Lane.

When Mama and I burst into the den, where my handsome hubby was already deeply absorbed in the game, we must have brought with us a surge of intense energy.

"So the concert was that good," Greg said, without shifting his gaze.

"The concert was just okay," Mama said. "It's the pirate who's put the wind back in my bloomers."

I cringed. "Mama!"

"You have to admit it, Abby, he was really a hittie."

"The word's hottie, Mama."

"That's what you think. I meant what I said. If he was twenty years younger, I'd hit on him."

"Mama!"

Despite the fact that my mother, who stands all of five feet tall, is trapped in a 1950s time warp along with June Cleaver, she at times displays disconcerting flashes of lust. If it were not for the fact that my minimadre is still a virgin — two children notwithstanding — and will forever stay that way, I assure you, I would have been really creeped out. As it was, I felt nauseous.

"Abby, I'm only human."

"No, you're not. Besides, he wasn't all that cute."

Greg pressed the mute button on his remote and jumped off the sofa. "What's all this about a pirate? Or did you say 'parrot'?"

Meanwhile my sweetie pie jumped off the sofa as well, ambled toward me, and rubbed his cheeks against my calves. This sweetie pie, by the way, is my ten-pound orange tabby, who sometimes responds to his name, Dmitri. Greg, on the other hand, seldom rubs his cheeks against my calves, and never responds to Dmitri.

"We saw a ghost," Mama said. "A really cute pirate."

"We saw an Apparition American and he was ugly enough to turn a train down a dirt road."

Dmitri purred loudly.

Greg smiled. "As ugly as that?"

"Even uglier. I bet that when he was born his mama had to borrow a baby to take to church."

"He was six feet tall," Mama said. "Just like Greg. And he had a huge black beard." She gasped. "I bet it was the ghost of Blackbeard."

"He was no taller than you, Mama. And he didn't have a beard; only stubble, and a scar that went from his left ear to his nostril. And those beady dark eyes — I'll never forget them. He even had a wooden leg, Greg, just like the stereotype."

"Yes, he did have a wooden leg." Mama agreed reluctantly. "But it was cute."

Greg laughed before kissing me on the mouth and then pecking Mama on the cheek. "Well, at least you two finally agree on something."

I bristled at what amounted to a dismissal. "I didn't say his leg was cute."

"But both of yours definitely are." Greg winked before plopping back on the couch.

He works long hours as a shrimper and is no couch potato. I certainly did not begrudge him his method of relaxation.

"What about mine?" Mama demanded.

I pushed her gently from the room. For much of the time since Daddy died nineteen years ago, hit in the head by a seagull with a brain tumor the size of a walnut, Mama has been competing with me for the attention of men. I'm happily married again, and no longer competing, but I'm not sure the message has really gotten through to Mama.

"Abby, are you trying to get rid of your dear old mama?"

"Absolutely."

"Why I never!" She stamped a petite pump and stalked dramatically to her very comfortably appointed room. One that I pay for, I might add.

Greg waited until we could no longer hear her. "So, Mrs. Ghostbuster, what are your plans for the rest of the evening?"

"Well, I thought we would get ready for bed and then I'd read this book on antique canes while you finished the game, but with all the excitement, I forgot to get the book from my shop."

"I have a better idea. What if we get ready for bed, and then instead of me watching the game, we come up with creative ways to

11

use the bed that don't involve sleep?"

Both Mama and the pirate were soon forgotten.

There is nothing like a good fruit cup to start the day right. Greg gets up at five on days he takes the boat out, and since Mama invariably sleeps in now that she's retired, I had the kitchen to myself.

Officially I open the Den of Antiquity at ten, but there are always things to be done beforehand, so I'm usually there by eight-thirty. My assistant, C.J., is a brilliant salesperson and an asset to the business, but a liability to my nerves, so she isn't permitted to show up until just before opening time. For the record, she also leaves an hour after I do.

I'm usually a cheerful person, but today I arrived at work in particularly fine fettle, eager to carpe diem. But both my fettle and diem were ruined the second I stepped into my showroom. C.J., bless her oversized heart, had strewn walking sticks in the clear space in front of the register. Apparently she'd been showing the canes to a customer at closing time, but still, that was no excuse to just let them lay there. If I hadn't flipped the lights on first I might well have broken my neck.

Of course I picked the sticks up, and by the time C.J. showed up, I was ebullient as always, the matter almost forgotten. In fact, it was such a busy day that the matter was forgotten, until the next morning. This time the canes were in a pile, and the faux elephant foot that held them had been up-ended.

I left the evidence where I'd found it and was busy cross-checking an invoice when C.J. arrived. I didn't know she was there until she tapped me on the shoulder. I don't mind sharing that I jumped a foot off my chair and used a few words unbefitting a lady.

"C.J.! You about scared the life out of me."

"Sorry, Abby. You drink too much coffee, you know that?"

"I drink just the right amount."

She tossed her dark blond mane in dis-agreement. "My Granny Ledbetter up in Shelby was jumpy just like you, and then she switched to powdered caribou. It made all the difference in the world. The only problem, it's really hard to find."

"That's carob, I believe. It's a seedpod that tastes more like chocolate than coffee. And you can find it in just about any health food store."

13

The mane got a good workout. "I know what carob is, Abby. What Granny drinks is powdered caribou antlers. Ones that fell off naturally, of course. She said that not only did the switch calm her down, but it ratcheted up her sex life something awful."

"TMI!"

"What's that, Abby? Another kind of health food drink? Because Granny doesn't need —"

"The letters stand for too much information. I'd really rather not hear about your grandmother's sex life."

She nodded and then her eye caught the pile of dumped canes. "Abby, someone could stumble over that and get hurt."

"I was about to say the same thing."

"I'll pick them up for you, Abby."

"As well you should. It is your mess, after all."

"It is?" She was staring at me without guile.

"Isn't it?"

"I thought you made it. Face it, Abby, you're not the neatest pin in the sewing box."

"I think I resent that. But never mind, if I didn't do it, and you didn't do, then who did?"

"Maybe a customer did it just before I

locked up yesterday. Sometimes after locking the front door, I head straight for the bathroom, and then go out the back. Especially if I already have my purse with me."

"Yes, but I found the same thing yesterday morning."

"Abby, it's possible you have a mutiny on your hands."

"A *what?*"

"You know, like on a ship. But instead of the *Caine Mutiny*, with an *i* like in the movie, it's the cane mutiny. Get it?" She chortled. "Of course it was a book first."

I sighed several times as I picked up the wayward walking sticks. It should have been C.J. doing it, but she was too busy impressing me with her vast store of knowledge. Meanwhile customers were gathering outside the locked doors. Finally, I'd had enough.

"C.J., it's time to get to work."

"Okay, Abby. You don't have to get so cross."

"I'm not cross!"

"Yes, you are." She sauntered over to the doors and unlocked them.

But whatever differences C.J. and I were having at the moment took a back seat when we saw the gentleman who was the first to come through the door.

2

Colonel Beauregard Humphrey is a legend in his own mind, as well as the mind of a great many Charlestonians, even though he's only lived here a few months. Tall, with leathery tanned skin, silver hair, and aristocratic features, he is the epitome of the Southern gentleman. He is never seen without his blue and white seersucker suit, bow tie, and white buckskin shoes. His most distinguishing feature, however, is his mustache, which is so long that the drooping ends come to rest on his bow tie. It has been said that the colonel stopped eating soup in 1963.

Nonetheless the Colonel — he is not a military colonel, but a Kentucky colonel, like the chicken magnate — had yet to enter my shop. Frankly, I was awed by his presence. But as both a lapsed Episcopalian and an Anglophile, I get my genuflections and curtsies mixed up. Even I have more sense than to genuflect to a legend in his own mind.

"Good morning, sir," I said loudly in compensation.

He was still a ways off and I had to repeat it — several times.

"Good morning," he finally rumbled.

"How can I help you today?"

"I'm a looking for a walking stick."

"Then you're in luck. I just happen to have a barrel of them right here. Actually, it's an elephant's foot, and not a real one at that."

Stooping slightly, his mustache dangling, he took a monocle out of his pocket and peered at the cane stand with his right eye. "This is terrible," he said.

"I beg your pardon?"

"Antique sticks should never be treated this way."

"But that's how I bought them."

He picked out a cane and held it to eye level, and then lowering it, stroked the wooden shaft. "This is a nice one, but the others are crap. Junk, if you prefer a nicer word."

I was stunned, beside myself — which, contrary to rumor, *does* add up to one whole person. He continued to stroke the staff while I sputtered.

Finally I was able to spit out some coherent words. "Did you come here just to insult me?"

The look in Colonel Beauregard

Humphrey's eyes was one of genuine bafflement. "Insult you? How have I insulted you, madam?"

"I do not carry crap in this store."

"Ah, but you do. With the exception of this eighteenth century, hand-turned piece, the rest are junk. Made for export somewhere overseas. But probably not in Indonesia; they have wonderful craftsmen there. They sure as shooting didn't make these."

"I bought them at a locked trunk sale," I said, coming to my own defense when no apology was needed.

"A what?"

"A locked trunk sale — although, strictly speaking, this was a locked storage unit sale. You know those places where you pay to keep things in storage? Sometimes the renters die, or move away, and don't take their stuff, so after a certain length of time, and after posting announcements in the local papers, the owners sometimes sell the contents of those spaces sight unseen. Most often you get a lot of junk — *real* junk — but sometimes you hit the jackpot. My friends, the Rob-Bobs, found a three carat flawless diamond in the bottom of a barrel of old clothes. You just never know."

"Clearly you were not as fortunate as your friends."

Trying to salvage at least a shred of my professional dignity, I pointed to the stick in his hands. "But you like that cane, right?"

"What's not to like? The shaft is good quality malacca, and as for the head, it speaks for itself."

"Uh — I hope you don't mind me asking, but what is malacca?"

"I should have known you weren't familiar with that term. My dear, malacca is the lightweight, but very sturdy, stem of the rattan palm. In the past it was often used for the finest walking sticks and umbrellas. The name comes from one of the principal cities in Malaysia, the country where this palm is found. I have actually been to Malacca. It is a charming city, situated, as it is, right on the coast. St. Francis Xavier was buried there for three months, you know. When he was dug up, to be shipped off to Goa, a workman hit him with a spade. It is said that not only had the body not decomposed, but blood and water gushed forth."

"How fascinating. Colonel Humphrey, you said the head of the cane speaks for itself. What is it saying?"

"Jade."

"The gemstone?"

"Burmese jadeite. Look at its translucency and luster. And that color, like new blades of grass."

There are times to keep one's mouth tightly shut, and this was one of them. I'd taken the shiny, intensely green knob on the end of the cane for a synthetic of some sort, possibly even plastic.

"Madam, are you aware of this walking stick's value?"

"A lot?" I squeaked.

"Several thousands of dollars, I imagine. The jadeite is superb in every way except for the obvious bands of darker color that cut diagonally across the stone. They give character to a cane head, but make it somewhat useless for jewelry. If the color was consistent, the stone could be cut down to a number of sizable cabochons worth several hundred thousand dollars."

First the silence, then a squeak, and now a gasp. I clapped a tiny hand over the offending aperture, and then just as quickly removed it.

"I had no idea that canes were made from such valuable materials."

"My dear, then what on earth are you doing running an antiques store?"

"One can't know everything. Why even my assistant, who practically *does* knows everything, thought the knob on this cane was some type of polymer."

Colonel Beauregard Humphrey snorted, an action that set his mustache to flapping. "I tell you what. I'll give you five for the whole shebang."

"Five what."

"Thousand, madam."

I'd already placed a price tag of fifty dollars on each cane, and there were ten of them on display. Even if the one with the jadeite was more valuable than the Colonel was letting on, I still stood to make a huge profit. Easy come, easy go, as they say. Besides, the canes on display were only the tip of the iceberg. In my storeroom, wrapped in plain brown paper, were at least a dozen more. Several of those were a bit unusual, and I'd intended to do some research before putting them out.

"You have a deal, sir," I said quickly, before I could change my mind.

"Oh, by the way," he said in parting, "that's a real elephant's foot you've got there. You should be ashamed of yourself, madam, for trafficking in endangered animal parts."

I was more stunned by this latest revelation than I'd been by the good news regarding the jade.

There is no one quite as capable at derailing a good day than a mother on a mission. Mine literally blew in off the street, propelled by a stiff spring breeze that had connected with her crinolines. Mama, you see, only wears dresses with full-circle skirts puffed up by enough starched slips to keep all of England's upper lips stiff for years.

Mama barely glanced at C.J., who was with a customer, and sailed right over to me. "Abby! We have to talk."

"I'm all ears, Mama."

"No, privately."

"Can we do this at home? I have a business to run."

My petite progenitress recoiled in well-rehearsed shock. "This is how you talk to the woman who endured thirty-two hours of excruciating pain to bring you into this world?"

"It was thirty-six, Mama. Last time you said it was thirty-four. One of these days I'll just pop right out of you like bagel halves from a toaster."

Mama tipped her head in C.J.'s direction and waggled her almost nonexistent eyebrows. "It's about her."

I sighed. "Five minutes. And this better be good."

"It's a matter of life and death."

I led her into the storeroom and offered

her the use of a Louis XIV gilt chair that was awaiting refurbishment. When she refused, I was happy to sit instead.

"Spill, Mama."

"Ivory," Mama said.

"Ivory? Make sure that it comes from a source that guarantees it hasn't been poached. Better yet, stick to very old ivory — pre-1950 — or a good imitation."

"Not that kind of ivory. I mean the color. C.J. wants to get married in an ivory white dress with a ten-foot train!"

"Good for her."

"Abby, you can't mean that. She'll be the laughingstock of Charleston."

What C.J. wears to her own wedding is not my mother's business, although *whom* she will marry is — well, to a certain extent. My younger brother, Toy, spent only six hours inflicting pain on our mother, a fact of which she is quick to remind me. At any rate, Toy and C.J. are to be married at Grace Episcopal Church in downtown Charleston this August. I'm going to be the maid of honor and Mama's going to be a nervous mother of the groom. As far as I know, that's the limit of Mama's involvement in the upcoming nuptials.

"Mama, I'm sure a lot of Charleston brides have gotten married in ivory gowns, and I bet some have had even longer trains than that."

"Yes, but C.J. isn't a — well, you know what. She shouldn't be wearing white. Even ivory white."

"So what if she's not an Episcopalian?"

"That's not what I mean. She isn't a —" Mama waggled the scant brows in what, after much pondering, I understood to be a suggestive manner.

"How do you know, Mama?"

"She told me."

"She did?" It's not my place to judge C.J., and it wasn't the extent of her involvement with my brother that bothered me; it was the fact that my friend and colleague had shared this information with my very prim mother, and not me.

"C.J. tells me everything, dear, just like a good daughter."

"Mama, if I told you everything I did, you'd have both hands over your ears while screaming la-la-la-la-la. Anyway, times have changed. I mean, you don't expect her to wear a scarlet dress, do you?"

"Of course not, dear. What I have in mind is a very nice pastel skirt suit with dyed-to-match pumps. I was thinking baby blue. I saw just the thing at Dillard's last week."

My patience was wearing thin. "Mama, if

every bride in Charleston County who wasn't a virgin — there, Mama, I said the word — wore something other than some shade of white, the bridal shops would go out of business. This is C.J.'s special day, and with any luck, it will be her only wedding day. She has a right to wear what she wants."

"Then I have a right not to be a part of this." Her eyes puddled up.

If it were not for the fact that my minimadre was a master at manipulation, I would have felt sorry for her. Instead, I felt wary, knowing full well that there was another shoe about to be dropped, perhaps one of those with the long pointed toes that come in so handy for killing roaches here in Charleston.

"I suppose you'd like me to tell her, right? I mean, there is no use in her worrying about a corsage for you if you're going to be a no-show."

The tears somehow managed to disappear into thin air. "I will most certainly not be a no-show at my only son's wedding!"

"Suit yourself, but you're not going to do to her what you did to me."

"What did I ever do to you, dear?"

"You sewed a black thread into the hem of the dress I wore when I married Greg."

25

"That's because it was your second marriage, Abby."

I hopped out of the Louis XIV. As beautiful as that chair is, it lacks in the comfort department and can lead to irritability. No wonder the royals in those days were forever lopping off heads.

"Sorry you have to run, Mama."

"I don't need to do any such thing." She started picking her way down along the right side of my storeroom, the area where I keep my new purchases that have yet to be marked. Even though she lives in my house, Mama frequently raids my storeroom for home furnishings. "What's this, Abby?" she said, pausing at the brown paper package that contained the rest of the canes.

"Nothing. Just some junk I picked up at a locked trunk sale."

"What fun," she said, and began unwrapping the contents.

"Mama!"

"I'm only trying to help, dear." But when she saw what the parcel contained, she immediately lost interest. "How can you sell such ugly things, dear?"

"Because people buy them."

"Sachets tied up with silk ribbons, and fancy soaps, that's what people want to buy. And scented candles."

"Not everyone is Donna Reed."

"Did you know that there is a shop in Mount Pleasant called Nose Stoppers where you can create your own scent? Suzy Tutweiler said she had them reproduce the smell of her pot roast. She said it keeps her husband home in the evenings, even when she serves him TV dinners."

"No offense, Mama, but Suzy Tutweiler needs all the help she can get to keep her husband home."

"One cannot work too hard on one's marriage," Mama said pointedly.

"Greg and I are doing just fine, Mama. Now if you'll excuse me, I've got work to do."

"Well, I never! Dismissing your own mother, like she was a servant."

"At least a servant would leave when asked."

"Ha!" Mama would leave when she was good and ready, and not a minute before. To remind me of this, she pulled a cane from the parcel, using just her index finger and thumb. "This is disgusting."

The walking stick she'd selected was disgusting, but in an interesting sort of way. The shaft was ebony and tipped with ivory, and frankly rather elegant, but the handle was carved from some hideous material that

I could not identify. At first I thought it might be the horn of a large animal, such as a Cape buffalo, but now, seeing it for a second time, I'd changed my mind.

"That's dried hippo hide," I said. "At least I think it is."

Mama dropped the stick, which clattered to the floor.

"Mama! That's my livelihood."

"All right, dear, I'm leaving. You don't need to get so bent out of shape."

She fluffed her skirts, hoping to catch a breeze, but finding none, was forced to exit the storeroom on her own power.

No sooner did the swinging door close behind her than it swung open again, admitting an even stronger personality.

3

Wynnell Crawford is my oldest and dearest friend. When I moved to Charleston two years ago, she sold her antiques shop up in Charlotte and followed me down to open a shop west of the Ashley River. Unfortunately, Wynnell's new store, Wooden Wonders, has not met with the same level of success that the Den of Antiquity has enjoyed. I'm sure a lot of that has to do with the fact my business is located on lower King Street in the prestigious heart of peninsular Charleston. As a result I have to work really hard to keep the green from appearing in my friend's normally brown eyes.

"Hey there," I called cheerily.

"What's that all about?"

"You mean Mama?"

"She looked fit to be tied."

"That's because I evicted her. Not to mention she's upset that C.J. wants an ivory white gown."

"It's C.J.'s wedding. She should have what she wants." Wynnell picked up the cane Mama had dropped. Without being

29

told, she slid it back into the partially open parcel. "But on the other hand, if she wants to have friends — well, enough said. I'm sure you can take it from there."

"What?" I wasn't sure if I'd heard correctly, and if I had, I was very sure I didn't like what had just been said.

"She adores you, Abby. She'll do anything you say."

"Were not talking about dress color, are we?"

"Next to you, Abby, I'm her closest friend."

I nodded. "I thought so. Wynnell, you shouldn't take it personally. C.J. has invited her entire clan to come down from Shelby. As it is, she's having six bridesmaids, so as not to offend anyone."

"That's easy for you to say, because you're her maid of honor. Besides, her Cousin Zelda isn't even a woman, but a goat."

"We're not sure about that; the DNA report is inconclusive. Look Wynnell, I know for a fact that C.J. feels really bad about having to exclude you from the wedding party. That's why she wants you and Ed to sit up front with Mama on the groom's side."

"She said that?"

I nodded vigorously. The truth is that C.J. *would* have said that, had it occurred to her. And it was *going* to occur to her just as soon as I got the chance.

Defused, Wynnell extracted a different cane from the bundle. "Abby, this is exquisite."

"You know about antique canes?"

"Just because I sell used dressers and armoires, some of them barely old enough to qualify as antiques, doesn't mean I'm ignorant about other areas in this business. Take this seemingly plain walking stick. Did you know that it's also a pistol?"

"Get out of town! You're joking, aren't you?"

"No. Look." My buddy turned the handle until I heard a click, and then gently pulled it back, slowly revealing the barrel of a pistol.

"Well, I'll be dippity-doodled. How did you know to do that?"

"Ed's granddaddy had one of these. Said he got it from *his* daddy who fought a duel over a woman in downtown Charlotte. He won, by the way."

"How romantic," I said, dripping enough sarcasm to ruin my four hundred dollar Bob Ellis shoes.

"Actually, it was. You see, the guy Ed's

31

great-great-granddaddy killed was a carpet-bagger. The man had made a pass at Ed's ancestor's wife. Great-Great-Granddaddy Crawford had already lost his first wife from cholera during the War of Northern Aggression. He said that while he had no regrets in laying down his wife for his country, he'd be damned if he did it again for a Yankee."

"Wynnell, that's an old joke."

"Maybe. Anyway, this pistol —" She set the weapon down gently. "Abby, what's in that barrel?"

The barrel was one of the items in the locked storage shed. It, the canes, a broken space heater, two lawn chairs in need of reweaving, a painting of dubious quality, and boxes of old magazines, dried-up pens, balls of string, and assorted junk too useless even to remember: that's what I'd received for my winning two thousand dollar bid.

"It's part of a locked trunk sale. That's where I got the canes."

"Abby, how come nobody ever tells me about these sales? I'm a dealer too. Why is it I'm always left out of the loop?"

The truth is that my buddy is not intentionally being left out of anything. She is privy to the same newsletters and sale information that I am; she just chooses not to pay attention. Some days, like today, she doesn't even open her shop, although she can ill afford not to do so.

"Wynnell, who's minding the store?"

"Ed."

"Really?"

"It was your idea, Abby, remember? You said I should ask him to help because he was bored with retirement. Well, I did, and he loves it. Not only that, but he's better at it than I ever was. So, now guess who's retired? Unofficially, of course. Anyway, that's why I'm here — to see if you want to go to lunch later."

"That, and to ask me to intercede on your behalf with C.J."

"You know me too well." She walked over to the barrel, which had a padlock on top. "Just how do these locked trunk sales work, Abby? I mean, this isn't exactly a trunk."

"Touché. Well, I can't speak for all locked trunk sales, but this one advertised that the contents of a storage shed were being sold sight unseen. Apparently the person renting the facility was many years behind in the payments. Anyway, we submitted bids on slips of paper, like at a silent auction, and then the five highest bids were put in a drum — the kind they use at bingo games — and the one pulled was the winner. I won, of course. Wynnell, it was in the *Post and Courier*."

She ignored my last comment. "Abby, if you didn't know what you'd be bidding on, why did you even go to this sale?"

"Because I thought it would be fun. And it was a chance to meet other bargain hunters."

"Other gamblers, if you ask me. Not you, of course."

"Of course."

Wynnell tapped on the barrel with her knuckles. "When are you going to open this, Abby?"

"Just as soon as I get the time to call a locksmith, or get Greg out here with his toolbox. But in any case, I'm not expecting to find a king's ransom. It feels practically empty, although you can hear something when you tip it. For all I know, there's a human skeleton in there, and nothing else."

"Would you like me to pick it open?"

"You can do that?"

She grinned lopsidedly. "Maybe you don't know me that well after all. My daddy was a locksmith, remember?"

"Vaguely."

"When I was a little girl he was my hero. During school vacations I went with him on all his house calls. Believe me, Abby, I can pick any padlock with a paper clip, and as for combination locks, I once opened one with my toes."

Wynnell, bless her heart, is a bit on the hirsute side. Her eyebrows are like hedges — make that one long hedge — and joint trips to the beach have made me painfully aware that this is one woman who eschews waxing. Just the thought of her hairy toes picking at a lock made me want to poke out my mind's eye. I dashed back into the showroom to grab a paper clip from my desk drawer.

My friend was true to her word. It took her less time to open the lock than it took me to retrieve the paper clip.

"What do you say to that, Abby?"

"I say you're a wizard, and that it's a good thing you're on the right side of the law."

She laughed happily. "Okay, Abby, go on and open it."

The truth be told, I would rather have opened the barrel when I was alone. Then I could have savored the thrill. But since Wynnell had just saved me a locksmith's fee, I couldn't very well exclude her from the event. But I'd be damned if she was going to get the first peek. I jokingly told her to stay back in case there was a live snake in there, and then, with hands trembling from excitement, released the metal band and pried off the lid with my fingertips.

Wynnell, who was supposed to have stayed back, somehow managed to stick her head into the barrel before I could react. "It's only a gym bag," she bellowed, her voice thankfully muffled by the barrel.

"Let me take it out." If it sounded like an order, so be it.

Wynnell stepped back obediently, but her prodigious brows puckered in the middle, displaying her true feelings. "I was only trying to be helpful."

"For which I am eternally grateful." I should have asked Wynnell, whose arms are nearly twice as long as mine, to hoist the bag out of the barrel. Instead I had to tip it, and unfortunately lost my grip. Fortunately, my Bob Ellis shoes were of the closed toe variety, or I might well have gone from a size four to a size two.

At any rate, it was indeed a gym bag, cloth with plastic handles, probably dating from the sixties. Unless it was stuffed with cash, or jewels from a safe heist, it was hardly worth getting excited about. Of course that didn't stop my heart from racing. We in the antiques business are, after all, treasure hunters.

Just to torment Wynnell, I unzipped the bag as slowly as I dared while still having it look natural. I even pretended the zipper was stuck.

"Abby, give it to me."

"No, I've got it." I yanked the bag open. When I saw what it contained, I dropped it immediately and sank to the floor in shock.

"What is it?" Wynnell clambered over me to get the bag. "Abby, you're acting really — oh my gosh, it's a skull!"

"Is it real?" Perhaps I'd jumped to the wrong conclusion.

Despite her sometimes annoying habits, Wynnell is precisely the kind of woman I'd want as a companion on an Indiana Jones–style adventure. In a few seconds she overcame whatever squeamishness she was feeling, and reaching into the bag, withdrew the skull.

"Feels real," she said nonchalantly, as if she were a beauty pageant director assessing the mammary glands of a contested contestant. She hefted it and slid her fingers along the dome. "If it's not real, then it's a darn good imitation."

"Wynnell, what should we do?"

"Call the police."

"Yes, but the odds are they'll send you-know-who out to investigate."

"You mean Tweedledum and Tweedledee?"

"Exactly."

Charleston's police force is one of the

finest in the world, headed as it is by Chief Greenburg, but not everyone on it is up to par. Officers Tweedledum and Tweedledee seem to share a brain that has, alas, been misplaced. They have, however, managed to keep track of their personalities, which are as abrasive as a bar of Lava soap. Those sad facts, along with their clear dislike of me, ensure that I avoid contact with them at all cost.

"Then you should call Greg," Wynnell said, stating the obvious.

"And he'll just tell me to call them."

"Looks like you have no choice, Abby. But just remember, I'm here for you, no matter what."

But as soon as I hung up with the dispatcher, Wynnell remembered that she had left her coffeemaker on and there was very little of the beverage left in the pot. If the liquid evaporated entirely, the element could overheat, cause a short, and burn down the Crawford house. I couldn't very well have that on my conscience, could I?

I said that I could, but she abandoned me anyway. It was either face the Dum-Dees alone or ask C.J. to close the shop as soon as she could herd the last customer out, and then join me for moral support. My employee and future sister-in-law was all too glad to be of service, which was exactly what I was afraid of.

"Ooh, Abby, can I hold it?"

Seeing as how I'd stupidly allowed Wynnell to get her prints all over the skull, what harm could there possibly be in letting C.J. amuse herself until the police arrived? The brain that arrived at this conclusion is the same brain that designed a transatlantic bridge for my Seventh Grade Science Fair project. The model was almost four feet long and broke into a dozen pieces before I could get into the auditorium.

Anyhow, C.J. seemed even more at home with the skull than Wynnell had been. She whipped out a miniature caliper — you'd be surprised what that gal keeps in her pockets — and measured various things, grunting each time she switched to a new location. After what seemed like an hour, she put the skull reverently back in the bag.

"It's not human, Abby."

"Excuse me?"

"It belonged to a female gorilla. She had an abscessed tooth. Probably died of blood poisoning, which is just as well, because otherwise she would have starved to death. Gorillas eat tough vegetation that requires a lot of chewing. She wouldn't have been able to do that with this tooth."

"C.J.! It's not respectful to joke about the dead."

"I'm not joking, Abby."

I stared at the big galoot. The cheese may have slipped off her sandwich, but hers was an awesome mind that could think circles around even Marilyn Vos Savant, reputedly the world's smartest woman. C.J. spoke seventeen languages fluently, and solved differential equations during TV commercials.

"C.J., how could you possibly — I mean, how do you know it's a gorilla skull, as opposed to an orangutan skull? And how do you know it's female?"

"Ooh, Abby, gorilla and orangutan skulls look nothing alike. And the females of both species look nothing like their male counterparts. You can tell this one was a female because her skull lacks the prominent bony ridge that a male would have, as well as those formidable incisors."

"I suppose you can tell me how old she was and how many baby gorillas she produced."

Sarcasm is lost on someone as sweet as C.J. "I'd say she was about thirty-five, which is old for a gorilla living in the wild, but not so old for one living in a zoo. And she had seven babies, give or take one. You can see how much calcium is missing from her jawbones."

"That's nice, but you mean *imprisoned* in a zoo, don't you?"

"Oh no, Abby. Zoos aren't as awful as most people think. Animals don't wake up each morning thinking, 'Oh goody, I get to walk twenty miles today through beautiful scenery while searching constantly for things to eat, and at the same time keeping a watchful eye out for predators, but being free in this beautiful place is worth it, so I don't mind.' "

"Bless your heart, C.J., was that run-on sentence sarcasm?"

The big gal has no guile. "No, Abby. What a lot of people don't realize is that most animals just want to eat, be safe, and reproduce. The only reason they roam so far in the wild is to find food, not because they want to sightsee. In zoos their basic needs are met, and these days most zoos are making a huge effort to duplicate an animal's natural surroundings, but without the predators, forest fires, and floods that would kill them in the wild. You really should read *The Life of Pi*."

"Can we agree to disagree?"

Her response was drowned out by the pounding on the back door to the storeroom.

4

Tweedledee recoiled when she saw me. "It's you," she said.

"Half the size of life, and twice as beautiful."

"What?"

Tweedledum edged his partner aside. "There's been a report of a possible homicide."

"Actually, that's not what I said to the dispatcher — oh, what the heck. Come in. But brush the Krispy Kreme crumbs off first."

To their credit, they did what they were told. Tweedledee, who has a shelflike bosom, took longer.

"Now, where's the body?" she demanded.

"It's a skull, not an entire body. And there's really no need for y'all to get involved, because it's only a gorilla skull. And an antique gorilla skull at that. So you see, it's not a police matter. Calling you was my mistake."

Tweedledum had his own shelf, a mite

lower down, and he unabashedly brushed it clear as well. "Ma'am, that's for us to decide, not you."

C.J., she-who-cannot-tell-a-lie, had been standing in the background. Now she insinuated her broad shoulders and planet-size head into the picture.

"Technically, Abby, it's not an antique unless it's a hundred years old, or older, and this one isn't."

I shook my head. *"Et tu, Brute?"*

"No foreign languages," Tweedledee barked. "This is my crime scene, and we're going to speak only English."

I nodded. "Forsooth."

The busty sergeant scowled. "Is that foreign?"

"Unequivocally not."

Tweedledee was linguistically challenged. "Is it, or isn't it? That's not rocket science, ya know. Either something is English or it's not."

"Me he," C.J. said. "That's both foreign and not."

Sergeant Tweedledee pivoted. "What did you say?"

The big galoot didn't even flinch. "I said 'Who is she.' That's Hebrew."

"She speaks seventeen languages," I said proudly.

"Me who," C.J. said. "That means 'Who is he.' You see, me is who, and who is he, and he is she, except they're not really, because they're not spelled like that —"

Tweedledee snapped her fingers, but they were both sweaty and stubby, and the gesture made no sound. "The body. Show me the body."

One of the blessings — it's also a curse — of being so small and perky is folks expect me to act perky no matter what. As a result, I can get away with glowering, and no one's the wiser.

"The *skull* is this way," I growled.

It's been my observation over the years that most folks cannot resist touching beautiful things. Dee and Dum were no exception. As we threaded our way between walls of stacked treasure, plump moist fingers and long gnarled ones trailed along, feeling everything in their paths. If anyone dusted my stuff for prints, the two cops would have a lot of explaining to do.

Before I'd opened the back door, C.J. had returned the skull to the bag and the bag to the barrel. I asked her to retrieve it.

Tweedledee nearly had kittens. "Nothing doing. This is a crime scene. From now on my partner and I will be taking over." She turned to Tweedledum. "Call the boys at

Forensics. And get an ambulance over here. Stat."

A snicker or two may have parted my wee lips. "An ambulance? She's been dead for decades, for goodness sake."

"Mrs. Washburn — or is it Timberlake again — if you don't stay out of police business, I'm going to arrest you for interfering at the scene of a crime."

"Moi?"

Out came the cuffs.

My name *is* Abigail Louise Wiggins Timberlake Washburn. I was born in the textile mill town of Rock Hill, South Carolina, and attended Winthrop College. During my senior year of college I met a law student from UNCC by the name of Buford Timberlake. What I didn't realize was that Buford was a timber snake in Timberlake clothing. Two children and two decades later he traded me in for a woman twice my size and half my age.

Tweetie, the new Mrs. Timberlake, experienced an untimely death, and Buford has since remarried. He and I have buried the hatchet (and not in his neck) for the sake of our children, Susan and Charlie. I too have moved on by marrying the very handsome, and only occasionally annoying, Greg Washburn.

We used to live in Charlotte, North Carolina, where I owned and operated the Den of Antiquity, an antiques shop on Selwyn Avenue. Then Greg, who'd been a detective, retired and got a hankering to move to the coast and pick up shrimping, something his family has been doing for generations. Not only did I decide to keep my shop, but I opened one just like it on King Street in Charleston.

It has been both a terrible and wonderful life. I am currently in a wonderful patch — knock on wood — and I aim to do everything in my limited power to keep it so. The last thing I needed was to be arrested and hauled off to jail. After all, when one is only four feet nine inches, horizontal stripes can make one look like they've practically melted into the concrete floor.

The actual charge was obstructing justice, and even though everyone involved knew it wouldn't stick, I got to see the inside of a jail cell close up. C.J. got thrown in the slammer with me, and we briefly shared quarters with two prostitutes and a pickpocket.

Both of the hookers appeared bored and indifferent, and after ascertaining that C.J. and I hadn't encroached on their turf, left us alone. The petty thief did not.

"My name is Geraldine," she said. "My parents named me after President Ford. Can you believe that?"

"Actually, I can," C.J. said. "Cousin Georgette Ledbetter was named after —"

"Charleston is a great city. I'm from Jackson, Mississippi. Pickings are pretty slim there." She laughed at her own joke. "Pickings, get it? But man, this place is da bomb. All you have to do is stand down there by the dock, where those cruise ships come in, and you can rake in the cash.

"The best time to do it is at the end of the day. The tourists are tired and in a hurry to get back to the ship. There's not a passenger on those ships that doesn't worry about getting left behind. Anyway, they're always loaded down with plastic bags filled with crap they bought at the Market, or better yet, really expensive things they splurged for on King Street.

"They're feeling the weight of those bags, see? At that point they aren't even thinking of their purses. If they're thinking about anything, it's the fancy dinners back on the ship and the show they'll see that night. So what you want to do is walk right behind them on the right side — a woman always carries her purse on her right, unless she's a leftie — and then you cut the straps of her purse with one hand and catch it with the other. Then you fall back and let the crowd surge around you."

"Hey," one of the hookers called from her corner of the cell, "how much can you make in a day?"

Geraldine smiled. "It's not just the cash, but the credit cards. Some I use, others I fence. But I'd say it averages out to a thousand bucks a day."

"No way," the hooker said.

"Caroline," her pal said, "maybe we oughta switch professions."

Everyone laughed, myself included. I was surprised at how well-spoken all three women were. The prostitutes were dressed in provocative clothing and wore excessive makeup, but toned down they could easily have passed for middle-aged housewives. And that's exactly what Geraldine appeared to be.

All three of them were more normal in appearance than Mama in her crinolines, pink gloves (it was not yet Easter), and flowered hat. But it was Mama who bailed me out of jail.

"Mama, promise me you won't tell Greg."
"Don't be silly, dear. You have a hearing

scheduled for next week. Besides, he'll probably read it in the police briefs."

"Thanks, Mama, you really know how to comfort a gal."

"You're being sarcastic again, aren't you, Abby?"

"You think?"

She drove, silent for a few minutes. The police station is not that far from my house, but the volume of tourists in azalea season can bog up traffic so bad that walking is sometimes quicker. A friend of ours flees the city with the first onslaught of spring tourists, not returning until well after Labor Day.

"Darling," Mama began, "just listen to me for a minute, will you?" The D word is how Mama prefaces her requests, as well as how she issues her demands.

"Mama, I'm tired; both physically and emotionally."

"That's exactly what I'm getting to, dear. You need someone to help you."

"C.J. is all the help I need. And she's taking a three day honeymoon. Is that what you're thinking of, Mama?"

"Gracious no, Abby. My feet would kill me if I had to stand around all day like you do. I'm talking about helping you with your investigation."

"My *what?*"

"Abby, need I remind you that I gave birth to you?"

"Mama —"

"Don't whine, dear. It's not becoming a lady. My point is that I know exactly what you're going to do next. You're heading straight out to Johns Island to interrogate the owner of Safe-Keepers Storage."

"I am?"

"Certainly. And then you're going to track down the owner of the barrel that contained the skull. I know, C.J. says it is just a gorilla skull, but you got arrested for having it in your possession because the Tweedles, who are dumber than dirt, say it's human. Darling, is there the slightest chance they could be right?"

"Not the slightest — well, maybe a minute chance. We were watching *Jeopardy!* together once and she got a question wrong. But Ken Jennings missed that one too."

"There, you see? We have to proceed as if it was the worst case scenario, because I can't have you watching your brother's wedding from behind bars."

"Mama, they won't send me to prison for finding an animal skull in a gym bag."

"You're not so sure. That's why you're headed to Safe-Keepers Storage. You plan to drag the owner to the police station and make him swear to the fact that he sold you the gym bag containing the skull. This gets you off the hook, the hearing is canceled, and Greg will be none the wiser."

I stared at the woman who'd given me thirty-six hours of her undivided attention. How disconcerting to realize that she could read my mind, as small as it was. I'd hoped the fine print would have been an impediment.

"Mama, if I let you tag along, will you promise you won't breathe a word of this to Greg? Not even one of your famous hints."

"What famous hints?"

"Like the time I'd planned a surprise cruise for his birthday, and you gave him a guidebook to the Caribbean."

Her face turned pink, but she wasn't bothered enough to apologize. "The first thing we'll do is take you home and give you a nice hot shower. No offense, dear, but you smell a bit ripe."

"I was in jail for two hours, Mama."

"In that case, let's quit burning daylight."

She turned right on Broad, followed it into Lockwood, and then left across the Ashley River.

River Road on Johns Island, just south of

51

Charleston, retains much of the charm that has brought thousands of people to the area. The irony is that these people need houses, which results in the cutting of ancient trees and encroachment on the salt marshes, so that the vistas that were once part of the main attraction no longer exist. Here, at least, are reminders of how Charleston County used to look.

Safe-Keepers Storage, however, is a blight on the landscape, a boil on the face of Mother Nature. It makes me cringe every time I drive by it. Even Mama knew exactly where it was, and her pink pump pressed the pedal to the metal, covering the distance from downtown in what had to be record time. Thank heavens she was driving her own car, because gravel sprayed against the sides as we skidded to a stop upon arrival.

"Mama, aren't you worried about damaging your finish?"

"Don't sweat the small stuff. Haven't you learned that yet, Abby?"

"I have," I said. I didn't dare tell Mama it was an expression I'd told myself whenever my ex-husband, Buford, demanded sex.

Mama got out and plumped up her crinolines before looking around. "So how do we find the owner?"

"Fortunately — although I would have

guessed otherwise — he lives in the house over there." I pointed to a dwelling that was as ugly, if not uglier, than the storage units.

Without further ado we crunched our way to the home of a Mr. Darren Cotter. Mama has a thing for ringing doorbells, so I let her do the honors. She had to mash it twice before anyone answered. Unfortunately, on the drive over I hadn't had time to warn her about Mr. Cotter's unusual appearance; his eyes were every bit as blue as a Siamese cat's. Shaped a bit like a cat's eyes as well.

When he came to the door, Mama overcorrected. "Hello. My name is Mr. Cotter," she said.

"Somehow I don't think so."

I nudged Mama gently aside. "She's actually Mrs. Wiggins. I'm Abigail Washburn. Although Timberlake is my business name. I'm the one who bought the contents of shed fifty-three."

"Ma'am, there are no returns on locked trunk sales. The ad made that very clear."

"Oh no, I'm not intending to return what I bought — or keep it, for that matter. But I would very much like to find out who the previous owner is."

"Sorry, ma'am, but that information is confidential. Besides, it won't do you any good. I've been trying for years to get in touch with this guy. If I knew where he was, I wouldn't have had to go to the bother of setting up an auction."

It was Mama's turn to elbow me aside. The three inches she has on me, plus a few pounds, give her an advantage.

"From what I heard, Mr. Cotter" — she pronounced the t's sharply — "you had about twenty dealers, plus a crowd of eager fortune hunters bidding on that shed. That's a lot of publicity for your storage business. One would think you'd be in an expansive mood after having sold my daughter a shed full of junk for two thousand dollars."

His eyes danced. "Your husband is a lucky man, Mrs. Wiggins."

"I'm a poor widder woman, Mr. Cotter. That means my sweet daughter here is half an orphan. Perhaps you can find it in your heart to help a poor widder and her sweet, semi-orphan child."

He had a crooked smile. "Perhaps I can. Wait just a minute."

The second he turned his back, I was on Mama like white on rice. "Mama! What on earth was that all about? And whoever heard of a semi-orphan?"

"Shhh, dear. Just you wait and see."

We didn't have to wait long. Mr. Cotter returned with two pages that appeared to be fresh from his printer. He started to pass them to Mama around the side of the screen door, but then opened it wide.

"The information you wanted is on this first sheet. But like I said, it won't do you any good. The second page contains the names, addresses, and phone numbers of everyone who signed up to bid. I took the liberty of circling the names of the top five bidders, not counting the young lady here. Don't know why, but they might come in handy. My phone number is on the masthead as well, in case you get the widder woman blues and need a little company."

"Thank you," Mama twittered, sounding every bit as coquettish as she might have had Brad Pitt handed her his unmentionables.

I waited until we were in the car and Mama had stopped twittering. "Mama, don't you think you went a bit far, throwing yourself at him like that?"

She patted her pearls. Mama's emotions are obvious when one observes the manner in which she handles those mollusk secretions. When they start spinning, you know you're in deep doo-doo.

"Why Abigail Louise! I most certainly did

not throw myself at that impossibly hand-some man."

"I'd need a crowbar to pry you loose from him."

The pearls began to move. "Don't be ridic-ulous."

"So, how long are you going to wait until you call him?"

The pearls made one full rotation, then stopped. "I think I'll call him right now, dear. Thanks for the suggestion."

"But Mama, we're still in the parking lot."

"Then I won't have to worry about a signal, will I?" she said, and dialed.

5

There are few things more embarrassing than having one's mother engage in wanton phone flirtation with a man whose house you can see. I closed my eyes to keep him from seeing me and pressed my hands against my ears. The only thing that kept me from singing "Ninety-nine Bottles of Beer on the Wall" at the top of my lungs was my consideration for Mama. She doesn't hear quite as well as she used to, particularly when there are background sounds. *Finally* she flipped her phone closed and revved the engine.

"Don't let me forget, dear. We're meeting at McCrady's, a week from Thursday, for dinner. Seven o'clock. We would have made it this week, but *Survivor*'s on, and we both think the teams are being merged. Isn't that exciting, Abby?"

"That you watch the same TV shows? I'm sure that's more than a lot of couples have in common, Mama, but there's a catch: you don't watch first-run television. You haven't since *Father Knows Best* went off the air."

Mama shook her very gray but well-coiffed head. "Abby, I'm beginning to think that as a mother I failed you. It's not what a man believes that's important, but what he thinks he believes. That's why it's always important to get dressed and undressed under the covers."

"That didn't make a lick of sense, Mama."

"Life is one long allusion, dear."

"Don't you mean illusion?"

"I know what I mean, dear." She jerked the gearshift intro reverse, and we exited the parking lot in a shower of gravel. Just as long as Mama maintained the illusion that her car was undamaged, and didn't allude to the fact that her car needed a new paint job, one for which I would somehow be held accountable, what did the truth really matter?

We drove back up River Road while I gathered my thoughts. Perhaps the smart thing was to hire a private detective to track down the elusive storage shed owner. If that didn't pan out, then maybe I'd try calling some of the names on the list Mr. Cotter had given Mama. *Maybe*.

But I'd only managed to gather a few of my thoughts when Mama made a sharp left on Plow Ground Road. For a second or two my stomach remained behind on the road more traveled.

"Mama, where are we going? This isn't the way back to the city."

"We're going to hobnob with the rich and famous — well, at least the rich."

"There are plenty of rich people in town. In fact, downtown Charleston, the area south of Broad, has the fifth highest concentration of wealth in the country."

"Yes, but those folks advertise their wealth just by being there. We're going to see a rich woman who doesn't care about showing off. It's what she would want with the contents of a storage bin that makes her interesting."

"Mama, you don't make a lick —"

Mama tossed the papers from her lap into mine. "That's because I'm making two licks of sense. Read the top name."

"Claudette Aikenberg. So what?"

"Well, he circled it, didn't he?"

"Yes, but —"

"Now read the address."

"It says 2513 Major Moolah Road. So?"

"That's on Wadmalaw Island. Sudie Pridgen lives on Wadmalaw Island. She had our Sunday school class out there for a cookout last summer. There was a vacant lot next door, one with a marsh view. Someone asked her the price, because the view was really stunning. She said a million five. Abby, she wasn't talking rubles. And you know what else? A lot of the houses out there can't even be seen from the roads. Believe me, that's where the serious money lives."

"Mama, a lot of really rich people enjoy the thrill of the hunt. Miss Aikenberg probably read about the auction in the paper — same as I — and thought it would be a fun way to spend a Saturday."

"We'll see."

Mama stomped harder on the gas. I checked my seat belt. I also checked the rearview mirror. The last time Mama got a ticket, she invited the issuing officer over for a home-cooked meal. You can imagine my horror when, after a hard day's work, I opened the front door only to find Tweedledum sitting on one of the Louis XIV chairs, eating a miniature quiche with both hands. Tweedledee, thank my lucky stars, had been assigned different duties for the day.

Things went from bad to worse when Tweedledum wiped his fingers on the silk damask seat of his chair. Had it not been for the arrival of Greg, I might well have experienced the inside of a jail cell a whole lot sooner. Mama, of course, pretended to be utterly oblivious to Tweedledum's bad manners. During the meal that followed, Greg sat beside me, instead of his usual place at the head of the table, and squeezed my knee every time he sensed that I was about to explode. Mama might well have gotten seriously involved with the miscreant had he not, at the meal's conclusion, let loose with a belch that sounded like a sonic boom. Even that might have gone unnoticed if the tremendous force of it hadn't knocked Daddy's picture off the sideboard and onto the floor.

At any rate, once my minimadre is on a mission, there is nothing, short of divine intervention, that can stop her. Having decided to give up prayers of petition for Lent, I was totally at Mama's mercy. I double-checked my seat belt, gritted my teeth, and hung on to the overhead handhold.

Major Moolah Road is unpaved, and as rough as a dragon's back, but it's mercifully short. Claudette Aikenberg lives at the very end, on a wooded peninsula that juts out into the Wadmalaw River. At the end of her drive an understated sign announces the name of her house: THREE BEARS.

We hadn't called, so I was both relieved and somewhat panicked to see a Jaguar sitting in the circular drive. Mama parked immediately behind it and then tooted her own horn.

"Mama! What is that for?"

"I'm just giving her a heads-up, dear. What if she's in the middle of putting on makeup and has only one eyebrow stenciled on? She might be too embarrassed to come to the door. I thought we'd give her about five minutes before we ring her bell. I'm sure she'll appreciate it."

"Maybe. And that's *penciled* on, not stenciled."

"Oh, not for me, dear. When you get to be my age and have nothing left, it's just easier to use a stencil."

"I never heard of such a thing."

"They're called 'The Eyes Have It.' They come in eight different shapes. I like the one called Cupid's Bow the best. See?" She turned her head so I could see both sides in profile.

Her brows were exactly matched. Why hadn't I noticed that before? And why hadn't I noticed that her skin hung in textured ribbons, like flesh-colored orange peels? Mama was getting old, and since the distance between our ages has pretty much stayed constant, that meant I too was getting older. I glanced at the backs of hands: still smooth, but several of the freckles were morphing into age spots.

"Looks nice, Mama."

"Thank you, dear. Do you think there's any chance we could talk Wynnell into shaving off those hideous eyebrows of hers and using the stencils?"

"I seriously doubt it. Wynnell needs those brows the same way a cat needs whiskers. They help her judge spaces. You wouldn't want her to get her head stuck in a cupboard, would you?"

Mama laughed, even though I was half serious. We chatted pleasantly for a few more minutes before Mama got out to fluff her crinolines. Then she had me honk the car one last time.

Thanks to our generous warning, Claudette Aikenberg answered the massive front door looking like a million bucks. I recognized her immediately from the auction, even though then she was wearing an Hermès head scarf and Versace sunglasses. It was clear by her expression that she didn't have the slightest recollection who I was, despite my rather distinctive size, which is usually a surefire giveaway.

"Hey," Mama said, ever the smooth operator. "I'm Mozella Wiggins, and this is my daughter, Abby. We'd like to invite you to church with us."

I would have gasped in surprise, but Mama, anticipating that, kicked me in the shin with the heel of her pump. I gasped in pain instead.

"Yes, come to church with us," I managed to say.

"What church is that?"

"Church of the Holy Confection," Mama said, without missing a beat.

"Father Baker teaches a mean Sunday school class," I said after just one beat.

"Is it Catholic?"

Mama smiled coyly. "Are you?"

"Baptist."

"Oh well, this church is intensely Catholic. I'm sure you'd be happier at a Baptist church. But a celebrity, such as yourself, probably already belongs to a church . . ." Mama let her voice trail off. Clearly she was up to something; something diabolical.

Claudette Aikenberg swung the door wide open. "Ladies, would y'all like to come in and sit a spell? Maybe have a glass of tea."

"Don't mind if I do," Mama said, and sailed in like she had a stiff breeze to her back.

I followed meekly, apologizing out the wazoo.

"Nonsense," Claudette said. "You ladies are most welcome. Confidentially, between you and I, and my four hundred walls, it can get a mite lonesome here."

Her house, like all homes in this area that are built close to water, was on stilts. She led us across gleaming hardwood floors, into a large room fronted by an immense bay window. Ancient spreading oak trees framed views that were stunning: first marsh, then the sparkling waters of the Wadmalaw, and then more marsh, followed by more woods. There was an abandoned barge in the middle of the river, and on it perched a lone blue heron. The furniture in the room was contemporary, and comfortable without detracting from the view.

"Please have a seat," our impromptu hostess said.

"Don't mind if I do," Mama said, and settled her skirts into an armchair.

"Sweet or unsweet?"

"Sweet," Mama said.

"Unsweet," I said. I was trying to be good. At my height even a pound or two makes a huge difference.

Claudette Aikenberg stared at me in horror. "I'm sorry. I only have sweet. But it will only take me a few minutes to make some fresh."

Much to my chagrin, I realized I'd committed a cardinal sin of the Deep South.

Only diabetics and Yankees ever set lips to a glass of unsweetened tea. Claudette had offered me a choice out of pure politeness; she hadn't, for a second, dreamed I would take her up on it. My only excuse, if it is one, was that a dear friend of mine, Bob Steuben, hails from north of the Line. He drinks the unsweetened variety — in secret, of course — and in private has been touting it as a weight loss solution, given that on a normal day I can drink a gallon of the sweet stuff.

"Did I say *un*sweet? Silly me. Of course I meant sweet."

The instant Claudette disappeared to carry out her hostess duties, I pounced on Mama like a cat on a vole. "Mama, what's this about her being a celebrity? This isn't another of your sniffing claims, is it?"

Some years ago Mama started saying she could smell trouble coming. She meant that literally. From there her amazing nose progressed to being able to detect future events of all sorts. She even predicted the results of the last national election. From the very beginning of this phenomenon I went on record as being a skeptic. But if she's right an additional six or seven more times, I will be seriously tempted to lay money on her nasal prognostications.

"And you call yourself a sleuth," Mama said. "Tsk tsk tsk."

"I don't claim to be anything but a put-upon antiques dealer. Now spill it, please, before she returns with our sweet tea."

"Well dear, there's a console table in the foyer. Just opposite the door. And right smack dab in the middle is this huge trophy. I didn't get a chance to read any of the fine print, but it looked like a beauty queen trophy to me."

Our hostess returned bearing a tray of tea glasses and a bowl of cheese straws. We thanked her and then Mama got right down to business.

"What's your exact title, dear?"

"Mrs. James Aikenberg."

"Yes, of course. But I was referring to that stunning trophy in the foyer."

Claudette giggled and blushed. Even my regular nose could tell it was an act.

"Oh *that*," she said. "Big Jim always insisted that I keep it there, and who was little ol' me to argue? But to answer your question, I was Miss Sugar Tit, South Carolina. We have a Bubba festival every year. It's a lot of fun. Y'all really ought to come."

I strained my brain trying to recollect where Sugar Tit was. Was it up near Spartanburg? Maybe outside of Greenville?

67

And what exactly was a Sugar Tit, besides a great name for a porn star? Something to do with babies. That's right, a sugar tit was a rag soaked in sugar water that was given to an infant to keep its mouth busy in the days before pacifiers.

"Sugar Tit," Mama said knowingly. "What a lovely little town. I'm sure you were the most beautiful Miss Sugar Tit ever."

Claudette glowed. "Thank you, ma'am."

I peered at the former beauty queen from behind the concealing safety of my tea glass. She was a tall, natural redhead whose alabaster skin was lightly salted with the faintest of freckles, the kind that are almost impossible not to get at this latitude. Although she'd presumably been alone when we came calling, she was decked out in a flowing hostess gown of lavender silk that had a frilly collar composed of shredded ribbons that were lime green — slime green, Buford used to call it. Her long red locks were piled high on her small round head, exposing a graceful white neck and displaying to their best advantage the most ostentatious pair of diamond chandelier earrings I'd ever seen. But perhaps her most distinguishing characteristic, despite her fiery hair, was the surgeon-enhanced bosom.

The implants had been placed so far apart that they almost pointed in opposite directions.

"Mrs. Aikenberg," Mama said, in a tone that was practically purring, "tell us all about yourself."

The former beauty queen tossed her head, rewarding us mortals with a thousand flashes of color from the diamond mines suspended from each ear. "Well, there's not much to tell, really. My parents moved to Sugar Tit from Shelby, North Carolina, back in —"

"The short version, please," I said.

Mama glared at me.

Claudette smiled. "I was raised up poor. Mama took in other folk's washing. She was a redhead like me. Daddy worked on a peach farm. He had one leg shorter than the other. Polio. My parents were so poor they couldn't buy hay for a nightmare. I didn't think I was ever going to get out of Sugar Tit, until I won the title. Never was very popular. Then this rich lawyer, Big Jim, came along — saw me win the title — and asked me to marry him that very same day. Said we were going to raise some fine-looking kids. But we never had any, see, because Big Jim was really Little Jim, and what there was of him was shooting blanks. Do you think I ought to have stayed with him, or what?"

"What," Mama and I said in unison.

"I guess it doesn't matter, does it? Because Big Jim's out on his ear now. We moved down here on account of Big Jim has his practice here in Charleston. This house was his idea. It's not my style, but all this water sure is pretty, even though two workmen drowned when they were putting up the dock. Anyway, after we'd been married ten years, Big Jim had himself an affair with his secretary. Make that three secretaries in a row — but I didn't find out until the last one. He had it in his head that the doctors were wrong, and that he really could produce children. Well, the last secretary did get pregnant, but the baby was black, so it wasn't his."

She paused to take a breath. "Don't stop now," Mama pleaded. "This is better than *All My Children*."

"That's just it. I told Big Jim my life was turning into a soap opera, and that if he didn't make peace with the fact that the Lord hadn't seen fit to deal him a winning hand, I was going to leave him. He said he'd shape up, quit trying to spread his seed around, but of course he didn't. So I sued for divorce, and won this house, the Jaguar, and over a million in stock. Not too bad for a skinny little gal from Sugar Tit, if you ask me."

"Not bad at all," I said. "My husband was a lawyer, and when we divorced he got everything, including the dog."

Claudette fiddled with the fortune worth of diamonds that dangled from her left ear. "That might well have happened to me, but the last woman Big Jim fooled with was the wife of the senior partner. He had more connections than a bag full of clothespins. When it was all said and done, Big Jim was on his knees begging for mercy."

"You go, girl," Mama said.

As beautiful as her house was, and as fascinating as that story was, I had a job to do. The problem was how to get from small talk to shop talk without arousing suspicion. But then again, I'd totally underestimated the usefulness of Mama.

"Tell me, dear," she said to the former beauty queen, "what did you think of the locked trunk sale at Safe-Keepers Storage last Saturday?"

Claudette clapped her hands together in a girlish gesture. "That was fun. I'd never bid at one of those, so my bid was way too low. You see, it's a silent auction — hey, how did you know I was there?"

"You're a celebrity, Mrs. Aikenberg —"

"I am? I mean, I *am!* So you're saying people recognized me because I was Miss Sugar Tit?"

"They'd have to be twits not to," I said, taking it from there. "Are you a collector, Mrs. Aikenberg?"

"Oh, yes! I've been collecting since I was fourteen. I was hoping to add to my collection Saturday, but no luck."

I glanced around the room. The furniture was Drexel Heritage. Good stuff, but not antique. There were two floral paintings on the walls, which, although hand-painted, were probably executed in a painting school in China.

"They're not in here," Mrs. Aikenberg said, popping to her feet with enviable vigor. "Come, I'll show you."

We followed her down a wide, airy hall to a secondary bedroom, also with a water view. But one would have to have her head in traction, and pointed at the window, to concentrate on the view. That's because the walls, bed, and most of the floor were covered with Beanie Babies. There must have been a million.

"How many are there?" Mama asked.

"Fourteen thousand three hundred and sixty-four," Claudette said proudly. "Of course they're not all authentic Beanie Babies. Not by a long shot. But I collect the rip-offs too. Look at the shelf over there; those are all made in Senegal. Who would have thought they made bean-filled dolls there?"

"Where is Senegal?" Mama asked.

"Somewhere in South America, I think."

"It's in Africa," I said.

"No, I'm pretty sure it's in South America."

There was no point in correcting her. There was also no point staying even a second longer.

"Well, this has been a delight," I said. "But like they say, all good things must come to an end."

Miss Sugar Tit arranged her lips into a very convincing pout. "Are you sure you can't stay longer?"

"Maybe another time."

"Abby, we're not in a hurry," Mama said, thrilled that someone as rich and famous as Mrs. Aikenberg desired her company.

"Yes, we are. We're shopping for outfits, remember? Clothes without stripes."

"Oh, that."

"Yes, that. Now come on, Mama."

"Well, I'm not going to let you go," Claudette said.

6

"I beg your pardon?"

The Sugar Tit queen tossed her head imperiously, setting free a hair comb, which released a torrent of red locks. It was like watching hot lava spill over the sides of a volcano.

"I am just a country girl," she said spitting out each word, "but I'm not stupid. Y'all didn't stop by just to invite me to church. I bet the little one doesn't even go to church."

A rich beauty queen *and* a mind reader? Jeepers, but life could be unfair. I wrestled with the truth, and unfortunately it won.

"You're right, I am a bit lapsed. But maybe only half."

"Half lapsed, my eye," Mama said. "You only come for funerals and weddings."

I held up a petite pinkie. "Nonetheless, Mrs. Aikenberg, we owe you an apology. We did come here with an ulterior motive. You see, mine was the winning bid on shed number fifty-three, and when I went through its contents, I discovered something a bit unsavory."

"A bit?" Mama exclaimed. "That's like saying Osama bin Laden is mischievous. Mrs. Aikenberg, there was a —"

My pinkie and its four companions found their way over Mama's pie hole. "A dead rat in one of the containers."

Two perfectly plucked eyebrows assumed impossible arches. "And what does a dead rat have to do with me?"

"Well, nothing, I guess. But besides the dead rat, there was a rather large collection of walking sticks."

"Say what?"

"Canes." I mimicked leaning on a fine specimen, one with an inlaid handle. Lapis lazuli and eighteen carat would be nice.

"Ma'am, are you all right?"

"Yes!" I snapped to my maximum height. "I thought maybe you had an interest in canes. Collecting them, I mean."

"I don't. Besides, it was billed as a locked trunk sale. Nobody was supposed to know what was in there. Did *you?*"

"Absolutely not."

She began herding us to the front door by injecting her sculpted body, with its wayward parts, into our comfort zones. "I could call the police, you know."

My heart froze. As small as it is, it doesn't take much.

"She's married to a detective," Mama said, rising to my defense. After all, she goes to church every Sunday and makes a public confession of her sins. She can afford to tell a white lie.

Miss Sugar Tit smiled tightly. "If you're looking for canes, then it's my neighbor you want."

I edged in front of Mama, risking contact with two of the woman's most obvious assets. "Your neighbor?"

"He's an expert on them. You should see his collection. I think he said he has over a thousand."

I couldn't believe my luck, for that's what it was.

"What are the odds?" she said.

"Excuse me?" If this got any more clairvoyant, I'd have to come back, toting a crystal ball.

"He was at the auction as well."

"Oh, really?" I snapped open my purse just wide enough for me to glance at the printout Mr. Cotter had given me. Sure enough, it listed two houses on Major Moolah Road. The numbers were consecutive.

"Just turn left out of my driveway," Miss Sugar Tit said, without me asking. "First house on the right — if you can call it that.

His name is Mac, as in macaroni. I forget what his last name is. That's the thing about living out here: we're too far apart to see each other on a regular basis. Oh, don't get me wrong; there is a bunch that gets together and has dinner, but they drink too much for my taste. They call themselves the Dead Sheep's Club. You see what I'm up against?" She didn't wait for an answer. "Yes sir, having money can make you mighty lonely. Don't ever wish to be rich. Wish for happiness instead."

We thanked her and took our leave, cowed by an onslaught of wayward silicone.

Mama and I had a devil of a time locating the correct house. That was because we — silly us — were looking at the ground. Neighbor Mac lived in the treetops. Literally. This arboreal residence was not just a tree house, but a tree mansion. Recall, if you will, the rustic, but romantic, dwelling built by the Swiss family, Robinson, in the Disney movie by that name. Double that in size, add air-condition ducts, modern plumbing and wiring, and a satellite dish.

This fantastic domicile was spread over several levels, each supported by the massive horizontal branches of a live oak. *Quercus virginiana,* as this species is known scientifically, is called live oak because it keeps its dark green leaves until late winter, a time when many other hardwoods are barren. Even then, the species drops its leaves in stages, as it is putting out new ones, so that it is never lacking foliage. On adjacent Johns Island there is an ancient specimen called angel oak, which has been estimated to be around fourteen hundred years old. This venerable giant has a trunk circumference of twenty-five feet, and its canopy covers seventeen thousand square feet.

Although the Wadmalaw Island oak was certainly smaller, it was still mighty impressive. There was, however, no need to climb a rope ladder or wooden slats to reach the tree house, which loomed overhead like an island in the sky. One had a choice between a glass-enclosed elevator or very sturdy stairs. We chose not to climb due to the arthritis in Mama's knees, a beguiling disease that comes and goes according to how badly she wants to avoid exercise.

The elevator opened at the top onto a solid wood platform, a front porch of sorts. Faux terra-cotta containers, brimming over with impatiens, delineated the door. I mashed the doorbell.

"She said she couldn't remember his last

name," Mama said with a giggle. "If it's Keebler, I'm asking him for a cookie."

"Just one?"

The door opened, catching us by surprise. Even more startling was the fact that the man standing before us was very small; not a millimeter taller than Mama, which put him at about five feet. His face was lined, to the extent that one might expect on a man in his middle years, but there was a boyishness about his features that made him look — well, a bit like an elf. One would think I would have remembered such a vertically challenged man, but auctions have a way of getting my blood racing, and I pretty much stay focused on the prize.

"What do you want?" he snapped, his voice both high-pitched and reedy.

"Cook . . . canes," I said.

"I don't sell drugs," he said, and tried to close the door.

Unfortunately for him, a sudden gust of wind blew Mama's skirt and its attending petticoats into the doorway, preventing it from closing. When Mama pushed on it to clear her crinolines, I went on the offensive.

"We're not here to buy anything!" I shouted. "We just want to speak to the owner."

The door opened wide enough for Mama to tug loose. "The author or the architect?"

"The author." I had no idea what he meant.

"Miss Aida isn't here at the moment." He paused, licking exceptionally pink lips. "Did you bring books for her to sign?"

"Tons of them," Mama said. Once she figures out the game plan, she's usually more than happy to play along.

The door opened all the way. "I don't see any books."

"They're in the car," I said. "We had to see if you were home first."

"So which is your favorite?"

"The latest one." My feet may be small, but sometimes I can think quick on them.

"Ah, *The Poisoned Druid Libel*. What did you think of the ending?"

"Very satisfying."

"Me too," Mama gushed. "It was very powerful."

The tree-dwelling gnome nodded. "Did you find the shaman a likable character?"

"Absolutely," I said quickly. Mama has been known to take our charades too far.

"There is no shaman in that book," he said, "because there is no book by that title." He made no move to close the door. "Now tell me why you're really here."

"I'm a dealer," I said, relieved to finally be telling the truth. "I own the Den of Antiquity. I'm here to —"

He didn't even wait long enough to learn the nature of our visit. "Come in. But watch where y'all step. The floor isn't exactly even."

He was right; it wasn't even. It was, however, spectacular. We could see immediately that the tree house wasn't just sitting on the branches, it incorporated them. In what appeared to be the main room, there were places where the limbs rose above the floor like serpentine couches. Custom-made cushions, with muted leaf patterns, created soft, safe places for resting one's bottom. Across one corner an overhead limb swooped down almost to the floor and up again, disappearing into the walls. A shelf had been built in the bottom of this natural U, and upon it sat a television, a VCR, and a DVD machine.

"There are no nails connecting this house to the tree," he said, the pride evident in his voice. "No invasive devices of any kind. I don't mind telling you that this is an original design, and that it won the International Tree House Association's Golden Bough Award. I'm sure you saw it on the news. Plus HGTV did a special segment on it that airs just about every week. Of course it usually comes on at three in the morning." He chuckled.

"What's it like in a hurricane?"

"So far so good. This tree's been weathering them for a millennium. And believe me, this house isn't going anywhere without this tree. Of course I do have to trim any dead branches before storms. There's no point in asking for trouble."

"No point, indeed." As fascinating as the house tour was, I'd come to talk to Mac about shed 53, and his motive for bidding on it. "Uh — sir — is someone named Mac here?"

"That would be me. Mac Murray. I was the thirteenth child; by then my parents had run out of names."

"Then Aida is your wife," Mama said. It was clear to me that she didn't think that was the case. She is, incidentally, forever scouting for unmarried ladies to match up with the bachelor sons of her friends.

"Aida is a friend," Mac said. "Please tell me why it is you want to see me."

"Mine was the winning bid in the locked trunk sale at Safe-Keepers Storage last weekend."

"Congratulations," he said.

"Thanks. I'm not here to rub it in your

face, Mr. Murray. I'm just curious why you bid."

"Why did you?"

"Touché. I realize this must sound bizarre, but you see, I'm writing an article for *Antiques* magazine about the thrill some collectors get when they acquire unitemized estates, or real locked trunks, or even just abandoned storage sheds. My theory is that these situations bring out the treasure seeker in us. That it's sort of like guys who salvage shipwrecks, only we don't have to worry about sharks, or getting the bends."

"Good save," Mama mumbled.

"I just think you answered your own question," Mac said.

"So you collect?" I asked.

He nodded. "Not me, but Aida. And not canes. Oh, she's had a few laying around, but that's not her specialty."

"What is? If I might ask."

"Rare books."

"How exciting. Is it possible to view her collection?"

"Follow me."

I trotted expectantly after him, with Mama at my heels. She was every bit as annoying as a street urchin hawking knockoff souvenirs at well-known tourist sites.

"If I'd known you were that good of an actress, Abby, I would have insisted that you get the lead role in my community theater's spring production."

"You don't belong to a community theater."

"Well if I did, I would."

Mac Murray stopped unexpectedly, and I narrowly missed running him over. The only reason I didn't is because Mama stepped on the back of my sandal.

"Is everything all right, ladies?"

"Fine as frog's hair," I said. "Except for the fact that my mother is worried you might be an ax murderer."

"Tell her not to worry; I gave that up for Lent," he said.

I turned to Mama. "He says to tell you —"

"I know what he said, Abby. Mr. Murray, please don't believe a word my daughter says. I dropped her on her head when she was just a month old. We were in Germany at the time, enjoying the sights from the balcony of our hotel room. Anyway, the doctor said she would always be subject to spells of paranoia."

He chuckled, then, no doubt seeing the expression on my face, stopped. "Please, step this way. Mind the bump."

The "bump" was the top of a limb that

protruded about six inches above the floor. It also served as the doorsill to another room. He opened the door inward, holding it with one hand, as we filed past him. The air that greeted us was as dry as an Arizona summer.

It took me a few seconds to realize that we had entered a climate-controlled room and were surrounded entirely by glass cases. Then I saw the books. Dozens of them — maybe hundreds — many of them open, like books on display in a museum.

"My manuscript collection," Mac said. "Actually, it's Aida's manuscript collection, but since this is my house, and I pay the electric bills, it may as well be mine. Not to mention it was me who figured out how to make this setup. I got the idea from the mummy room in the National Museum in Cairo, Egypt. I figured if it was good enough for mummies, it'd work on Aida's books."

I stepped over to the nearest case. It contained early German Bibles. I scanned the available text for Gutenberg's name. Mac read my mind, an occurrence that was getting to be scary. If it happened again, with someone else, I was going to start wearing a motorcycle helmet.

"The one you want is on the left. It's a slightly later version — well, at least I'm required to say that for insurance purposes."

I turned just in time to see Mama sniff the air. She was not the least bit impressed.

"Old books?" she said. "I thought you collected canes."

The little man smiled. "What makes you say that?"

"Your neighbor."

"Which one?"

"Miss Topsy-Turvy — or whatever her name is. The one who looks like a floozy."

I was mortified. "Mama!"

"Well, Abby, in my day a woman who dressed like that was advertising her wares."

Mac Murray was still smiling. "Or her availability. Claudette Aikenberg — and I assume that's who you are referring to — killed her husband. From what you say, it looks like she's on the prowl again."

7

Mr. Murray definitely had our attention. Mama, bless her heart, moved closer to me, as if I would somehow be able to defend her, should a crazed pageant killer burst into the room and attempt to pummel her to death with pompoms.

Panic can be highly contagious, but I was determined to remain rational. "Are you saying she murdered him?"

"I don't have any proof, but the circumstantial evidence speaks for itself."

"Such as?"

"They fought all the time." He held up a tiny, well-manicured hand. "Yes, I know that's not uncommon, but please allow me to finish. The nights out here tend to be very quiet; you hear only the insects and tree frogs. And the occasional owl. Anyway, one night several years ago I was enjoying the stars out on my deck, and I heard their car pull into their drive. When they opened the doors I could hear them shouting horrible things to each other; things I will not repeat. I went inside and put on some Italian opera to drown them out. When I went to bed an hour later I could still hear them going at, even though they'd gone inside. Eventually I fell asleep, but about two in the morning I woke with a start. I mean, something had wakened me up. A second later I heard a gunshot — the *second* gunshot."

"Did you call the police?"

"No ma'am. Not just then. This is all private land, and some of my neighbors hunt at night. At the time I didn't have proof of anything. Besides, I'm from L.A. We mind our own business back there."

"My son, Toy, used to live in California," Mama said proudly. "He was an actor, but now he lives in Tennessee and is studying to be an Episcopal priest."

"Toy was never an actor, Mama. He parked cars for actors."

"That may be, but he has a cigarette stub that was Mel Gibson's. How many other mothers in Charleston can say their son owns a genuine Hollywood artifact?"

Mac dispensed another of his enigmatic smiles. "I've never been to Los Angeles. For me L.A. stands for Lower Alabama. Anyway, I got up after the second gunshot and went back out on the deck again. It was a full moon, and the river looked like mercury, it was so shiny. I must have been sitting there about an hour when I heard a boat engine. I didn't need three guesses to know it was the Aikenberg boat. I went inside and got my telescope, and sure enough. But I thought it would be him steering it, not her. She gets way out into the middle of the Wadmalaw and then stops just long enough to roll this thing over the side. Like a carpet, maybe, with something in it. Made a huge splash. From then on I didn't see hide nor hair of Mr. Aikenberg. Shortly after that word got out they were divorcing. You be the judge."

"And *then* you called the police?"

"Actually, I called them right after she dumped that thing — his body — into the river. The police came out, interviewed me, interviewed her, but that was it. I couldn't get any information out of them except that she had an alibi; she was talking on the phone to her sister all night after the fight with her husband."

"Yes, a cell phone — from the boat," Mama said, and patted her pearls. "If you ask me, those things should be banned."

I was bewildered. "She said her husband was a lawyer and works downtown. Surely that can be traced."

Mac shrugged his narrow shoulders. "Like I said, I'm from L.A. I did my civic duty, and now I'm minding my own business."

"Did Miss Aida witness the body being dumped?"

"Excuse me?"

"You know, the author who lives here. Was she able to verify your story to the police?"

Dark eyes flitted from me to Mama and back again. "No. Miss Aida was away on a book-signing tour. Naturally she was horrified when I told her what happened. But now I think she's going to use it in an upcoming book. And speaking of which, I should help you bring in the books you brought for her to sign. Either she or I will call you when it gets done. It shouldn't be more than a day or two."

"Books?" Mama said.

Mama might be a trooper, but sometimes she needs a general to give her a swift, but gentle, kick in the crinolines. Being out of range, I had no choice but to develop a sudden and fatal-sounding cough.

"I'm sorry," I said when I could finally speak, "but my *Ficus pumila* is acting up. I forgot to take my meds this morning. We'll have to come back another time — if that's all right."

Mac was more garden-savvy than I would

90

have thought. "You take medication for your creeping fig?"

I don't always think fast on my little feet. "I meant to say my creeping crud."

"She's delirious again," Mama said. She grabbed my arm and pulled me, not unwillingly, back to the elevator.

Once inside, we exploded into gales of laughter. We didn't stop laughing until we reached May Bank Highway and it was time to think about lunch.

Wynnell and C.J. are my two closest female friends, but it is the Rob-Bobs to whom I turn when the going gets really tough. Rob Goldburg is tall, handsome, and debonair, and Bob Steuben is tall. The life-partners own The Finer Things, an upscale antiques shop, also on King Street. Of course all the antiques shops on King Street are upscale, but The Finer Things is the sort of place where one must be buzzed in, and once having gained entry, one is plied with champagne and pâté.

But a word to the wise: Bob fancies himself a gourmet cook, and the pâté served is likely to come from a farm-raised emu. When I called suggesting we meet for lunch, Bob insisted that we eat at their house. He had a coconut-alligator salad just waiting in the fridge. I told him alligators were very patient, as were some coconuts, and the salad wouldn't mind waiting another day or two.

At any rate, my buddies met us at Thai Two, a fabulous new eatery on upper King Street. By then the front room, with its views of passing tourists, was taken, so we opted for a seat in the back by a splashing fountain overseen by a smiling Buddha.

"So how was your morning?" Rob asked as we unfolded our starched napkins.

"Other than finding a skull in a gym bag, getting arrested, meeting Miss Sugar Tit and a tree-living gnome, it was nothing out of the ordinary."

Bob, a lapsed Catholic, formed a cross with his index fingers. Rob, a nonpracticing Jew, glanced around, searching for the nearest exit sign.

"Come on, guys," I said, "you're hurting my feelings. How do you know I'm not kidding?"

"Abby," Bob boomed in his basso profundo, "you weren't kidding when you said the ninety-five-year-old King of Banga Banga proposed to you, gave you a five carat emerald ring, and then asked you to sleep with his grandson in order to preserve the royal dynasty."

"Sheesh. That was back in college. But

wow, what a ring. Too bad I had to either put out or give it back."

I don't think Mama had heard that particular story before, but she was totally unfazed. "Where is Banga Banga?"

"Just east of Pago Pago," I said.

"Actually," Bob said, assuming his tutorial voice, "it's pronounced Pango Pango. Apparently the missionary who first transliterated the name in their language used a typewriter with an N key that stuck."

"Fascinating," Mama said. She eyed the menu with apprehension; Donna Reed, after whom she models her life, never had to contend with Thai food.

"Tell us about the skull," Rob said, just as calmly as if he'd asked me to read from the menu.

I told them everything that had happened that morning, beginning with the cane mutiny. I left nothing out; at least nothing that seemed pertinent. Unfortunately, the staff at Thai Two are extremely attentive, and I was forced to interrupt myself several times. But by the time the satay arrived I'd pretty much said everything.

Rob, the big brother I wished I'd had, draped his arm over my shoulder. "There could be a very simple explanation for the gorilla skull. The previous owner might have been a zoologist."

"Or a Shakespearean actor who played Hamlet," Bob said. He trotted out one of three Yiddish words he's learned from his partner. "Oy, what an ugly Ophelia."

"Or an ax murderer," Mama said, "if that skull turns out to be human after all."

"Mama!"

"What? You always say that I'm out of touch with reality. I was just trying to keep it real, like you young folks say these days."

Rob let his arm slip off my shoulder, lest Bob, who was sitting across the table from us with Mama, should get jealous. Bob has absolutely no reason in the world to be jealous of us, but that hasn't stopped him in the past. Frankly, I take Bob's unwarranted concern as a compliment.

"Abby," Rob said, "may I please see the list of participants in this locked trunk sale of yours."

I handed him the much folded paper. He read it carefully, stopping to reread a couple of names too many times for my comfort. Before returning it he folded it one more time.

"Abby," he said, "have you considered the possibility that the owner of this storage facility, this Mr. Cotter, might have been trying to set you up so as to divert suspicion from him?"

"Him? I don't follow."

Bob nodded. "If C.J.'s wrong, and the skull really is human, it could belong to Mr. Cotter's dead wife. Maybe he killed her, cut her up, and kept her head in that gym bag. I saw something like that on *Desperate Housewives* — except that it was a toy chest, instead of a gym bag."

"You really think that could be possible?"

Mama poked at the grilled chicken on her appetizer plate. She sniffed at the peanut sauce that came with the satay.

"Don't be silly, dear," she said. "If Mr. Cotter had killed his wife, and he wanted to get rid of the evidence, all he'd have to do was put some stones in that gym bag and toss it off the Folly Beach pier. Besides, why would he have kept just her head?"

At my height, I don't even have to look at food to put on the pounds; all I have to do is read a menu. But if the conversation continued in this vein, I knew I might actually lose weight over lunch. Thank heavens Rob came to my rescue.

"Abby, you mentioned your wayward canes. Were you aware that two people on your list are serious cane collectors? That has got to be more than a coincidence."

I whipped the list out of my purse and unfolded it. "Get out of town!"

Rob pointed to the second name down. "Hermione Wou-ki. You've met her, right?"

"Uh — no. Should I have?"

The Rob-Bobs exchanged glances, all the while clucking dramatically like a pair of hens that had just laid their first eggs.

"Oh, cut it out. Tell me who she is."

"She owns The Jade Smile," Bob said. "Don't you read your newsletter?"

He was referring to the *Charleston Antique Digest*, affectionately known as CAD, a biweekly slip of a magazine that is supposed to keep us in touch with our fellow dealers. Mine usually arrives in the mail sandwiched between pizza advertisements and the Have You Seen Me bulletin. Given all the other things I have to pay attention to, CAD usually ends up in my circular file. I was, however, quite aware that a new store had opened on King Street. In fact, the buzz in the biz had been so good, I'd put off being a good neighbor and dropping by to extend my best wishes. And *yes,* I was a bit envious. When I started up the Den of Antiquity, not everyone had greeted me with open arms.

"Of course I read the newsletter," I said. I paused to push a piece of chicken off the wooden skewer, using the tines of my fork. When the recalcitrant tidbit finally broke free, it landed on the floor. I observed the thirty second rule. "Who else on this list collects canes?"

"This guy," Rob said, and tapped the name Marvin Leeburg with his forefinger. "He's bought from us in the past. Of course you wouldn't think it, to see him."

"You talking about Mr. Leeburg?" Bob asked.

Rob nodded. "He owns Leeburg's Gym over in Mount Pleasant. Nice guy, but very physical."

"Translation: Rob thinks he's cute."

"How do you know he collects?" I asked. "You don't sell canes."

"We sold him an eighteenth-century English breakfront," Rob said. "He was so pleased he invited us to a party. He has a cane collection that will knock your socks off. If you talk to him, try and catch him at home. It will be worth your time just to see his place."

My friend meant well, but nonetheless, I resented his suggestion that I make time to ogle a stranger's goodies while I had the threat of prison hanging over my head.

"It's been real, guys, but I've got to get back to work. Tweedledee and Tweedledum are not going to rest until I'm in an orange jumpsuit."

"I thought it was stripes," Rob said. To his credit, he winked.

"It used to be stripes, but then the chubby inmates complained that the stripes made them look too fat. So they made the stripes vertical, instead of horizontal, but then tall, skinny gals said the new stripes made them look like beanpoles. So now it's fluorescent orange. Everyone looks equally hideous in that."

They nodded far too seriously. I think they may have believed me.

"We can't leave now," Mama said. "We haven't gotten our entrées yet."

"I have to stop and get some gas," I said. "We can grab some candy bars. I read somewhere that a Snickers bar is just as nutritious as the average fast food meal."

Southern gentleman that he was, Rob stood when I did. Bob, a transplant from Toledo, Ohio, followed his lead.

"I'd like to come with you, Abby," Bob said.

I was taken aback by his request. "Well, I — uh — have Mama to keep me company."

"I'm not going anywhere until I get my entrée," Mama said, still sitting.

Bob looked at me intently, as if trying to

convey a secret message. "Rob won't mind covering for me. Besides, we could ask for a better assistant than the one we have now."

"Okay," I said, eager to be on the move again. It had seemed rather decadent, sitting down for lunch in my favorite new restaurant while my personal freedom or, at the very least, my reputation was at stake.

The address on my paper was for Leeburg's Gym, not Marvin Leeburg's residence. Partly because Rob had insisted I see the house, and partly because the gym was closer, I chose to visit the gym first.

To reach Mount Pleasant from downtown Charleston one had to cross the Cooper River on the most magnificent bridge ever constructed. The longest single span suspension bridge in North America, the Thomas Ravenel Bridge, resembles two pair of sails that have been lifted off the water by a strong wind and soar high above the harbor, brushing the heavens with their mast tips. On foggy days the tops of the spans actually disappear into the clouds. On clear days it takes concerted effort to drive from one bank to another without being dangerously distracted.

Less than half a century ago Mount Pleasant was a sleepy little village that depended on the shrimp industry. Today most of its workforce is employed feeding, clothing, and otherwise tending to the needs of thousands of retirees who have discovered this sun-drenched paradise. Whilst previous generations retired shortly before dying, many Boomers retired early, only to realize that, thanks to an increased life expectancy, they had more free time on their hands than they knew what to do with. Not wanting to spend this time in less than peak condition, they began exercising with a vengeance. Gyms replaced shuffleboards, and personal trainers took the place of bingo callers.

But the quest for healthy bodies and svelte waistlines does not always go hand in hand with logic. Drive by any gym in the country and you will observe that the parking places nearest the front door are invariably filled. Folks who are eager to pace both aimlessly and endlessly on treadmills are often loath to walk an extra hundred yards to get to their machines. Many of these people, who are content to jog in place for miles on end, must drive to the grocery store that is just up the street.

Thus it is that Mount Pleasant is chockablock with cars. Bob, who clearly had had something on his mind, took advantage of the congestion to unburden his soul.

"Abby, I'm trying to be as open-minded as I can about this, but I don't see it working."

"I'm not saying that I have much hope for it either. But what else can I do? If by the time Greg gets home tonight I don't have some plausible explanation, he's going to be one unhappy camper."

"Uh — Abby, I don't think we're talking about the same thing."

"No, I hear you. I really do. Every time I get in a tight spot, rather than waiting to be rescued, like any sensible woman would, I come out charging, rattling my saber."

"Would you be willing to rattle that saber in her direction?"

"What?"

8

"Rob's mom. We did tell you she's coming to visit, didn't we?"

Oops. Maybe we weren't on the same page.

"How long is she staying?" I asked. That was the most important question. I can take Greg's mom just about as long as it takes a fish to spoil. Any longer than that and we both get into rotten moods.

"Six weeks," Bob said.

"What?"

"Rob's sister, Rachel, and her husband are going on a South Pacific cruise. Rachel usually looks in after their mother — not that she needs a lot of care — so I can't blame her for wanting a break. But Abby, the mother lives entirely on her own, and is completely capable of looking after herself. The only reason Rachel is so involved is for her own peace of mind. But in that case, why doesn't she just hire a live-in companion? She can certainly afford it."

"Holy guacamole."

"Abby, what will I do? The woman hates

my guts. She blames me for turning her son gay. Never mind that he came out decades before we met."

"What does Rob think of this extended visit?"

"He's worried to death. He won't say anything about it, but I can tell. He's never been so solicitous. If I didn't know his mother was coming, I'd think he was having an affair. Abby, what shall I do?"

We were stuck at a traffic light behind an SUV that bore a perplexing variety of bumper stickers, including HONK IF YOU LOVE NOISE and SILENCE IS GOLDEN. I took my time in formulating a response.

"Use what you've got," I finally said.

"Great. I have a receding hairline, a bit of a gut, and arms and legs like matchsticks."

"You have a keen intellect, a love of classical music, and you're a whiz in the kitchen."

"I am? Abby, I thought you hated my cooking. You're constantly thinking of new excuses not to eat with us."

"True — and I mean that in all kindness. But Bob, it isn't your cooking per se, but those ghastly ingredients you use. Emu meat, duck embryos, locust butter — the kind of stuff they make you eat on *Fear Factor.*"

"Abby, emu is becoming very popular. It's low in fat, high in protein —"

"But not ordinary, right? And that's what Rob's mother likes; ordinary food. And she listens to elevator music, not the classics. So here's the deal: turn your dial to the classical music station and start cooking the weirdest — I mean most exotic — dishes you can think of. If you have any doubts, call me. I guarantee you that she'll be packing her bags again within a week."

"But where will she go?"

"Where not? The woman has more money than God and Fort Knox put together. Last year she went on four cruises, by *herself.* And you know she has more friends up in Charlotte than she can shake a stick at. Cousins, too."

"Six."

"I beg your pardon?"

"She went on six cruises."

"I stand corrected. So you see, Bob, the only reason Rob's sister checks in on her mother every day is because it makes her — the sister — feel good. If you play your cards as I suggested, you can get Mrs. Goldburg to leave on her own account. Rob won't be able to blame you for that — for just being yourself."

Bob leaned over and kissed my cheek.

"You're the best, Abby. I have a great new album, *Bland Bach* (*Sonatas for Sleeping By*). And I think I'll start by cooking some haggis. Do you know what haggis are, Abby?"

"Please don't remind me."

The light changed, and just past the intersection we turned right and into one of Mount Pleasant's unfortunate strip malls. Leeburg's Gym occupied what used to be a bowling alley. To the left was Bubba's Chinese Buffet, and to the right was Sweated in by the Oldies, an upscale clothing consignment shop. One could fill up on Moo Goo Gai Grits, pretend to work it off, and then buy a set of larger clothes, already broken in. The American dream in only three stops.

Sure enough, all the parking spaces immediately in front of the gym were taken. But as luck would have it, a car parked right in front the restaurant pulled out, drove twenty yards, and began to cruise the lot, waiting for someone in the gym to depart for the clothing store. We gladly took their spot.

Luck held with us and we located Marvin Leeburg at the reception desk. He smiled when he saw us, revealing teeth that only a dental supply company could make.

"Hi," I said, "I'm Abby Timberlake, and

I believe you already know Bob."

I could see how Rob would find Marvin attractive. In addition to perfect teeth, he had a strong profile, a thick head of hair, piercing blue eyes, and sported the Yasser Arafat beard that is so popular these days.

"Hey," he said. I could tell that he didn't remember Bob, but I think he recognized me.

"Mr. Leeburg, I was wondering if I might have a few minutes to discuss antiques with you."

His scowl was slight but unmistakable. "I don't solicit at your place of business, so please don't solicit at mine."

"I'm not here to solicit, sir. It's just that Bob here says you have an awesome collection of antique canes. I know this is very forward of me, but I was wondering if it would ever be possible for me to see them."

His scowl melted. "Well, why don't you step into my office. We can talk in there." He called to a young man with a mask of freckles who was helping a vastly overweight woman regain her self-esteem. The lad trotted over to cover the reception desk.

We followed Marvin into a long, narrow room that had undoubtedly once contained shelves of rental shoes. The lingering odor of feet only just overcame the smell of cheap Chinese next door.

106

"Please, have seats." He gestured to a pair of folding chairs. "Can I get you something to drink?"

"We're fine," I said, before Bob had the chance to request rare Tibetan teas picked from inaccessible Himalayan ridges by virgin monkeys wearing Hermès scarves and Versace sunglasses.

He nodded. "I have over three hundred canes in my collection," he said. "I know that sounds like a lot, and it is, but once you start collecting, it can become an obsession. It's like I live and breathe canes. I go to as many shows as I can. Forget what I said before. If you have something really special to show me, I might be interested."

It's hard to stay on one's toes when they are so tiny. "Uh — yes, I do have some canes. As a matter of fact they came from a storage shed sale on Johns Island. I believe you bid on that lot yourself."

He didn't even blink. "Yes. Didn't have much hope for it. But you say there were some canes? Any nice ones?"

"Mouthwateringly nice."

"Do you mind describing some?"

"Dark. Fine grain. Handmade." I felt like I was describing fudge.

"I assume your intent is to resell them?"

"Certainly."

"May I have first crack at them?"

"Absolutely, that's why I'm here. Mr. Leeburg —"

"Please, call me Marvin."

"I'm a relative newcomer to this business. At least when it comes to cane collecting. I was wondering how it is you knew to bid on that storage shed? I had no idea there were canes in there, or anything else in there for that matter. I mean, the shed could have been empty."

"What else *was* there in the shed? If you don't mind my asking."

"Junk." I'm sure that answer would have cleared a lie detector test. Nobody in their right mind would consider a dirty gym bag containing a skull to be anything but trash.

"One man's trash, another man's treasure," he said.

I keep my bottle-brown hair short. Nonetheless I reached up and tugged on what little bangs I have. If folks kept reading my mind, I would have to grow my hair long, possibly even wear a scarf. A Hermès scarf, of course.

"Touché."

"As a matter of fact, that's how I started collecting canes. When I was a young boy I inherited a walking stick my granddaddy always used. And I mean *always*. When he wasn't leaning on it, he was whacking me with it. The old codger was so mean he'd fight a circular saw with one hand and a camp meeting of wildcats with the other. Anyway, when the cane finally ended up in my possession, the first thing I did was run over to the nearest Dumpster and toss that sucker in. Well, somebody knew it was worth something. The next thing I knew, there was a front-page article on it, with a photo, in the *Post and Courier*. It said Granddaddy's walking stick — the same one he used to beat me with — was also a blowgun."

"What?" Bob and I chorused. His bass and my soprano sounded pretty good together.

"The staff was hollow. It also unscrewed to make two sections. The top section contained little darts. Poison-covered darts from South America, the kind some Amazon tribes use for hunting. The poison comes from frog secretions. At any rate, the bottom piece was the actual gun. Well, I did some checking with relatives — my mom was dead by then — and learned that Granddaddy was in a so-called import-export business that never actually imported anything. He spent most of his time away from home, and a lot of it in Europe.

Especially during World War Two. My uncle Bart, mom's older brother, said he'd heard a story that his father was an American spy whose mission it was to kill Hitler. Of course he didn't kill Hitler, but that doesn't mean the story isn't true. In fact, it made a lot of sense to me; a lot of things started falling in place.

"To make an even longer story shorter, I was able to buy the cane from the guy who found it in the Dumpster, but I had to top several other offers. But ever since I got that cane back, I've been fascinated by them. Unlike paintings, or statues, canes were actually used by the previous owners, and a lot of them — if they could speak — would have real tales to tell."

Bob, bless his Yankee heart, knew a tale when he heard one. As interesting as the poison dart cane was, its story had neatly diverted us from the question I had posed. Why did Marvin Leeburg bid on the shed, and did he have any inkling it contained canes?

"I saw the ad for the locked trunk sale," my friend said, "but I passed. It didn't seem that exciting — maybe just some lawn chairs and an old backyard grill. I'm with Abby; what made you think there might be canes?"

Again Marvin's gaze held steady. "I

didn't. But I have Saturdays off — one of the perks of being owner — and I try to get around to as many sales as possible. I even hit the yard sales if I'm up that early. You know what I mean; you have to get up at five these days to make it worth your while. If you're not there when they lay out the stuff, you might as well stay home." He paused to scratch his stubble. "You fish, Mrs. Timberlake?"

"My husband's a shrimper. He likes to stay on land on his days off."

"Not ocean fish," he said. "I mean pond fish. With a bamboo pole — Granddaddy whipped me with that too — and a bobber. Used to love to fish like that as a kid. Especially if the water wasn't clear and I couldn't see beneath the surface. That way you never knew when that bobber was about to jerk and you had something on the line. Maybe something really big and special. Been trout fishing, where you can see the fish, and that isn't the same. Well, that's what the locked trunk sale felt like to me. I love those things. But you were the lucky one this time and caught the fish."

His explanation seemed quite reasonable. The thrill of the hunt is something every dealer I've ever known well has admitted. One even said it was like going on safari, not to a game park where you knew there'd be payoff, but to some obscure dark jungle where at any moment a leopard could leap down from the branches. This dealer, by the way, had just acquired a Bengal cat, a rare breed that is descended from the Asian leopard cat, and seemed to have leopards on the brain.

I stood, and Bob hastily followed suit. "You've been very helpful, Marvin," I said.

"But don't you want to set up a date to see my collection? You could bring the canes from the auction with you."

Silly me. More and more it seemed like I had elephants on my brain. Literally. Youth is wasted on the young, and so are active brain cells.

"Certainly," I said. "How about Thursday evening?" Frankly, I was satisfied that Marvin was who he presented himself as, and that a visit to see his collection could wait until after I'd extricated myself from the jam I was in. By Thursday I'd have the entire mystery tied up with a bow, and if the ribbon was long enough, I'd tie up Tweedledee and Tweedledum as well. The nerve of them to threaten me with an ape's skull!

"Sorry, no can do. Not unless you're into watching *Survivor, the South Pole*."

I'd forgotten that was on. It was, in fact, my favorite show. Greg's too. We had a tradition: I'd make a huge bowl of white cheddar popcorn, he'd whip up a batch of chocolate martinis, and then along with Dmitri, our cat, we'd curl up on our California king-size bed, pull up the drawbridges, and utterly relax. It was not the kind of thing we could, or would, share with someone else.

"Forgot about *Survivor*," I said. "Tell you what. Here's my card. Call me sometime and let me know when it would be convenient for you."

"How about breakfast tomorrow?"

"Excuse me?"

"I'm taking the morning off — have to see my chiropractor. I live on the Isle of Palms, oceanfront. We could have breakfast on my deck and watch the container ships come in." Since Marvin Leeburg could read my mind, reading my face was child's play. "Rob is welcome to come as well."

"That's Bob," my companion said, clearly annoyed.

"Yes, of course. Well, Mrs. Timberlake, how about it?"

Breakfast by the sea, watching ships and dolphins, what could be nicer than that? Given all the stress I had on my plate, salt air might just be the tonic I needed. Of course Bob had his own shop to run, so it wouldn't be fair to ask him. But I wasn't about to breakfast with Marvin Leeburg without a chaperone present.

"My last name is Washburn, by the way. Timberlake is my professional name. Mind if I bring a friend?"

"Not at all. The more the merrier. Real coffee or decaf?"

"Definitely real, and stiff enough to stand a spoon in."

He smiled and handed me a card bearing his address. "Eight o'clock."

"Abby, I can't believe you did that," Bob said, the second we were out the door.

"Did what?"

"Agreed to meet that horrible man for breakfast."

I tugged him by a spindly arm until I was certain we couldn't be overheard by anyone inside. "Why Bob Steuben, shame on you. That's not like you at all — calling him a horrible man." I paused just long enough to allow curiosity to take over. "What's so horrible about him? I found him both attractive and pleasant."

"Abby, he was all over you like white on rice."

114

"He was not! I mean, was he?"

"Totally. If Greg could have seen him, he would have punched that bundle of muscles in the nose. With both fists."

"Greg knows other men flirt with me — well, sometimes they do. Bob, it almost sounds like you're jealous."

I'd meant my tone to be affectionately teasing, and vaguely ambiguous, but it didn't appear to have gone over that way. "Jealous? Of what? Maybe Marvin Leeburg tries to come off as charming, but he's really just smarmy."

"For what it's worth, I'm not in the least bit interested in his smarm — I mean, charm!"

"Abby, who's your guinea pig?"

"My what?"

"Because if I were you, I'd take a canary instead. That's what they carried down into coal mines to see if the air was safe to breathe."

"Mama doesn't know it yet, but she's going to be my canary."

9

On the way back into Charleston, with a game plan in place to foil his partner's mother, my friend was much more relaxed. In fact, he was positively ebullient. To say that Bob babbled excessively is to be kind in the extreme.

I learned all about his life growing up on the poor side of Toledo, the scholarship he won to Kent State, *and* the fact that he was married. Fortunately, we had just exited our sky-scraping bridge when he dropped that bombshell on me, otherwise we might have ended up in the Cooper River, inadvertently feeding next year's crop of shrimp.

I slammed on the brakes. "You're *what?*"

His face was ashen. "I can't believe I told you," he whispered.

"Are you serious?"

"I wish I wasn't."

"Does Rob know?" I had a gut feeling he didn't.

"Not yet."

I pulled into the parking lot of an apart-ment building. "Why not? Who is she? How long have you been married? Details. I want details!"

"Her name is Carol. We got married right after college. I hadn't come out yet — not even to myself. I thought that maybe the feelings I had for men would stop if I got married. But they didn't. Abby, I really tried — and Carol was such a nice girl — but I couldn't . . . you know. I never even was able to get things off the ground, so to speak. We separated two months later and applied for an annulment. It was a mutual decision, but then suddenly she changed her mind and said divorce was against her principles."

"She's still in love with you, isn't she?"

"Yes. But Abby, it's been years. From what I hear from family back home, Carol's been mooning around like I jilted her at the altar just yesterday. My mother still has hopes that we'll get back together."

"Did you love Carol?"

"As a friend, yes. I thought it could turn into more than that if I just tried harder."

"Why haven't you told Rob about this?"

"It's hard to explain."

"Try me."

"Abby, you won't understand. It's complicated."

"Robert Vaughn Steuben, if you don't tell

117

me, I'm going to rip your tonsils out."

He laughed nervously. "Okay, here goes. When we first met, I didn't want Rob to think I could be so stupid. I mean, he knew who he was ever since he hit puberty. Anyway, after we were dating awhile, it seemed kind of awkward bringing up something that maybe I should have mentioned in the beginning. Then the longer I kept it secret, the harder it got to tell. I started thinking he might get angry if he ever did find out — not angry about the fact that I was married, but because I hadn't shared. Abby, you're the first person I've told since I left Ohio. It just kind of slipped out, and I'm sorry. I didn't mean to dump this on you. You couldn't possibly understand."

I unbuckled my seat belt so I could hug him. "Bob, believe it or not, I do understand. I have *All My Children* to thank for that."

"The soap opera?" He said it in the same tone he would use to describe a TV dinner.

"Yes, and it's not a dirty word. The characters on *All My Children* are always keeping secrets from each other. Invariably the secrets come out and the lies are exposed. Of course that makes the people who've been lied to extremely angry. They claim that if only they'd been told the truth up front, they could have handled it. But the thing is, those characters who *do* learn the truth up front don't handle it any better than the ones who've been lied to. I've actually thought a good deal about that, and the conclusion I've come to is that bad news will always have a bad reaction, no matter when it's shared. That being the case, one may as well hang onto the bad news as long as possible — as long as no one is getting hurt. Especially children."

He burst into tears. "Thank you, Abby," he said between sobs.

I patted his scrawny back. "But you do realize that there is still a bomb ticking away in your cellar, don't you?"

He nodded.

"If you ever do decide to tell Rob, I'll do all I can to help him understand."

He squeezed me so tight I found it hard to breathe. "Abby, you're the best."

I struggled free. Bob had enough on his plate, bless his heart. If he accidentally suffocated me, it might send him over the brink, and they'd ship him back to Ohio. That would be South Carolina's loss as well, because Bob, his marital secret aside, is truly one Yankee we are happy to have living in our midst.

"Fasten your seat belts," I said, as I did

just that. "Hermione Wou-ki, here we come!"

The Jade Smile has its own parking lot in back, but Bob asked to get out just as I was pulling in. "I need to get back to the shop, Abby."

"I thought you wanted to hang out all afternoon."

"Well, I do, but —" He shrugged, looking as sheepish as any ram.

"But now that you've used me as a sounding board, you no longer have time for me? Is that it?" I was only half kidding.

He cringed. "Abby, how could you say that? You're my friend. I wouldn't do that to you. The truth is, if you must know, Ms. Wou-ki kind of scares me."

I checked to see that my car doors, which lock automatically when the vehicle is in motion, were still secured. Bob wasn't going to bolt without spilling even more of his guts.

"Scares you? How?"

"She has this way of looking at you that makes it feel like she's looking right into your mind. That she can read your thoughts."

"Uh-oh."

"How so?"

"Lately it seems like everyone can read my mind. I'm almost surprised that strangers on the street don't confront me with what I've thought about them."

"You think bad things about strangers?"

"Not *bad* things. Just things like, 'Wow, if those shorts rode up any higher, people might think you're wearing nothing but a thong.' Or, 'If I were you I'd dump the rest of that ice cream cone in the nearest trash bin.' Or — and this is really bad — 'Did you ever hear of shampoo?' That kind of thing."

"Trust me, Abby, those are pretty mild thoughts."

"Really?"

"Toodle-doo, Abby," my friend from Toledo said as he punched the unlock button and leaped safely out of reach.

"I hope she loves your cooking," I hollered after him, only half in jest.

One has to ring in order to gain admittance to The Jade Smile. I used to think this was pretentious, but that's before my friend Kim had a car full of women double-park directly in front of her shop. Before she could think clearly, they barged through the door, two at a time, grabbed every single piece off a rack of vintage clothing, and then skedaddled before Tweedles Dee and Dum could be summoned. Since then I've been thinking of replacing my cow bells with a buzzer.

At any rate, having seen Ms. Wou-ki's picture in the paper, I knew that the dour woman who finally opened the door for me was not the owner. When I asked to see Ms. Wou-ki, Mrs. Crabcakes expelled a lungful of stale air in my face.

"My employer is busy," she snapped.

"Tell her that makes me very happy. Busy is good, right?"

"If you say so. What do you want?"

"I want you to give Ms. Wou-ki a message for me. Please tell her that her assistant has a nasty disposition, bless her heart, and is as homely as a toad in the high speed lane."

"*I* am her assistant."

"Are you sure?"

"Positive."

"Don't be silly, dear, you're very nice. I could tell that right away. But her assistant — wow, Ms. Wou-ki needs to rethink that decision."

The woman mumbled something about me having it all wrong, but she immediately headed for the back. I took advantage of her absence to poke around. The shop was short on space but high on value. Everywhere I looked museum-quality merchandise met the eye. From stunning rosewood carved furniture to the finest porcelain vases. I could just hear Ms. Wou-ki's register go ca-ching with the sale of each Ming.

When an uncomfortable length had passed since the assistant had disappeared into the back room and not returned, I stood on my tiptoes, cupped my hands to my mouth, and hollered. "I'm no one important. Never mind that I have a bundle of cash with me that could choke a horse."

Immediately Ms. Wou-ki swooped out of nowhere. "How may I help you?" she said, her voice as clear and delicate as a crystal bell.

"I'm Abigail Timberlake," I said, and offered to shake hands.

She regarded my hand with some distaste, but took it nonetheless. "Hermione Wou-ki." It was very much apparent my name didn't ring a bell, crystal or otherwise.

"Yes, I know. I understand you're an expert on walking sticks."

She was a beautiful woman, perhaps in her late fifties, with flawless ivory skin and dark brown hair that fell beneath her shoulders. Her smile seemed genuine enough, and if she could read my thoughts, perhaps she'd chosen not to look into the wasteland that is my mind.

"I don't consider myself an expert on anything," she said. "But I do have some lovely canes I could show you."

Without waiting for a response, she led me to a nook that was lighted from above and roped off with a golden cord. The walls of the nook were covered in blue velvet and mounted with clear Plexiglas rings that were not in the least bit obtrusive. Lining the walls of the nook, like soldiers on parade, were canes of every description. At first glance even my untrained eye could tell that these walking sticks were a step above even the finest I'd recently acquired.

There were canes with highly glazed porcelain handles, enameled handles, ivory handles, pewter handles, silver handles, vermeil handles, even jeweled handles. The designs ranged from brightly painted flowers to three-dimensional lifelike animal heads. Even the simplest were works of art. I strained to read one of the tiny price tags without having to lean forward or touch it.

"Sixty-nine hundred."

I tried not to show my reaction. She'd read my mind through the back of my head, which was pretty darn unnerving.

"It's very beautiful," I said. And it was. The handle appeared to be carved from ivory or bone, and it depicted what looked like a water buffalo.

"The handle is vegetable ivory, which really isn't ivory, but made from palm nuts. This cane comes from the Philippines and was commissioned by a veterinarian. Inside the shaft is a long, sharp piece of metal, like a large needle. He used it to poke the stomachs of domestic water buffalo to relieve them of excess gas."

"You don't say." I found it both gross and engrossing.

"It's both gross and engrossing."

I clapped a hand to the back of my head. I still had hair, but it wasn't doing a very good job of covering my mind. Maybe I should consider converting to the Amish way of life. My soul could use a dollop of gentleness, and the bonnet might help protect my meager mind from rearguard readers.

"Is everything all right, Ms. Timberlake?"

"Everything's peachy." I concentrated on a new cane. It had a straight silver handle that was entwined by silver vines that terminated in fleur-de-lis, which were surmounted by a vermeil lioness's head. The lioness's tongue was hanging out, and her eyes were closed. The tongue appeared to be carved from a pink sapphire of exceptional clarity. Good pink sapphire can demand a hefty price, but even so, the price was a staggering twenty big ones.

"I know that twenty thousand might seem like a lot to pay for a cane, but this one has a fascinating provenance. The story is that this walking stick belonged to the executioner who cut the head off Marie Antoinette. The lioness represents Marie, and the closed eyes and protruding tongue portray death. The sapphire used for the tongue was supposedly plucked from Her Majesty's crown. The small amount of gold to gilt the silver came from one of the dead queen's teeth. I am still working on gathering the physical evidence to support this claim, but the word of mouth comes from a very dependable mouth." Crystal bells tinkled as she laughed.

"Wow, you really have some interesting things."

"Ms. Timberlake — do you mind if I call you Abby?" For the first time I detected a slight British accent.

"I insist."

"Well then, Abby, is there one cane in particular I can show you?"

I steeled myself for the moment of truth. "Ms. Wou-ki, I'm not here to buy anything — not today, at least. You see, I own the Den of Antiquity, just down the street."

Her eyes brightened. "Lovely! I've been

in your shop several times."

"You have?" I'm not claiming to remember every face that walks through my door, but encountering a woman as classy and beautiful as Hermione is not an everyday occurrence.

"Your assistant, C.J., and I have become quite good friends. Did you know she speaks perfect Mandarin?"

"Actually, I did know that. She speaks seventeen languages, in fact. Do you speak Mandarin as well?"

"Abby, do you have time for a cup of tea?"

Did I ever! Skipping out on my lunch entrée had been a bad idea. If possible, I'd load that tea up with milk and sugar.

"With biscuits, of course. Cookies to you, I guess."

"Call them anything you want," I said gaily. "They all go down the same."

"Indeed. Please, this way."

She ushered me over to a pair of heavy red velvet drapes trimmed with gold tassels. Pushing them aside, she opened a door and stepped through into the most unusual storeroom I'd ever seen. While the back half appeared to be fairly typical of an inventory storage area, the front half had been roped off and, with the use of lacquered Chinese screens, in simple black and red geometric designs, turned into a cozy, albeit exotic room. Deeply carved rosewood divans upholstered in yellow silk damask were arranged around a mother-of-pearl inlay coffee table that was centered on a Kazakh rug that was predominately bottle green. The somewhat odd juxtaposition of cultures and colors worked beautifully. I actually gasped in appreciation.

"Do you like it? It's based on my father's office in Hong Kong — although his was a much larger space. Not to mention that it had a breathtaking view of the South China Sea."

I was about to babble something inane when I noticed that at one end of the room within a room was yet a third room, an alcove that contained a table-mounted microwave, a coffeepot, and a hot-water-making machine. Standing still as a statue, a mug in her hand, was the less than gracious assistant I'd encountered out front. Her expression was one of controlled antagonism. I had a feeling that if Hermione were to abandon me here, her assistant would leap on me like a rabid cat and scratch my eyes out. I stared back at the sullen woman, willing her to disappear.

"Natasha, please go back up front. Ms. Timberlake and I will be having tea."

The banished employee glowered as she slipped out of the alcove and within striking distance of me. I leaned back unconsciously.

When the door closed behind the sullen woman, Hermione sighed softly. "She's a hard worker and knows her antiques, but she rather lacks in the social skills. I'm afraid that's off-putting in a gracious city like Charleston. Tell me, Abby, do you have any suggestions?"

"Well, I — uh — I'm not sure what to say." My friend Wynnell would accuse the acerbic assistant of being a Yankee insurgent, or at the least as being from "up the road a piece." But I've met many surly Southerners in my time, and more than a few fine Northerners. I was sure Hermione Wou-ki did not intend it that way, but I felt like she'd put me on the spot.

"Oh dear, I shouldn't have put you on the spot like that," she said, moving toward the alcove. "Which do you prefer, lemon or milk?"

"Milk, please."

"One lump or two?"

"Three, please." I was too hungry to be ashamed.

She reached under the microwave table and produced a brightly colored tin. "These shortbread cookies are to die for. If you like Walker's, you'll love these. You don't even need to swallow; all that butter makes them melt in your mouth and slide right down your throat." She procured a saucer, also from beneath the table, and started piling on the rich treats. "Just say when."

I didn't say when nearly as soon as I should have. If she didn't already think so, Hermione was bound to conclude that we Americans were gluttons.

"Now then," she said when we were both settled in our respective divans, our teacups balanced carefully on our knees, our biscuits beside us, "what really brings you to see me?"

"Would you believe the desire to give you a warm, Charleston welcome?"

"Absolutely not. I know you feel threatened by my shop."

"Why that C.J.!"

"There's no need to blame her, dear. I would have read it in your eyes, anyway."

For once she was wrong! "I don't feel threatened; I'm jealous."

The cookies didn't interfere with her tinkling laugh in the least. "Jealous? Of me? I'm the last person on earth you should be jealous of."

"Well, not you, exactly. I'm jealous of the

130

reception you've received. When I got here — well, it was a total nonevent."

"Abby, don't you see? That's because you're one of them; a fellow Southerner, a regular American. I'm the exotic thing that blew in on the trade winds. They'll tire of me soon enough. Do you know that I have yet to set foot inside a private home?"

I'd like to think it's General Sherman's fault, but we Southerners, famous for our hospitality, are reluctant to invite folks we don't know well — i.e., went to grade school with — into our inner sanctums. We are, however, quick to bake them a peach pie, and deliver it with "Ya'll come on over sometime, hear?"

"I'm sure it's just because everyone is so busy," I said, "but I'd be honored to have you over sometime, hear?"

Dark eyes twinkled briefly. "Thanks, Abby." She leaned forward, her features hardening, turning to jade. "Now, tell me the truth: why are you here?"

Sometimes, not only is truth the best policy, it's the only one available. "You bid in the locked trunk sale. So did I; mine was the winning bid. I want to know why you participated in such a rinky-dink auction."

"Rinky-dink?"

"Insignificant. A woman of your taste and

sophistication interested in a musty old storage shed — it doesn't add up."

Her stone visage began to crack. "What about you, Abby? Why did you bid?"

"The thrill of the hunt." My visit to the oak-dwelling gnome had not been a total waste.

"Touché. I once bought a real locked trunk that contained a museum-quality eighteenth-century kimono. My ten dollar buy netted me ten thousand dollars. That kimono, by the way, was featured in a sushi western titled *Show Gun*. Did you see it?"

I shook my head. "I prefer spaghetti westerns."

"So Abby, what *was* in the storage shed?"

"Some canes. That's another reason I came. I'm going to need some help in evaluating them. One can't know everything, cane they?" I laughed at my own joke.

"Uhm. My instincts tell me that you know a lot more than you let on."

And my instincts told me that Hermione was hiding something a lot more interesting than a secret parlor. And she wasn't going to be an easy nut to crack. Thank heavens I hadn't wasted my formative years reading silly books, electing instead, over Mama's loud protests, to watch *Perry Mason* on our black and white Motorola TV.

"I think it's drugs," I said, just to see her reaction.

"What?" Her composure shattered altogether.

"White stuff in bags. Lots of it. What should I do?"

"What should you do? Call the police of course! Really, Abby, I'm surprised. I had you pegged as a very competent woman."

"But I am! Really. Just ask anyone I know. Ask the Rob-Bobs."

She took a sip of tea, her eyes speaking volumes over the bone china rim.

"And ask Mama," I blurted. "Her name's Mozella Wiggins. She calls it like she sees it. Believe me, I don't get any extra points for being her daughter."

"Your mother sounds delightful. But frankly, Abby, I have no reason not to trust you." She set her cup down without as much as a clink. "Now then, tell me what was in the gym bag."

10

I stared, open-mouthed. If a colony of bees had been present — perhaps clinging to an overhead rafter — they might well have flown down my throat, turning me into a four-foot-nine-inch human hive. Then when strangers called me "honey," which most of them do because of my diminutive size, they'd be right on the money. And speaking of money, for the right price I might even burp up some of the golden stuff and seal it in jars. "And what goes well with honey?" I asked aloud. "Milk, of course. Particularly goat's milk. I've always been fond of goats. Heck, I could get into the goat milk business and make my own cheese. After all, isn't feta the most popular type of cheese on the market today? Of course I'd have to sell my shop to get the capital for my new business. But it would be worth it. Who knows, maybe someday I'd write a best-selling novel about my experience and title it 'The Secret Life of Cheese.' "

"Abby, Abby!"

"What? I mean, yes?"

"Are you all right?"

"Certainly. Why would you ask?"

"Frankly, you seem knackered."

"I beg your pardon?"

"Knackered — don't you say that in this country?"

"Not in this part."

"Drunk. Sorry about that. You see, I grew up in Hong Kong; my father was Chinese, but my mother was English. I went to school at Berkeley. Anyway, sometimes I get English and American mixed up. But let's not talk about that just now." She flashed me a smile so bright that, had we been outdoors, it could have been seen forty miles out to sea. "Abby, I've been very patient. Now I want to hear about the gym bag."

Patient? She sounded like she had a right to know about its contents. The elegant, exotic newcomer, so gracious at first, now seemed menacing.

"Don't worry, Abby. I have no plans to tie you up and sell you into white slavery like in that movie, *Thoroughly Modern Millie*. A thoroughly enjoyable film, by the way, if you can get past the racial stereotypes."

"I've never seen it." I popped to my feet. "Tea has been delightful, but tempest fugit."

She jumped up as well, positioning herself

between me and the door. "The gym bag, Abby. I would very much like to hear what was in it."

"Who told you I had a gym bag?"

"That charming assistant of yours. Is it true, Abby, that it contains a skull?"

"Yes — Yes, it does. A cow skull." If I got the woman confused enough, or maybe even just irritated enough, she might blurt out something unintended. After all, it's when we blurt that we bare our souls, isn't it?

"But — But C.J. said it was a gorilla skull."

"Oh, no, definitely a cow. Moo-moo, and all that. Although come to think of it, this might have once been a steer. Like you see in dioramas of the Old West, or movies — you know, with a snake crawling out of an eye hole. Except, this didn't come with a snake. But there was a stuffed roadrunner. And some crushed tumbleweed."

"All of this in a gym bag?"

"A very large gym bag. And like I said, the tumbleweed was crushed."

"How fascinating. Abby, do you mind if I take a look at this skull?"

"Uh — why?"

"Just curious, I suppose. I've never seen a cow skull; except in films."

"Seen one, seen them all," I said blithely.

If looks could kill, I'd soon be dead, cremated, and my ashes scattered over the tops of a dozen cat litter trays. I could see the effort it took for her to produce civil words.

"If you will excuse me, Abby, I really must be getting back to work."

I grabbed a few of the buttery cookies before exiting. Following the fiasco that was Floyd — motorists fleeing that hurricane spent a dozen or more hours stalled along I-26 — I have it as my motto to eat whenever you can. Eliminating whenever you can is even more important; but that would wait until I got back to my own shop.

"Abby!" C.J. shrieked with glee as she embraced me in a bear hug. Given that the big galoot is larger than many bear species, I had to struggle to get loose, and quickly, if I were to continue breathing.

"Take it easy," I said when I was finally released. "You could crack one of my ribs next time."

"Ooh, Abby, that's what we say back home in Shelbyville to wish someone good luck. But what do you need good luck for, besides the fact that you've been arrested for murder and might spend the rest of your life behind bars, and might never get to see the nieces and nephew I'm going to produce for you?"

"C.J., you've not only put the horse before cart, but you've put the horse in another county. I have not been arrested for murder; the official charge is 'unauthorized possession of human remains.' And besides, the phrase is 'break a leg,' *not* 'crack a rib.' "

"Ooh, but you're wrong. Cousin Garth was a famous wrestler, and each time when he went into the ring, Granny Ledbetter would shout 'Crack a rib!' Poor Cousin Garth had his ribs cracked more than thirty times before he finally retired. They never did heal properly, and if he puts a mind to it, Cousin Garth can squeeze through a space smaller than his head. Now he makes a living spelunking. That's the sport of exploring caves, Abby."

"I know what it means, dear. And anyway, it seems to me that both your cousin and your granny should have noticed long before thirty cracked ribs that shouting 'crack a rib' wasn't bringing him good luck."

C.J. shook her massive head. "The good luck wasn't for Cousin Garth; it was for his opponent. That old bear never lost a round. Never cracked a rib either."

"Bear?"

She nodded vigorously. "Biggest grizzly in captivity, that's how he was billed. I saw him close up once. His head was bigger than all of you."

"How fascinating. C.J., how are things going here at the shop?"

Her eyes danced. "Abby, look around, and then tell me what's missing."

"C.J., please, I don't have time for games."

"Aw." Her quarterback's shoulders slumped. "You know that ninety-six-inch bookcase that you said would never sell on account it was too tall?"

I turned to look, my jaw dropping when I saw the empty space. "Who bought it? Anyone I know?"

"You sort of do. It was Colonel Beauregard Humphrey."

"Get out of town! He just bought a pile of canes from me this morning."

"Abby, I think he has the hots for you."

"What?"

"He asked if you were married. And" — she paused for dramatic effect — "he called you a 'pretty little thing.' "

Thanks to a slightly inactive thyroid, my blood merely simmered, rather than boiled. "Pretty," I'll take. With the proper protest, of course. And "little" is unavoidable. But I draw the line at "thing."

"I hope you didn't give him a discount," I said hotly.

"Abby, I didn't fall off the turnip truck, you know. I know that's just an expression, Abby, but Cousin Rudy Beggah really did fall off a turnip truck, and it was the happiest moment of his life."

"You don't say," I said, praying she wouldn't say more. "Can we please get back to the bookcase?"

"Okay, if you insist."

"Which I do."

"Anyway, I could tell the Colonel wanted the bookcase really bad, so I told him that if he paid an extra ten percent, I'd see to it that the ghost who lives in the top level doesn't follow him home."

"And he fell for that?"

"Yes. But it took me a good half hour to convince Mrs. Peebles to move into the highboy over by the window."

That C.J. believed in ghosts — Apparition Americans, as they prefer to be called — was to be expected. That she would know any of these hyphenated pseudocitizens by name was a bit unsettling.

"Did you help her move her luggage?" I asked, perhaps a bit unkindly.

"Ooh, Abby, you know that Apparition

Americans don't have luggage. But they do have baggage — emotional baggage, that is. That's why they're still earthbound. Either that or they don't realize they are dead."

"Did you tell Mrs. Peebles it was time to hit the highway in the sky?"

"Shhh, Abby, you're being disrespectful, and she can hear you. Besides, she already knows she's dead. She said she's not going anywhere until you tear down this shop and rebuild her house."

"What?"

My buddy, my coworker, nodded solemnly. "This is where her house stood before the great Charleston earthquake. Poor Mrs. Peebles was one of the fatalities of that quake. She was a childless widow then, and her estate was left to a nephew who sold the property to a shopkeeper. Mrs. Peebles has been hanging around ever since then, waiting to get her house back."

"But the earthquake happened in 1886!"

"Mrs. Peebles has been very patient — up until now. But she says she can't wait much longer. Her memory of her old house is starting to fade, and when it's gone, she will be too."

"C.J., I've been very patient as well. Back to Colonel Beauregard: do you trust him?"

"About as far as I can throw a sheep."

I knew for a fact that C.J. was Shelby's champion sheep-thrower in her weight division. "That far, huh?"

"Ooh, Abby, with that long, drooping mustache of his, he looks just like Aunt Alice. I trusted her with my life savings — of course she was a bank teller. Miss Business Shelby 1985. Or was it 1986? At any rate, it was the year Cousin Nefarious Ledbetter won the world's record for sewing on buttons. You know, Abby, if I wasn't about to marry your brother — well, being Mrs. Colonel does sound pretty posh, doesn't it?"

"C.J., haven't you heard? He's been married and widowed three times. And all three died in their forties of supposedly natural causes. Everybody in Charleston has speculated about what really happened to those women. Be very careful around that man, dear."

"I don't think he weighs as much as a sheep. I'm pretty sure I could take care of myself."

"What about Hermione Wou-ki?"

"Don't be silly, Abby. I don't want to marry a woman — not that there's anything wrong with that."

"I mean, do you trust her? Apparently the two of you have hit it off, chatting up in Chinese."

"Abby, there is no such thing as the Chinese language; China has many languages. For your information, we did talk in Mandarin. My Cantonese is not all that great. But, to be honest, I don't trust her. She asked too many questions about you."

"About me? She hadn't even met me until a few minutes ago."

"She said you have a reputation of being a very astute dealer who knows her stuff. She wanted to know if that was true."

"What did you say?"

"I told her that yes, you were pretty good. But then she wanted to know if you dealt much with Asian antiques. And if you had a family here. And what kind of boss you were."

"What did you tell her?"

"I said you were pretty good."

My cheeks were smarting. "Just 'pretty good'?"

"You didn't want me to lie, did you?"

"No." I swallowed my pride; it took two gulps. "C.J., can you hold down the fort for the rest of the afternoon?"

"Sure, Abby. Mrs. Peebles and I need to talk anyway. She says she has a friend who died playing with matches. She's thinking of getting him over here to do his thing if you don't hurry up and tear down this shop."

"Tell Mrs. Peebles she doesn't want to take me on. She doesn't stand a ghost of a chance when it comes to a battle of wills. I don't have proof, but family legend has it that Margaret Mitchell based Scarlett O'Hara on my grandmother, Prunella Wiggins."

As I was closing the front door behind me, I saw the faint figure of a woman sweep across the face of the highboy by the window. I swear I did.

Colonel Beauregard Humphrey not only lived south of Broad Street, the dividing line between Charleston and *Charleston,* but his three-story Greek Revival had a commanding view of the Battery. I'd walked by the Colonel's house many times, and even peered through the wrought-iron gates and into a garden lush with subtropical plants and soothed by the splashing of fountains. So picturesque is the Colonel's abode that it is a rare occasion when one does not find a knot of tourists having their pictures taken in front of his steps.

A newcomer to town, Colonel Beauregard remains ignorant of some local taboos, of which paying attention to tourists is the most offensive. Ever since he bought the mansion, the Colonel has been known to stand at the top of his steps, so as to have his likeness — or at least his feet — included in the photos. Last month there was a notable blip on Charleston's social screen when it was discovered that the aging gent sometimes hired stand-ins, theater majors from the College of Charleston. Sometimes the actors showed up on their own, apparently just for the fun of it. Of course heavy greasepaint is needed to replicate the Colonel's time-etched face. At any rate, what might have eventually disappeared into the annals of idle gossip became front page news when one of the aforementioned youths was found dead, floating facedown in the newly formed Atlantic Ocean, just off the Battery. The young man was in full colonel regalia. Outside of a moderately high alcohol level in his blood, no definitive cause of death was ever released to the public.

As luck would have it, there was no copycat Colonel on the steps that day. I must admit, however, that I felt a slight thrill as I politely, but purposefully, wound my way through the throng of tourists outside the mystery mansion. They were there only to gawk, whereas I, a bona fide, albeit recent, Charlestonian, had business to attend to. Although I faced straight ahead, I possess exceptional peripheral vision, and could see the looks of envy that swept over the tourists' faces.

"Ask her," a woman said, her remark quite clearly directed at me.

"I ain't gonna ask," a man responded.

"Harvey, you always chicken out. I have to do everything myself."

"Yeah? You make me take out the garbage."

You can bet I'd rewound the spring in my step so as to slow my pace. How often does one get to be the object of so much attention, yet have their shoes entirely free of toilet paper?

"Harvey, ask!" the woman ordered.

I turned and smiled. "Is there something I can help you with?" To add to the occasion, I affected an accent so Deep South, it made Vivian Leigh's accent sound like that of a Brooklynite by comparison.

"Yeah," Harvey said, "the wife wants to know where we go to catch the boat over to Fort Sumter."

I was tempted to steer them wrong, but nonetheless gave them impeccable directions. Then holding my head high, I ascended the remaining steps and pressed the yellowed plastic doorbell. A second later, when it opened, I gasped in shock.

11

"You're a woman," I managed to say, after an embarrassing length of time.

"There's no denying the fact," she said with a laugh. She was, by the way, fully made up to resemble the old codger, but was still dressing. Her unbuttoned weskit vest revealed unmistakably feminine attributes.

"Neat getup," I said. "How much does he pay you?" It was undoubtedly a rude question, but it just sort of slipped out.

"Ten bucks an hour, and I don't have to pay taxes. Of course I don't fool everyone. Sometimes when the tourists catch on they give me tips. But sometimes they're just pissed. Once, a man gave me a hundred dollar bill and asked me if I was interested in working in Hollywood. Of course I knew that was a come-on."

I smiled. "It sounds like fun. Is the Colonel here?"

"Oh, I'm afraid he doesn't come to the door for tourists."

"I'm not a tourist; I'm a local. I'm here on business."

She frowned. "Is he expecting you?"

"No, but I'm sure he wouldn't mind if I popped in for just a minute or two."

"He would mind; he's upstairs napping."

Seeing that she majored in drama, and was probably a darn good actress, there was no way I could tell if she was speaking the truth. Except to call her bluff.

"Yoo-hoo, Colonel Humphrey! Abigail Timberlake Washburn calling Colonel Beauregard Humphrey!"

The young woman reacted by straightening her back, thrusting out her assets, and frowning. Her frown lines, by the way, did not match with the greasepaint wrinkles on her forehead. All that posturing would merely have been annoying had she not also whipped out her cell phone.

"I'm calling 911 if you don't get out this minute."

Technically, I wasn't inside, but on the threshold. A proper lady would have apologized for not having called first and then backed out gracefully. I'd like to think that I would have done just that, had not a gentleman from one of the square states — his pleasantly flat accent gave proof to that — decided to involve himself.

"Hey lady, don't you know it's rude to bother the locals. This isn't a zoo, you know. The locals aren't animals on display."

"Yeah," a woman from Tennessee said.

"She's probably from New York," a man with distinct California diction said.

"Hey, I resent that," a woman from Lower Manhattan intoned.

Rather than turn and face my linguistically diverse detractors, I chose to have it out with the college girl. More precisely, I appealed to the old man upstairs.

"Colonel," I called, "I just got a lovely collection of antique canes in, and something else you will undoubtedly find very interesting."

Before the girl's itchy finger could hit the numeral 9, the real Colonel stepped out of nowhere. "Melissa, she's fine," he said.

Melissa growled as she palmed the phone and stepped aside.

I smiled graciously at her. There was no point in holding a grudge. After all, she'd only been doing her job. Besides, the smattering of applause from the assembled at the foot of the steps was both heartening and informative. In fact, it gave me an idea for a business venture, should the antiques business ever bottom out. What is it folks enjoy most when visiting a historic city? Not the history; that comes in second. What they enjoy above all else is the *sense* of history, that something happened here, that there were real-life Scarlett O'Haras and Rhett Butlers running around.

What if I updated that concept a bit? Tourists, I've noticed, are fascinated by us locals — even newly transplanted locals like myself. What if there was a tour that one could take that would offer a glimpse into the lives of contemporary Charlestonians? Warts and all. Of course the warts would be carefully scripted and the authentic Charlestonians would be paid actors. The drama students would prosper, as would I, and the tourists could return home with tales to tell, which would undoubtedly bring in even more tourists, and the service industries and area merchants would thrive. I could call the venture "A Peek at Charleston's Private Parts" — or maybe not.

The rumbling of a male voice disturbed my reverie. "Earth to Miss Timberlake, I believe the expression is. Are you in there?"

"W-What?"

Thank heavens Colonel Humphrey seemed more amused than irritated. "Please come all the way in." He addressed Melissa. "You may go now, young lady. And please close the door behind you. We don't want to let flies, or tourists, into the house. They're the two things I can't stand."

Melissa closed the door as the shocked tourists gasped. I couldn't blame them. Wasn't the Colonel famous for mingling with their ilk? Well, he certainly wouldn't be on my tour of the Holy City.

"I know what you're thinking," he said as he motioned me to follow him. "Yes, it's an act. But if I didn't have a little fun with them, I'd be tempted to run them over with my car. Did you know they climb my garden gate and peer into my windows? I've even caught them going through my garbage. And this was *before* I started putting on my little shows."

Even at home, behind closed doors, the Colonel was a showman. He was still dressed in his blue and white seersucker suit and his trademark bow tie. Completing his regalia was the jade-topped cane I'd let go for a song — well, a very pleasant song.

"We have a garden tub," I said ruefully. "It looks out on what we thought was a very secluded part of the yard. I used to love looking out at real gardenias whenever I took a gardenia bubble bath, but not since the time I looked up from my bubbles to find a family of four staring at me. Well, three of them were staring, at any rate. The father was too busy taking my picture."

He chuckled briefly. "Doesn't surprise me. Please, Miss Timberlake, take a seat."

I glanced around to see my options. He'd led me into a large room with dark paneled walls and a stamped tin ceiling. The furniture was Victorian, the upholstered pieces in dusty rose velvet. On the floor was a pair of very large animal skins. One was zebra, the other that of a large antelope, maybe a kudu. On the walls, intermixed with electrified sconces, were the mounted heads of other unlucky beasts, most of them in ratty condition. I recognized a lion, a leopard, a rhinoceros, a Cape buffalo, a warthog, and more antelope species. The latter had widely varied horns; some short and to the point, and others twisted into astonishing shapes.

"Shot every one of these myself," he said proudly.

"Uh-huh." I didn't know what else to say. I'm a Southern girl and hunting is an important part of our culture, although I personally am not into it. But we primarily hunt deer, of which we have an overabundance, or pigs, which are an introduced animal that uproot the forests and devour the eggs of ground-dwelling birds.

He pointed to the rhinoceros with his cane. "That's a white rhino. Northern white rhino from the Congo, to be exact. Shot him back in the day when there were plenty of them. Now they're almost extinct. Maybe only fifteen left."

"Fifteen?"

"Yes. The southern white rhino is faring much better, but even then, there are less than twelve thousand of them."

"Hunters," I said, no longer masking my disapproval.

"Poachers, young lady. Not sport hunters like myself, who pay fees that help run the game parks."

I had not come to debate conservation with him. But if an argument was what he wanted, who was I to disappoint him?

"A rhinoceros is a large animal," I said. "You really can't blame the native poachers. They probably have no source of income, and an animal that large would supply a lot of meat. Even feed a small village."

"You're quite right, my dear. Quite right, when you're not wrong, which in this case, sadly you are. Rhinos are poached mainly for their horns. Often their carcasses are left to rot in the bush, where they become dinner for hyenas and vultures."

I looked more closely up at the rhino head above me. The horn was ugly when compared to many of the antelope horns. It was impossible to believe someone would kill a magical creature like the white rhinoceros, second only in size to the elephant, for its horns.

"If what you say is true," I said, "then the antelopes on these walls must also be endangered by now."

"Some are, but most aren't. You see, young lady, an antelope horn is just a horn. A rhino horn isn't a horn at all, but a tightly packed bunch of hair. For centuries ground-up rhino horn has been used in Asia as an aphrodisiac, as well as for other medicinal purposes. In the Near East — Yemen to be precise — rhino horns are used as dagger hilts and convey status to the owners." He pointed to the long sweeping horn on the rhino head above us. "That, my dear, isn't even a real horn, but some kind of plastic. I sold the real McCoy to a Chinese merchant in the Kivu. Got almost a thousand dollars for it, and that was back in the 1950s."

"Oh."

He sighed. "Well, enough about rhinos. Let's talk about what you're really here for."

"Yes, of course. You see, Colonel —"

"Allow me to save us both time, young lady. You are not getting that cane back. Not the one with the jade head. That's mine. No offense, ma'am, but what caliber of antiques dealer are you? Surely, even a fair one would possess a basic knowledge of semiprecious stones. Not all antiques are made from wood and porcelain."

"Then I guess I'm subfair. But to be fair, I have a lot on my plate now."

"Everyone does. For all you know I could be dying of heart disease."

"Are you? Uh, because — I'm sorry, if that's the case."

His eyes were small, not unlike the rhino's, and all but hidden in the folds of time. But they twinkled now, as bright and blue as any I'd seen.

"Young lady, we all start to die the second we're born."

"Cliché." I tapped my mouth gently for having misbehaved. "I meant to say touché. French was never my forte — which, by the way, is really supposed to be pronounced 'fort,' because it refers to one's strong point, like the garrison type of fort. When pronounced 'for-tay' it becomes a musical term. Unfortunately hardly anyone gives it the preferred pronunciation these days."

"Well said. You've got spunk, little one. If

I was ten years younger I'd ask you to be my fourth wife."

"Was that a joke?"

"Indeed not. I never joke about marriage." He tapped the tip of the cane on the hardwood floor a couple of times. "Oh, what the hay, as they say in polite circles. Are you spoken for?"

I waggled my left ring finger.

He leaned forward, his mustache ends swinging like ribbon curls, and squinted. "Seems to me a feller would be wanting to make more of a statement if he had a fine filly like you in his stable. That little chip would be plum lost in a sugar bowl."

Lost in a sugar bowl? I'd never heard anything so rude — at least not directed at me. I was tempted to show him the fine filly's backside as I headed for the door, but that meant leaving empty-handed. Instead, I decided to drag out the Southern woman's best friend: Miss Bless Your Heart. The Colonel was from Kentucky, one of the border states, whereas I was from the Deep South, where charm dripped from lips just as surely as dew dripped from the overhanging boughs of oak trees. If sugar was what was on his mind, that's what I'd give him. The man would never see it coming.

"Why bless your little old heart, Colonel," I said, opening up the sugar valve. "I can't imagine what it would be like to be blind."

"Blind?"

"This is a two carat stone, sugar pie. VSI, G color. A feller, as you put it, would have to be blind not to see this rock."

"Hmm. Still, I would have done better by you."

"I choose to take that as a compliment. Colonel, do you mind if we get down to business now?"

"I thought we had. My answer, by the way, is still no. The cane stays."

Too much sugar can be bad for one's teeth — mine were certainly on edge. Who knew it could be bad for the eyes as well? I could swear that I saw the warthog blink.

"Colonel, who did your bidding for you at the so-called locked trunk sale on Saturday?"

He swayed with surprise. "Bidding?"

"Well, I know you weren't there. No offense, sir, but you don't exactly blend into the background. But someone was there on your behalf, bidding in your name."

"Young lady, I haven't the foggiest idea what you mean."

"But you do. I know it for fact, Colonel. I have a list of names."

He took a step forward. "Miss Timberlake, let's keep our voices down, shall we? These walls have ears."

"And eyes, Colonel. They would have legs and tails as well if you hadn't seen fit to slaughter them."

He nodded. "Good one, if I do say so myself." His voice dropped to barely a whisper as he crossed the room. "Yes, I did send a representative to the sale Saturday. And you can be sure that young feller who runs it is going to get a piece of my mind for having shared that information. As to what my representative was doing there — well, I'd have to say he, or she, was doing the exact same thing you were."

"I disagree. I'm a dealer. I get my inventory from sales like that. And, of course, auctions. But surely you didn't expect your rep to find any stuffed animal heads in that shed. Then again, given that it was a storage shed, maybe you'd gotten wind of some pack rat trophy heads —"

The Colonel's arm was as quick as a striking snake. In a flash his cane darted out, the tip of it punching the warthog's right eye.

"Ow! That hurt, damn it!"

Now I knew I was hallucinating. Dead warthogs seldom speak, or so I'd always been led to believe. And certainly not in English.

12

"Now make yourself useful," the Colonel ordered the dead beast, "and bring us mint juleps and some of those benne crackers."

"Yes, sir." The warthog sounded like a female to me.

The Colonel turned to me, his face breaking into a wreath of smiles. "This warthog normally has only one eye. The other, a glass one, of course, got lost when I moved down here from Louisville. I confess that I rehung the head over a hole in the wall, and that I have been known to observe my guests through the empty socket. But not very often, mind you. It's quite unpleasant in there."

Since the Colonel had previously offered me a seat, I saw no reason to put off sitting. My poor legs just barely got me to the nearest chair, so weak and rubbery had they suddenly become.

"There was a lady in there? Behind the warthog head?"

"Not a lady, my housekeeper. My representative, as you just called her."

"Colonel, you could have blinded her."

"Hardly. This thing has a rubber tip, and besides, it didn't go in all the way. Trust me, I've been practicing."

"So she does that a lot?"

"More and more, it seems."

I couldn't help but laugh. Perhaps it was the absurdity of it all, perhaps it was the banana peel syndrome. At any rate, as long as the housekeeper was well enough to serve us refreshments, there was no real harm done.

The Colonel laughed as well. "Serves the old biddy right," he said. "Last week she put Exlax in my chocolate pudding. I couldn't leave the house for two days. That's why I couldn't make it to the sale."

"Colonel, I just remembered I'm on a very strict diet. I'm afraid I'm going to have to pass up the refreshments."

"What kind of diet?"

"It's called the Sundown Diet. I'm not allowed to eat anything during daylight hours."

The Colonel roared with laughter. He laughed so long and hard that I began to fear he might go into cardiac arrest. Anxiously I fumbled around in my purse for my cell phone. It had been years since I'd taken a CPR course, and frankly, I'd rather that the paramedics be the ones to give him mouth to mouth.

"I like you, little lady," he said, when he could finally speak. "You're a pistol. You sure you don't want to dump that feller of yours?"

Mercifully, for everyone's sake, the sudden appearance of the housekeeper put an end to his proposal. It also left me speechless for a minute. The woman was the spitting image of Julia Child; tall, slightly slumped at the shoulders, and with a twinkle in her left eye. Her right eye, however, was blinking rapidly.

"You don't need to worry about the mint juleps," she said, looking directly at me, but by no means whispering. "I only mess with the old goat's food, not his drinking. I don't believe in wasting alcohol. As for the benne wafers, they're still sealed in their original wrapper."

I adore benne wafers. The word benne means "sesame" in Mandingo, a West African language. Slaves from that region brought the recipe with them to America, and today the crisp little treats are enjoyed throughout the Deep South, but perhaps nowhere more so than in Charleston.

Since eating sesame wafers is said to bring good luck, and drinking enough mint juleps helps one not to notice bad luck, I decided that it would be in my best interest to accept the proffered snack.

"By the way," the housekeeper said as she held the tray out to me, "your drink is on the left."

"I heard that," the Colonel growled. However, he sounded more amused than irritated.

The housekeeper was still looking at me. "Ma'am, can you do me a favor?"

"Certainly — if I can."

"Tell the old goat I'm going to the movies tonight, and if he wants any supper he's going to have to fix it himself."

"Tell the old goat yourself," the Colonel growled again.

"No need now," the woman said. She set the tray on the coffee table — a very bad resin replica of an elephant topped by glass — and strode from the room.

"Uppity old witch," he said.

"Conceited old coot," she said.

"Mighty fine mint julep," I said, and took a gulp of my drink.

"Well," the Colonel said, when it was just the two of us again, "where were we?"

"I was here, sir, watching you flirt with your housekeeper."

"How's that?"

"Shame on you, Colonel, for asking me, a

happily married woman, to be the fourth Mrs. Humphrey, when there is another woman so desperately in love with you she can't see straight. Literally. The good news is that you love her too."

I could see anger and embarrassment battle for dominance on the battlefield that was his face. "This is outrageous. Miss Timberlake, I'm afraid I'm going to have to ask you to leave."

I took a second big sip just in case he meant what he'd said. "Believe me, I've seen this a hundred times; boy and girl fight constantly because they're both too proud to put their true feelings on the line. But then by seventh grade they usually sort things out. Except that by now they've moved on to other people. Colonel, you don't want your charming housekeeper to turn to someone else for affection, do you?"

Uh-oh. I'd done it now. The Colonel was puffing with rage. He trembled as he steadied himself enough to lift the cane high and poked at the air above my head.

"Get out of my house, young lady. Get out now."

I grabbed my purse from the floor beside my chair. "But I was hoping to see your cane collection."

"Out!" he roared.

★ ★ ★

If there is status to be gained by being ushered into one of the mansions south of Broad, then there has to be something that is lost when one is thrown out on one's ear. That thing is dignity. You don't realize it's there when you have it, but you sure know when you don't. The fact that a new clump of tourists now clustered at the base of the stairs only made matters worse.

"Shame on you," a sweaty woman hissed. "You can't just go into people's houses like that. You must be from up North."

"I most certainly am not," I said, gathering my shreds of dignity as if they were scraps of cloth to cover my nakedness.

"Hey, I resent that remark," a second woman said. "I'm from Pittsburgh, and we are some of the politest people on earth. It's you Southerners who need to learn manners. Why just this morning a woman with a Mississippi license plate stole the parking space I saw first."

"So that was *you!*" the first woman said. "I'll have you know I circled through that parking garage three times. I saw the space about to open and before I could circle back around you zipped in out of nowhere. Didn't you see me waving my arms?"

"I saw you almost crash into me, that's

164

what I saw. Just because you drive an SUV doesn't mean you can bully your way into a spot that isn't yours. Is that what you call Southern hospitality?"

The woman from Mississippi put her hands on her hips. Her forehead was beaded with sweat and it ran in rivulets down her neck. Given that it was a somewhat balmy spring day, I concluded that she must have been in the middle of a hot flash. If indeed that was the case, she should be granted some leniency.

"Yankee go home," she said, spitting each syllable out like a watermelon seed. Given her Deep South accent, that totaled seven seeds.

"This is the *United* States of America," the woman from Pittsburgh said. "This *is* my home."

"That's easy for you to say, ma'am. Y'all won the war. As far as I'm concerned, the United States of the Confederacy is an occupied nation."

"Did everyone hear that?" the Pittsburgher yelled. "This is treason!" Without further ado she attacked the Biloxi belle by swinging a handbag the size of a small suitcase.

The belle fought back, swinging her purse, which was the size of a large suitcase.

I had no choice but to join the fracas in order to achieve peace. Alas, my pocketbook was barely larger than a pocket, so I was forced to do the old Timberlake one-two. Balling my fists, I flew at the nearest lady, the one from Mississippi, and socked her in the soft spots behind both knees. The belle buckled, bawling with rage as she toppled directly across the Pittsburgher, provoking a plethora of profanities.

I drew myself up to my full four-foot-nine inches. Aided by two-inch heels, I must have been a formidable sight.

"Ladies," I said sternly, "look over there, just beyond the spot where the two rivers come together to form the Atlantic Ocean. That's Fort Sumter out there. That's where the War Between the States began. But here is where it's going to end. Do I make myself clear?"

The women exchanged glances, then they both glared at me. "I ought to sue you," the Pittsburgher said. "My husband is a well-known lawyer who specializes in personal injury cases."

"My husband is an orthopedist," Mississippi said. "He'll testify that you've given me whiplash."

"So sue me," I said, and forced a little

166

laugh. "It's obvious you don't know who I am."

"Who is she?" a bystander whispered.

"I think she's Sarah Brightman," someone else said.

"No, Sarah is much prettier than that. Taller too."

A man jumped into the discussion. "I know I've seen her somewhere. On television, I think."

"It's Katie Couric," a second man said. "I'm almost positive."

"Katie is prettier too," someone else said.

"Yeah," the first man said, "but that's with her TV makeup. No, Ed is right. That *is* Katie Couric. I did the *Today* show once. It was a segment on my new book, *How to Catch Your Dream Man in Ten Days.*"

The woman from Biloxi gasped. "You wrote that?"

"Get out of town," the Pittsburgher said, as she too turned her back on me.

I scurried away unnoticed. But I hadn't gotten as far as East Bay Street when I felt a tap on my shoulder. I whirled. Had I been a cat, I would have led with my talons. The tourist women were taking their lawsuit threats too far.

"Listen ladies — oh, it's you. The Colonel's housekeeper."

The woman, who towered over me, was breathing heavily. Her large, flat face was red from exertion.

"I need to talk to you," she gasped.

Not knowing her intentions, I kept walking. "Then talk."

"Is there somewhere we can sit?"

Relenting, I led her over to the seawall. Steps, half hidden by flowering oleanders, open to an elevated walkway that offers spectacular views of Charleston harbor. She settled herself on a concrete ledge and leaned back against a metal railing. Behind her an enormous container ship, like a floating skyscraper — no, make that a floating city — glided by.

I tried to keep my attention on her and not the handsome Greek sailors that scurried about on deck. "What is it you'd like to talk about? But first, just so you know, I am not in the competition for Colonel Humphrey."

Her mouth opened and closed rapidly several times in mute surprise, then she cackled. "And you think *I* am?"

"Without a doubt. It's written all over your face."

"Why that's just downright cheeky of you Miss — uh —"

"Call me Abby."

"Roberta," she said, and tapped a chest so speckled with age spots it gave the illusion of a deep tan. "Roberta Stanley. That's my maiden name. Unlike the Colonel, I've only been married once, but I'm not going to tell my ex's name. He was a real slimeball."

"Been there, done that. My ex was the slime on the ooze on the muck at the bottom of the pond. However, I still use his name for business purposes. I figure I've earned the right to benefit however I can from that fiasco of a marriage."

She cackled again. "I like you Abigail. I'm a good judge of character, and I think I can trust you."

"Roberta, if you saw my husband, you'd know you could trust me."

She waved a hand impatiently. "I'm not talking about men now. I'm talking business."

"Excuse me?"

"I understand you sell antique canes."

"Well, yes, but — who told you that?"

"The Colonel. He came back from your shop with a bunch of them, gloating like there was no tomorrow. Said you wouldn't know an antique cane if it rose up and hit you. Had himself a good laugh."

"He did?"

"Novice, that's what he called you.

Anyway, as it happens, I have a special cane I'd like to sell, but not to the Colonel."

"Why is that, if I may ask?"

"Because the Colonel wants to buy it so darn badly."

"I don't understand."

"That's the way we do things, Beauregard and I. Been that way ever since the beginning, thirty years ago when I first started working for him. He was married to the first Mrs. Humphrey at the time. A real slob, if I may be so frank. A slut too. Cheated on the poor man more times than I care to remember. Anyway, he and I started teasing each other all the way back then. Fool that I am, I didn't see it for what it was."

"You were attracted to each other?"

"Yes. Did you ever see the movie *Who's Afraid of Virginia Woolf?*"

"Richard Burton and Elizabeth Taylor?"

"That was us. Loved each other fiercely, but couldn't stand each other at the same time."

"You were better off than I. I thought I was happily married — for twenty years — until my husband traded me in for a younger model. One with bigger headlights, I might add."

She snorted her laugh. "I married my slimeball as a way to make Beauregard jealous — I guess that makes me a slimeball as well. Anyway, Beauregard upped the ante by acquiring two more wives."

What a pair of idiots, I thought. Why didn't they just marry each other and get it over with?

"Bless your heart," I said. "So, if you sell me this cane, you can stick it to the Colonel?"

"Exactly."

"It must be very special. But why me? Why not sell it to any number of area dealers that have a higher profile than myself? Like, for instance, Hermione Wou-ki who owns The Jade Smile."

"Because Beauregard didn't flirt shamelessly with her in front of my eyes."

"Actually, only one of the eyes was yours. The other belongs to a warthog."

"A small point, but one taken. There is another reason, as well. But I can't discuss it here. I have tomorrow afternoon off. Could you meet me at Magnolias restaurant for tea? Say, four o'clock?"

"Actually, I'm very busy right now. Something unexpected landed in my bag — I mean, on my plate."

"Abby, this is extremely important. I can't emphasize how much."

"I understand, but sometimes a gal just

171

has to say no." That, I believe, is one of the most difficult life lessons I've had to work on to date.

"Did I mention tea was on me?"

Now that irritated me. Magnolias is a fine restaurant, and the chef is guilty of making the world's tastiest crème brûlée, but one doesn't have to sell one's firstborn to afford taking tea there. Frankly, I was a mite offended by her offer. Did I look like I couldn't afford even dinner at Magnolias? I may not buy couture, but I do buy most of my things at Dillard's and Neiman Marcus.

"I can afford to pay for myself, thank you. But you still don't understand. I don't have time at this point in my life."

"Abby, it's a matter of life and death. You must do it."

13

The "must" word rattled my teeth like a Yankee saber. "I think I heard wrong."

"No, you didn't. Abby, it is imperative that we meet somewhere more private. Tomorrow afternoon at the latest."

"Roberta, I don't have time for any more of y'all's shenanigans. The two of you should be ashamed of yourselves for dragging a stranger into your bizarre War of the Roses. And to think I missed out on a perfectly good opportunity to watch some Greek eye candy go by."

"They weren't Greek, they were Albanian."

"You sure?"

"Positive. I know that ship's registry. I even recognized some of the crew."

"From this far away?"

"I have a thing for faces, Abby. I never forget one, even if I just see it at a distance. That's really why I'm here."

"Really, Roberta, I've got to get going."

My answer was to walk away. Unfortunately a tour bus had just disgorged a horde

173

of pale panting bodies from one of the square states, and a quick, graceful exit was out of the question.

"Excuse me," I said as I tried to squeeze my way out of a fortress of hot flesh.

"Okay," she called at my retreating back, "I'll tell you now! Some of those canes Beauregard bought from you are contraband."

I turned, but so did the tide of tourists. Apparently someone had spotted a pod of dolphins farther up, toward the Charleston Yacht Club. What had begun as a group of sweaty individuals was now a giant sweaty cell, of which I was the nucleus. The cell swept me along with it until it reached private property and couldn't go any farther. Then it melted like a snowball in Dixie, depositing me on the sidewalk like the product of an unleashed dog. By the time I got back to where I'd left Roberta, she was nowhere to be seen.

I was so frustrated, and angry at myself for having started to walk away from the woman, I could have kicked myself. A few minutes later that's exactly what I did. But first I walked across the street to White Point Gardens and sat on a bench, under the spreading branches of a live oak tree. It was near the spot where the notorious pirate

Stede Bonnet and thirty-nine of his men were hung in 1718. At any rate, before kicking myself, I removed my sandal.

"It would be more effective if you kept your shoe on."

I whirled. The love of my life was standing there, having materialized out of nowhere, like the ghost of Stede Bonnet. Other than his ability to appear unexpectedly, my beloved shares very little with your average Apparition American. Greg is flesh and blood, and the flesh is very well shaped in my opinion: long and lean, but still muscular. His features are reminiscent of Cary Grant, but his hair is blacker, and his eyes like the finest Kashmir sapphires. He was dressed now in a shirt the color of his eyes, white chinos, and rawhide sandals. It was immediately clear that he had just showered, otherwise the odor of fish would have announced him — either that or a flock of hovering seagulls.

"Darling! What are you doing home so early?"

"Goober got sick," he said, referring to a nephew who sometimes goes along as a cabin boy. "Abby, how about an early supper?"

"At this hour? It's not even four."

"Then how about a mid-afternoon snack?

There's a crème brûlée at Magnolias that's calling your name."

"Why did you say that?"

"What do you mean?"

"Why Magnolias? And why crème brûlée?"

"Because that's your favorite restaurant, and that's your favorite item on the menu. Or have you changed it again?"

"No, no. I thought maybe you'd overheard."

"Overheard what?"

I hate lying to the love of my life, but sometimes it just makes life a whole lot easier. "Uh — just some tourist. Darling, don't you hate it the way tourists show up in our white-tablecloth restaurants wearing shorts and tank tops?"

"Men tourists, or sexy young women tourists?"

"Beep, you got the wrong answer."

"Yes dear, I hate it. How about supper somewhere else?"

"Greg, I need to get back to work."

"Come on then, I'll drive you back. I'm parked —"

"I have my own car. Thanks."

"Hon, we need to talk."

"Later, dear? I'm really in a hurry."

"Abby, I have a confession to make.

Goober did get sick, but that was last night. I came back into port because your mom called."

The hair on my neck stood up. I stood up to keep it company.

"She *what?*" Mama knows she is not allowed to bother Greg when he is out shrimping unless there is a genuine emergency, or when she has gift ideas to give my husband. Since it wasn't anytime near my birthday, or Christmas, she could only have called about one thing.

"Hon, we can talk about it here in the park, where my emotions can run wild, or we can discuss it civilly over dessert, in a posh restaurant where I wouldn't dare make a scene."

"Crème brûlée it is."

Normally, whenever we go to Magnolias we request a window seat so I can people watch. Now I asked for the seat so people could watch Greg. Not that Greg is a bully; he can, however, blow things out of proportion.

We settled into our usual spot. I ordered coffee with my crème brûlée. Greg opted for a fudge cake and ice cream concoction and an imported beer. Under normal circumstances I might have pointed out that I thought it an odd combination. Now I simply smiled and asked to taste the beer when it came.

"Hon," Greg said, almost before the waitress was out of earshot, "did you really think you could sneak this one past me?"

"Hope can spring eternal in even the smallest breast, can't it?"

"Apparently. Now let's hope that I can help you clear up this mess. Please, babe, start at the beginning and don't leave out anything. *Anything.*"

I did as he asked. Magnolias has excellent service, so I'd finished my dessert before I was done with my tale. Greg, listening intently, interrupted only a few times, and never once pontificated.

"Those two are acting like idiots," he said, referring to Tweedles Dee and Dum. "They don't have a case and they know it. I'll speak to the chief and have this whole thing dropped by suppertime. I'll make sure Reuben assigns someone competent to investigate the skull, but frankly, it's a nonissue. Gorillas may be one of our closest kin, but they are just animals in the eyes of the law. And even if C.J. is wrong, and the skull proves to be human, there are any number of explanations for it, from *Hamlet* to a first year medical student. Sure, they'll run a computer check, but the odds are that they'll end up giving it back to you."

"Did you say *Hamlet*?"

"Yeah. I handled a case like it up in Charlotte once. The skull in question had been a prop for a high school drama department for as long as anyone could remember. Then one day some squeamish parent called the police, but there was nothing for us to do. At least not after the principal found a record saying that the skull had been donated by an alumnus in medical school — almost sixty years earlier."

"Wow. I never realized — *give it back?*"

Greg grinned. "I was wondering how long it would take for that to sink in."

"I don't want it back!"

"Then donate it to the College of Charleston Drama Department. They do a fair amount of Shakespeare. Sixty years from now some other squeamish parent can report it."

I shook my head. "That doesn't seem right. That was once a real person — or a real gorilla, or whatever."

"If it makes you feel better, we can have it buried. However you want to play it is fine with me."

Tears filled my eyes. How stupid I'd been for not calling Greg within seconds of opening the gym bag. But how could I have known he'd be so reasonable; more like a friend, or a husband, rather than a stern, bossy parent?

"Thanks, darling," I murmured.

He reached across the table, grabbed my hand and squeezed it. "My pleasure, hon." He paused, massaging the back of my hand with a thumb as coarse as sandpaper. "But you have to promise me two things."

I snatched back my hand. "Silly me. Of course there would be a catch."

"No catch, hon. I just want you to promise that you'll stop investigating this case."

Before promising I took time to blot the tears with a tissue. One of these days I'd learn my lesson and start wearing water-proof mascara.

"What's your second ultimatum?" I asked.

"It's not an ultimatum. I just want you to promise that you won't take any of this out on Mozella. She was just being a good mother. You'd do the same if you thought Susan and Charlie were getting in over their heads."

"I don't think so. I respect my children."

Shame on me. I knew that the use of "my" stung Greg. On the other hand, "our" would not have been appropriate since Greg had no part of raising my two children, who are now both adults. Two very nice adults, I might add. Yet someday I fully expected Greg to be the grandfather of my grandchildren. Remarriage, especially when children are involved, can be riddled with minefields, requiring one to tread carefully from time to time. Until now I'd always referred to my children as "the" children, hoping someday to slip in an "our."

Greg was silent for a time. "Well," he said at last, "do you agree?"

"Yes, sure, I agree. Greg, I'm sorry —"

"It's all right, hon."

The tears came again, this time in rivulets, and I had to sop them up with my cloth napkin. If I'd known I was going to cry, I would have asked for a back booth.

"I love you, Greg."

"I love you too," he said, and squeezed my hand so hard it hurt.

Mama felt so bad that she'd tattled on me to Greg that she stewed the dishrag — that is to say, she cooked up a storm. While I appreciated her effort to make amends, I was a mite put out by the fact that she invited my brother, Toy, and C.J. to dinner. Without asking me first!

181

"I didn't even know Toy was in town," I said, trying hard to keep the whine out of my voice.

Toy is my only sibling, and a good deal younger than I am. He is the Prodigal Son to a tee. Not only did Mama clasp this wayward child back to her bosom upon his return from the fleshpots of California, but she totally erased his slate of all his sins. Whereas my minimadre can tell you the exact date and time that I came in after my curfew that *one* time when I was a senior in high school, she has no recollection that Toy was repeatedly caught smoking pot in his bedroom, and that on two occasions she caught Cindy Lawhorn sneaking out of his window in the morning.

"Sewanee Theological Seminary just started their spring break. Promise you'll be nice to him, Abby."

"I promise," I growled. The absurdity of it all was laughable. Toy an Episcopal priest? That was like me trying out for the Olympic high jump team, for heaven's sake. I didn't for a minute believe that it was for Heaven's sake that "Wild Boy Wiggins," as his friends called him, had chosen this vocation. But whatever the real reason, Mama would never see it for what it was.

No sooner was I done growling than the

doorbell rang. A second later it opened, and Toy strolled in as if he had a right to be in my house. Hard on his heels was the irrepressible C.J.

"Ooh, Abby," she cooed when she saw me, "we were just talking about you."

"Nothing good, I bet."

"Of course — ooh, Abby, you're such a tease, you know that?" She gave me a bear hug — one she claims to have learned from a bear — and kissed both cheeks.

Instead of a kiss, Toy gave me a brotherly wink, which was a sure sign that high jinks would follow. "Abby, it was sheer genius what you did, suggesting to my sweetheart that she invite Wynnell Crawford to man the guest book at our wedding."

"But I didn't —"

He slapped me on the back. "Always so modest. That's my little sister."

"I'm your *older* sister," I growled.

C.J. was beaming. "I asked Wynnell, and she said yes. She's also going to make sure that the punch bowl stays filled. And the nut bowls. Ooh, and those little candy hearts."

I've heard that weddings up North are often followed by elaborate dinners and dancing. This is becoming a trend in the South too, but it used to be that folks were content with cake, punch, and a few finger foods. It seems to me that instead of spending twenty grand, or more, on a dress and a party, those footing the bill should spend the money on a down payment for a house. After all, fifty percent of all marriages end in divorce, and the chief cause of divorce is financial problems. But then who am I to comment, seeing that I am divorced? My divorce, however, had nothing to do with money problems, but everything to do with the fact that there were six inches of my ex-husband that could not be domesticated.

"C.J.," I said, "I'm really glad you've found something for Wynnell to do. And you'll have her sit up front in the church too, right?"

She nodded her leonine head. "Of course, silly."

"That's wonderful, C.J. Wynnell considers you her second best friend. Just between you and me, she was hurt to think you'd have a goat as a bridesmaid and not include her."

"Hey sis," Toy said with surprising sharpness, "you know that DNA test was inconclusive."

The next thing I knew C.J. burst into tears and commenced bawling up a storm. I'd never seen the big gal lose it, and I hope to never witness such a spectacle again. The loud rasping sobs drew Mama out of the kitchen, and Greg emerged from our bedroom wrapped in a towel. If only he had thought to bring an extra towel.

I have never in all my born days seen a continent human being lose so much water in such a short time. Fortunately my hardwood floors were sealed, and Toy was a practitioner of the manly, but disgusting, custom of using cloth handkerchiefs. He pulled one from his pocket that was the size of a small sheet and proceeded to mop his beloved's face.

"C.J., sugar," Mama said, patting her pal's broad back, "what did Abby do to you now?"

"Me?"

C.J. shook her head, but Toy was unable to keep up with her, so we all got soaked. To her credit, the big galoot was able to go from blubbering to lucid speech in two seconds flat.

"Mozella, it isn't your sweet daughter I'm crying about. It's Cousin Zelda."

"The goat?"

"That's just it; they did a second DNA test and it turns out she isn't a goat at all. She's one hundred and two percent woman."

"*And* two percent?" I asked.

"Don't even go there," Toy said quickly. "You don't want to know."

"I'm afraid I don't understand," Mama said. "If Cousin Zelda is a woman, then what's the problem?"

C.J. rolled her eyes. If I ever did that, Mama would slap me — gently, of course. I know that from personal experience.

"You see," she blurted, "it's an ancient Shelby custom to dress up a goat and include it in the wedding party. That way any bad luck will stick to the goat, and leave the bride and groom alone."

"You're joking," Mama said.

"Oh no, Mozella, I would never joke about something that serious. And now that we know for sure Cousin Zelda is a woman, I'm going to have to buy a real goat and teach it how to walk in heels."

Perhaps I should have minded my own business at that point, but I felt I couldn't. "C.J., I've been to Shelby, North Carolina, and know for a fact that most of its inhabitants are good, sane people."

Her lower lip stuck out so far it cast a shadow on her saddle shoes. "And what are you saying, Abby? That I'm not good? That I'm not sane?"

"No, no, of course not. What I'm saying is

that — uh, well —"

Greg, bless his heart, couldn't bear to see me flounder. "She's saying that she doubts the good, sane, folks of Shelby bring goats to their weddings."

"Yeah," I said.

C.J.'s lip retreated. "I can't believe Granny lied to me like that. She said it was a Shelby custom, and now I know it's just because she wanted Cousin Zelda to be included in all the family weddings."

"And so she can," I said.

"All's well that ends well," Mama said. "Who's ready for dinner?"

"I am," Toy said. "What are we having?"

"Lamb."

"Not a ba-a-a-d choice," I said.

14

On mornings he takes the boat out, Greg gets up promptly at four-thirty. I know this not because I hear the alarm ring, but because at 4:35 my sweet husband rolls our ten pound bundle of joy off his chest and onto mine. The bundle, by the way, is Dmitri. I'm nowhere as big, or generous, as Greg. After about five minutes of labored breathing I too roll over and make the poor cat sleep on the bed. Then I sleep until seven.

But the next morning I was awakened by Greg gently touching my shoulder. "Not now," I said. "I'm too sleepy."

"Hon, there's someone here to see you."

I sat bolt upright, simultaneously drawing the sheet up to my neck. "What is it?" I asked, panic racing through every nerve cell in my body. "Is it the kids? Which one? What happened?"

Greg managed a lopsided grin. "Relax, hon, it's not the kids."

"Oh God, not Mama! I told her not to stop taking her Lipitor."

"It's not her either. It's you."

"Me?" The older I got, the more realistic my dreams become. Okay, I wouldn't fight this one. To the contrary, I'd see just how far I could take it without waking up.

"Hon, I'm afraid I have some bad news."

"Greg, darling, scrap the bad news and bring me breakfast in bed, will you? My usual will be fine. Oh, and don't forget to put a yellow rose in the bud vase."

"Abby, you're dreaming."

"I know. This could be one of my better ones. Tell you what, when you bring my breakfast tray — oh shoot, I'm not dreaming anymore, am I?"

Greg sat on the bed and stroked my legs through the sheet. "I'm afraid not, hon. Detective Gaspar is waiting in the living room. He said that a woman named Roberta Stanley was found dead in her maid's apartment this morning. She'd been shot to death."

"That's awful! But what's this have to do with me? I don't know anyone named" — I gulped. "She's dead?"

He nodded. "Apparently you were seen talking to her by the seawall yesterday."

My heart skipped a beat. "And?"

"And the detective would like to ask you a few questions, that's all."

"Greg, I didn't do it! I swear."

He laughed. "That's one of the things I love about you, Abby. You're disarming, you know that?"

"Disarming, maybe. But certainly not diabolical. I don't understand why the detective would want to speak to me."

"Trust me, it's just standard procedure. They're trained to interview anyone who's ever known the victim. You never know what clues will turn up, and sometimes the clues come from the most unlikely sources."

"That would be me — the unlikely part, at least. I just met Miss Stanley yesterday. She works for Colonel Beauregard Humphrey. You know, the eccentric gentleman from Louisville who looks like Colonel Sanders, but his mustache drags in the mustard."

Greg's eyebrows rose a quarter inch. "Yeah, I know who he is. But you actually *know* him?"

"I only met him yesterday morning. He came into my shop looking for antique canes. It turns out he's one of the people who bid against me at the locked trunk sale."

"How did you meet the victim?"

The victim again! Greg has been off the force — he used to work up in Charlotte —

for a year and a half, and he still talks about perps and victims.

"I paid the Colonel a visit yesterday afternoon, to ask him why he bid in that auction — he sent her to bid for him — and when I was done talking to him, she followed me to the seawall. I told you that yesterday at Magnolias."

"I just wanted to be sure that was the first time you met her." I started to speak, but he lovingly shushed me. "In that case, you have nothing to worry about."

I never thought I did — until then. Moving quickly, I slipped into some capris and a T-shirt, washed my face, and dragged a brush through my hair. But I hesitated before putting on lipstick. Did I want to appear pitiful for this so-called interview, or as pretty as time permitted? I opted for pitiful. Let the detective know he'd roused me from the deep sleep that only comes with innocence. Besides, I certainly didn't want him to think I was vamping it up for his benefit.

I needn't have worried. Detective Gaspar was oblivious to any of my possible charms. He looked like he'd been up all night and was badly in need of caffeine. I coaxed him into letting me make a pot of coffee (strong enough to stand a spoon in), and after serving him, poured myself a cup. Greg, who'd asked to be present, preferred to nurse a diet cola.

"Fire away," I said pleasantly when we'd all settled in around the dining room table with our beverages.

"Abby!"

Detective Gaspar managed a feeble smile. "It's all right, sir. Your wife has a right to feel inconvenienced."

I kept my smug smile to myself. "What I meant to say, Detective, is that I'm ready for your questions."

He took a sip of black java. "This is really good, by the way. Not like the weak stuff I get at the station because we have to cut corners."

"Cutting corners results in an oval, in which case you should be drinking Ovaltine."

Greg groaned. "Sorry, Detective, she needs at least a cup before she comes to her senses."

"Make that a pot," I said. I have, in fact, had two-pot days.

"Ma'am," Detective Gaspar said, without wasting another second, "the first question I have is: what is your relationship, if any, to the deceased?"

Deceased? Greg was right after all. Victim was a much more descriptive term for a woman who'd been murdered. Decease was what one did when nature took its course.

"We had no relationship. I only met her yesterday afternoon."

Detective Gaspar scanned the sheet of paper in front of him. "Was this a business meeting?"

"No. She followed me from the Colonel's house to the seawall. She wanted to tell me something. She wanted us to meet at Magnolias."

"Do you have any idea what she wanted to talk to you about?"

"No — only that she said it was a matter of life and death."

I could hear Greg gasp softly.

"You didn't ask for any details beforehand?"

"She wouldn't give any. Look, Detective, this is a woman who hid behind a warthog's head to spy on a man she's been in love with since before you were born. Both of them are nuttier than pecan pies."

He jotted something down. "How long have you known the Colonel?"

"I've seen him around town a lot, but I only met him yesterday morning when he came into my shop looking for canes."

"Canes? What sort of canes?"

"Walking sticks. Apparently there are some very beautiful and valuable canes. I'm afraid that's something I didn't know anything about either until yesterday morning."

He jotted more things down. "Mrs. Washburn, how would you describe the Colonel's relationship with the deceased?"

"You tell me. You're the one with the spies." I put a hand to my face. "Oops. I didn't mean to sound quite that snide."

"Yes, you did," Greg said. He turned to Detective Gaspar. "That's one of the things I love about her."

"Yes, sir." The poor man looked anguished. "Mrs. Washburn, how long did you know that the deceased and Colonel Humphrey were — well, having an affair?"

"I learned that yesterday afternoon. From the deceased herself. Except that she was very much alive then. Detective, now I have a question for you. How is it that you know about my conversation at the seawall? Surely I wasn't a suspect then. I mean, that was before the deceased ceased to be, as it were."

I've no doubt that the detective squirmed inside his skin. "Uh — Mrs. Washburn, I'm sure you understand that I am not free to di-

194

vulge this information while the investigation is ongoing." He set his coffee cup on a stone coaster and stood. "But I do appreciate your time. And if anything occurs to you — anything at all — that may be useful to us, please give me a call. And thanks for some excellent coffee, by the way."

"She liked to flirt with sailors and knew some of the ships by registry."

"I beg your pardon?"

"We both like to wave at sailors. Sometimes they wave back."

Greg's grin dissolved with a quiver. "You do?"

"Well, it's such a harmless thing. It's not like winking at a man at a stoplight — not that I do that, mind you. I mean, a sailor can't very well jump off a ship and follow you home." Then, knowing that Greg was a teensy bit jealous, I added, "To make passionate love with you."

The detective, bless his heart, was clueless. "Are you saying that Miss Humphrey was a sexual addict?"

"Absolutely not!"

"Because I've heard of such things, Mrs. Washburn. And not just on Oprah Winfrey. These things do happen. I know it for a fact."

"Of course."

"Mama couldn't help herself — it's a disease, you know — but it like to tore my heart out every time I found a new one in the house. Imagine coming home from a ball game, and you're just a kid, and there's your mama with a complete stranger. It's no wonder Daddy left her. She always swore she'd never do it again, but then —"

"Detective Gaspar, I think Miss Stanley was only flirting with the sailors. She was deeply in love with the Colonel."

He quickly rubbed his sleeve across his eyes. "She was?"

"Does that surprise you? You've talked to the Colonel, haven't you?"

"I'm not allowed to discuss my investigation with a civilian," he said. Nonetheless he nodded to let me — and especially Greg — know that he had talked with the Colonel.

"Thank you for coming, Detective," I said. I meant it as a cue that he should leave.

Detective Gaspar needed no further coaxing. When he was gone, Greg came over and put his arms around me.

"You're amazing, Abby, you know that?"

"How so?"

"It's obvious that this Gaspar guy is a rookie, but still, you dispatched him like a pro. You sure you haven't lived a secret life of crime?"

"Pretty sure. Greg, do you think that's the end of it?"

He looked down at me with those azure eyes that are incapable of lying. "We'll see."

"That means no. It isn't fair. If Tweedledee and Tweedledum hadn't been so incompetent, I would never have ended up in the slammer with a hearing scheduled, which means I never would have met Roberta Stanley, and I wouldn't be connected with her grisly murder."

He squeezed me tight, and I could smell fish through his cologne. "The Tweedles are getting what's coming to them. You have my word on that. And as for this — well, you know I'll stand by you."

"Stand by your woman," I sang.

Despite what I've been told is a pleasant voice, I'm a terrible singer. Dmitri, who just emerged from the bedroom and had begun to wrap around our legs, took off to hide in the kitchen. My caterwauling also woke Mama, who stumbled out from her bedroom.

"What's going on, dear? Abby, are you all right? I heard the most awful sound."

"She started to sing," Greg said.

"Oh," Mama said.

It irritated me that Greg should betray me. At the same time I was grateful that he hadn't thought it necessary to reveal anything about Detective Gaspar's visit. But what really hiked my hackles was the fact that Mama had called my singing awful. She's a Mercy Member of Grace Episcopal Church. By that I mean every time she opens her mouth to sing, folks say, "Mercy, me."

"Whassup," Toy said, stumbling out of the guest bedroom, with C.J. on his heels. He was wearing only a towel, and all C.J. had on was an extra large T-shirt.

Whassup is that I was about to have a heart attack. My eyes bulged and my mouth hung open so long my gums began to dry. Finally I found my voice. Make that a mere fragment of it.

"What are you guys doing here?" I squeaked.

"Now Abby," Mama said, "don't go getting your knickers in a knot."

"At least I'm wearing knickers! Would anyone care to explain what's going on?"

"Go easy, hon," Greg said, which was like spilling gasoline on a fire.

"I said, 'Would anyone care to explain what's going on?' "

Mama grabbed her pearls and began rotating them around her neck. "Well, dear, you went to bed early last night, and the rest of us stayed up to play a couple hands of hearts. But I kept winning, and nobody wanted to quit, so we played longer than we intended. Then it got to be kind of late, so I asked C.J. if she wanted to stay over. And once I'd done that, I couldn't very well send my own son home that late, so I asked him to stay, and — say, dear, would you like me to cook breakfast? I'll make stuffed French toast, just like they serve at IHOP."

"I'll have some," Toy said.

I glared at my brother. "Stuff the toast! Am I to understand that you and C.J. shared a room?"

"Hey chill, sis."

I turned to Mama, the cause of this morning's fracas. "Mama, how could you?"

"How could I what, dear?" She knew darn well, or else her pearls wouldn't have been twirling at the speed of light.

"You never, ever, let me have a sleepover guest of the opposite sex. Not even Greg. Remember the time the ice storm trapped us at your house before we were married? You gave me the guest room and made him sleep on the couch."

"But that was different, dear."

"Yes, that was me, and this is Toy. He gets special dispensation."

"Why I never!" Mama tossed her head as

she gave her pearls a final fling.

Having spent nine months in her, and forty-nine years observing her from the outside, I knew that the final fling was a prelude to her flouncing off in a dramatic huff, her crinolines bobbing like buoys in a hurricane. What I didn't know, and never would have expected, is Toy would stick up for me.

"Mama, she's right," he said. "You do treat me differently."

Our mother's mouth fell open. "H-How?" she finally managed to say.

"All those years I wasted in California, parking cars for the stars, and never even getting close to becoming one myself, you sent me monthly checks. But when Abby got divorced and taken to the cleaners by that snake of a first husband, you made her get by on her own."

"I'm feeling faint," I said to Greg. He put his arms around me and literally carried me to the nearest Louis XIV chair.

Apparently Mama was also feeling light-headed because she crept to one as well. I love my mother dearly, and we are friends as well as relatives. Perhaps that's why I felt so betrayed by her obvious favoritism. And just how stupid can a woman — that would be me — be to not have suspected such a thing was going on all these years? That certainly would explain why, when I humbled myself one month and asked if she'd advance me some money for an overdue mortgage payment, she came up with a ton of excuses and finally refused. That was the day I decided to sell off my furniture, which, to make a long story short, resulted in me opening an antiques store. The Den of Antiquity.

From across the room I heard Mama's voice, but she sounded like she was talking into a tin can with a string through it. "— because Toy didn't have your survival skills, Abby. You always were so competent, so smart, so able to land on your feet. Toy, bless his heart, was always so — well, you know what I mean."

Toy frowned. "So incompetent?"

"Your words, dear, not mine. I prefer 'shiftless and irresponsible.' "

"Mama!" I'd never seen Toy this angry at our mother, not even during his bratty teen years. Then again, why should he have been? He'd always gotten what he wanted.

"But darling," Mama said, the panic rising in her voice, "you always seemed so needy. I was only trying to help. I was only doing it because I love you."

"You could have helped me by *not*

helping. You were enabling me, Mama. I'm forty-two years old and only just now finding out what I want to do with my life. By the time I graduate from seminary I'll be forty-five. I'd have a congregation and a family already if you hadn't loved me so much."

"Toy's right," C.J. said, which shocked me further. "Granny Ledbetter kicked me out of the nest when I was eighteen. Of course all them sticks and leaves were making my room kind of messy. Anyway, she gave me fifty dollars and told me I wasn't allowed back home until I'd gone around the world and had stamps in my passport to prove it."

"C.J.," I said gently. "Not now. Besides, even the tightest person I know, Ramat Syrem, couldn't go around the world on fifty bucks."

"That's what you think, Abby. I worked my way around the world. That's how come I know seventeen languages. The year I spent in Ulan Bator making yurts was the most fun I've ever had." She shook that massive head of hers and giggled. "Genghis — he's the first boy I ever kissed, if you don't count the cousins — taught me how to ride bareback across the steppes."

"C.J.," Greg said gently, "maybe you

should tell us about your horseback riding experiences some other time."

"Ooh Greg, don't be silly," she said. "It wasn't a horse I rode bareback, it was Genghis."

My friend and employee does speak seventeen languages, so she was probably telling the truth. Still, there is a time and a place for everything, and now was not the time to hear about nookie in Nepal, or Mongolia, or wherever Ulan Bator is.

"C.J.," I said firmly, "maybe it would be best if you waited for us in the den. This is a family discussion we're having —"

"She stays right here!" Toy was livid.

"Of course, dear," Mama said.

There was something in the way she said it that made me want to scream. Either that or grind my teeth to the gums. Since neither was an acceptable way to behave, I decided to slip outside for some fresh air.

I expected at least one person to protest my departure — no one did — but I certainly did not anticipate being tackled on my front porch.

15

Wynnell didn't mean to knock me down. She picked me up and brushed me off, apologizing profusely the whole time.

"It's okay, Wynnell. You had no way of knowing I was coming."

"Yes, but I should have been looking down."

"It's all right, already. Can we move on?"

"Where to?"

"Well, I'm off on another round of sleuthing. It seems that this time there's a body, and since I was seen with the deceased yesterday, I'm on the short list." I couldn't be sure of my list length, but I doubted it was long.

"Abby, I'm so sorry. I'm coming with you."

"Don't you need to be at your shop?"

"Ha! That's a laugh. Remember, last year you suggested to Ed that he might find helping out as a good way to fill some of his retirement time? Well, I thought so too at the time, but Abby, he's taken over. I would complain, but the truth is he does a far better job than I ever did. So far this year at Wooden Wonders sales are twenty percent more than last, and we've had zero complaints, and zero attempted returns. I hate to say it, but my husband could charm the drawers off a preacher's wife."

"I'll be sure to warn C.J.," I said. We both laughed. "Wynnell, I am so happy that things are working out. To be honest, I was feeling a bit guilty."

"Guilty? About what?"

"Well, I'm the one who lured you down here from Charlotte. I kept yapping about how Charleston was such a great place for antiques stores."

"Abby, I'm not a baby. Ed and I made the decision to move here as informed adults."

"Of course. I didn't mean to patronize you. So, are you ready for an adventure?"

"Ready and waiting."

"Eat breakfast yet?"

"No, I wanted to see you first. But come to think of it, I'm starving. How about you?"

"Good, I'm taking you to breakfast."

"Not IHOP again! Abby, I hate to have to be the one to break it to you, but what they serve at the International House of Pancakes is not haute cuisine."

"We're each entitled to our own opinion. But, just so you'll stop complaining, it's someplace I've never been, and it's on the beach."

"Great. It sounds like fun."

We drove in silence for a few minutes. "Abby," Wynnell said, "aren't you going to tell me who was murdered, and how you're connected?"

"Later. Maybe after breakfast."

"But —" she shook her head. "You know, Abby, after C.J., you're the weirdest person I know. And well, there's your mother."

"Me?" I was both startled and hurt by her comment.

"It's a compliment, Abby. I love you and your family. Ed and I come from such boring stock. We should change our last name to Normal."

"May I remind you, dear, that you once ran off to Japan to become the world's oldest geisha? You probably wouldn't have come back had you not encountered squat toilets."

Judging by my buddy's expression, she could dish it out but she sure couldn't take it. We rode the rest of the way to breakfast in silence.

The Island of Palms is a long, narrow, barrier island just to the northeast of Charleston, between Mount Pleasant and the Atlantic Ocean. True to its name, there are thousands of palms, and in the summer months thousands of tourists. But as it was still April, traffic wasn't bad, and we showed up at Marvin Leeburg's house just on the stroke of eight.

Judging by the size of the house, Mr. Leeburg's gym was doing quite well. Not only was the two-story house oceanfront, but it was set as close to the water as any house I've seen on that island. That resulted in a deep leeward yard with a horseshoe-shape driveway built around a multistoried fountain. Numerous landscape lights and lush sub tropical plantings promised dramatic nighttime vistas.

Wynnell peered intently out her window. "I've been here before."

"You sure?"

"This is Marvin Leeburg's house."

I stared at her in disbelief. "You know him?"

"I was at a party here once. The Rob-Bobs were here too. The owner, Marvin —"

"What kind of party was it?"

"Mostly antiques dealers. But a few celebrities: the mayor, some local authors, that really cute guy who does the weather — really, just anybody who is anybody."

"Thanks!"

"Abby, you were here, weren't you?"

"No."

"Sorry. I thought I remembered you being here." She tried to smile, but it seemed to stick on her front teeth.

"That's all right. It may have been just an oversight. I'm here now, aren't I? And for breakfast, no less."

"Does he know you're coming?"

"Wynnell! It's been a long time since I've done that." The trouble with having a friend who goes way back is that they remember way back.

"Just asking."

I won't deny that I felt a little bit redeemed by the fact that Marvin was indeed expecting us and didn't give the slightest indication of ever having met Wynnell. He was utterly charming, however, and had her eating from his manicured hand within minutes. And I mean that literally.

A well-appointed table was set on a screened porch from which we could both see, and hear, the waves. On a smaller table, set on casters, were several chafing dishes along with a bowl of fruit. Marvin picked out a bunch of enormous grapes, and before we could protest, popped one in each of our mouths.

"These are seedless globes. Fantastic,

aren't they? Well, if you ladies will excuse me, I need to dash in and get the coffee. Mrs. Crawford, how do you like your coffee?"

"Like I like my men — pale and weak. Oops, I can't believe I said that." Wynnell slapped a hand over her mouth.

Marvin Leeburg laughed, displaying deliciously white teeth. "And Abby, I do remember how you like yours; coffee so strong you can stand a spoon in the cup."

"Yeth," I said. Just one grape filled my mouth.

"Yummy," Wynnell said as Marvin's firm buttocks disappeared around the French doors.

"You don't mean the grapes, do you?"

She shook her head. "Just between you and me, Abby, Ed needs to see a doctor."

"What's wrong?" Ed had scared all of us badly, but me in particular, with a heart attack two years ago.

"Not his heart."

"What then?"

Wynnell's great brow waggled as she looked shyly down at her lap. There was a stiff breeze blowing off the ocean, and I feared she might become airborne, only to be dropped farther inland, like say in North Charleston, or Up Chuck, as some wag once called it.

"I don't get what winking at your napkin has to do with Ed being sick."

"He's not *sick* sick, Abby, he just needs help."

"Doing what?"

"Let's just say my shop's name doesn't apply to him."

Wooden Wonders? "Oh *that*," I said, finally getting her drift, before she drifted away.

"Sometimes it's hard for me to not look at another man."

"I hear you. Anyway, you've been married — like what — a million years?"

"It will be forty-two years in September. I can't remember what it was like before Ed started shaving his back."

"TMI!"

"What does that mean?"

"Too much information," a baritone voice said from the doorway. There stood our handsome host, a cup of coffee in each hand. "Don't mind me, ladies. I have no idea who Ed is."

"A talking horse," I said, thinking quickly on my petite patooty. "But that's before your time."

He handed us our coffees. "I don't drink the stuff," he said. "Always hated the taste.

But I keep a machine in the kitchen for guests." He gestured toward the serving table. "Please. Help yourselves. There's scrambled eggs, bacon, sausage, grits, hash browns, and broiled tomatoes. Oh, and biscuits."

We needed no further coaxing. Marvin proved to be an excellent cook, and until I'd eaten enough to satisfy a man twice my height from Dayton, Ohio, I kept my mouth busy with my fork. Meanwhile Marvin and Wynnell managed to discuss the relative benefits of Pilates versus water aerobics, while all the time feeding their faces. One of them talked through a mouth filled with food, but out of loyalty to an old friend I won't say who.

After receiving my second cup of coffee — which was pretty good, by the way — I got down to business. "I'm afraid I have some bad news," I said abruptly. They stared at me, silent for once, so I continued. "Roberta Stanley was murdered last night."

I thought I saw Marvin blanch. I'm almost positive I did. Then again, it could have been an extra sunbeam or two peeking from behind the clouds. Wynnell simply looked annoyed.

"I don't know why they make such a fuss about celebrities," she said. "I don't mean to be disrespectful at a time like this, but have you noticed that all the missing girls who make national news are young and pretty? And mostly white, as well? When is the last time you heard about a massive manhunt for an old, fat, ugly, African-American or Hispanic? Or just any of those things. I'm not familiar with the Roberta Stanley case, but I bet she was young and cute."

"Actually, she was not," I said. "And she didn't make national news. At least not yet."

"Roberta Stanley was Colonel Beauregard's housekeeper," Marvin said softly. "And probably much more."

"Probably," I agreed.

Poor Wynnell. She still didn't have a clue. Her face resembled a fallen soufflé — no, make that a soufflé that has fallen because a fluffy kitten landed on it. How does one tell her best friend she needs to pluck her eyebrows, unless she wants a career as a Mexican artist?

"Who is Colonel Humphrey?" she asked.

"A Charleston eccentric who is badly in need of a mustache trim," I said, grateful for the opening. "Don't you just hate it when people neglect their personal grooming?"

"I hear you, girlfriend. You might not believe this, Abby, but if I didn't trim and pluck everyday, I'd have big bushy eyebrows."

"You're right, I can't believe it. So, anyway, you do know who the Colonel is, right?"

"No. Abby, you forget, I'm merely a W.O.T.A. — a West of the Ashley nobody. You're the S.O.B. who knows everyone and everything." By S.O.B. she meant South of Broad.

"Sour grapes," I said.

"What?"

I picked up the bowl of grapes that had been sitting on the table throughout breakfast and handed it to Marvin. "You might want to stick these back in the fridge, before they turn sour."

He smiled briefly and set the bowl down again. "Abby, tell me more about Roberta. Who killed her, and why? How did it happen?"

"She was found dead in her apartment. She'd been shot."

"Isn't her apartment part of the Colonel's mansion?"

"I don't know. I've never seen it."

"Yeah, I'm right. I remember now. It's just off the kitchen house. Is the Colonel a suspect?"

I gave him what I hoped was an enigmatic smile. Having been thrust into numerous similar situations by fate, I have made it a point to study Mona Lisa's smile.

"Abby," Wynnell said, the concern in her voice palpable, "are you all right?"

"It wasn't the bacon, was it?" Marvin sounded equally distressed. "It was two days past the expiration date."

"I'm fine. I was trying to be enigmatic."

"Why would anyone want a disease?" Wynnell said.

"So," Marvin said, crisis averted, "are you going to answer my question? Is the Colonel a suspect?"

"I honestly don't know. But I think I might be."

Wynnell gasped. "Is that why I caught you fleeing your house this morning?"

"Yes. But fleeing might be too strong a word. I didn't take any clothes with me. Plus which, I left my cat." I turned to Marvin. "I came to see your legendary cane collection, but to be honest, I want your opinion on something."

"Shoot — oops, poor choice of words. Sorry."

"Yesterday I had a chat with Darren Cotter, the guy who owns the storage sheds. He gave me the names of the top five bidders, who, by the way, outdistanced any of the others. Two of those bidders just happen to have cane collections, and another sells them. Don't you find that a bit odd?"

He looked me in the eyes. His were, appropriately for the setting, green with specks of sea foam.

"No, I don't find that particularly odd. Cane collecting is a lot more common than you think. Darren comes across as an uneducated redneck, but he's really quite savvy. He knew the time had come when he could sell the contents, so he notified everyone he could think of. I bet he sent e-mails out to a hundred people. On mine he added a brief note: just the word canes and a question mark."

"I didn't get an e-mail; I had to read about the sale in the paper. But never mind that. You sound like you know Mr. Cotter."

"Every collector and dealer in the Lowcountry worth their salt knows Darren Cotter."

"I don't get it. Why?"

"Because Safe-Keepers Storage is the cream of the crop, as far as storage facilities go."

"But they're awful-looking. A blight on the landscape, if you ask me."

He nodded. "That part's a shame. But when Darren says his sheds are climate controlled, he means it. Each shed has its own thermostat and humidity controls. Want to store a mummy? He'll make it as dry as your mouth the day after a bender. Want to store some uncured carvings from a rip-off woodcarver in Bali? He can make that happen too." He paused to take a sip of fresh-squeezed orange juice. "Abby, did you count yourself among the five?"

"Excuse me?"

"You said the top five bids were put in by cane collectors. Does that number include you."

"No."

He smiled. "So let me guess who the other four are. The eccentric Colonel, the man-killer Claudette Aikenberg, the smolderingly beautiful Hermione Wou-ki, and the enigmatic Mac Murray."

I gasped. "How did you know?"

"Because I called Darren and asked him. I was hoping to make contact with other stick collectors. Turns out only the Colonel and Hermione are big on sticks. The Colonel, as you may know by now, is an irascible S.O.B., and Hermione's prices are through the roof."

"Are they also liars like you?"

"Abby!" Wynnell recoiled in horror.

"Of course since you're a liar, how would I know if your answer was true."

"Abby, apologize!"

Marvin chuckled. "No, it's okay. The lady has a point. Once a liar, always a suspect, right? But before I cop to being one, what lie are you accusing me of?"

"Yesterday you said you participated in the auction because of the thrill of not knowing what you might find. Something about fishing in murky water, I believe. But now you say you were tipped off that there might be canes in the shed. Which is it?"

He shook a long, deeply tanned finger at me. "You're really something, Mrs. Washburn. I swear, if you weren't married —"

"Forget about her," Wynnell snapped. "She already has a stud muffin for a husband." Then realizing that she had just spoken aloud her most private thoughts, she clapped a hand over her mouth in horror.

Lord knows I've been there. "Look," I shouted, pointing out to sea, "there's a whale."

Marvin jumped up so quickly he knocked over his chair. "Where?"

"About halfway to the horizon. To the left

of that container ship."

"I don't see it."

"It's there all right. Look, it just spouted."

"I'm getting my binoculars," Marvin said, and sprinted from the room.

He'd only been gone a second or two when Wynnell turned to me. "Thanks, Abby."

"No problemo."

"There isn't a whale, is there?"

"None that I can see."

Marvin returned panting. His was a large house, so he must have had a pair of the glasses close by.

"Has it moved?" he asked.

"I'm afraid so," I said. "It went under, and hasn't surfaced yet."

I waited patiently until he gave up trying to spot the phantom behemoth. "Okay, Marvin, which is it?"

"I don't know. I didn't see it."

"Forget the whale for a moment, Marvin. About the auction, were you tipped, or casting your line in murky water?"

"Both. You must have misunderstood me yesterday. I said I like to hunt — fishing might have been the term I used — but I didn't say that was the case on Saturday. I got the e-mail from Darren sometime last week, and *then* decided it was time to enjoy the thrill of the hunt again."

I wanted to call him a liar to his face, maybe even throw some scrambled eggs at him, but that wouldn't have been ladylike — oh the heck with acting like a lady. The truth is, honey really does attract more flies than vinegar. And I'd come to see Marvin's cane collection. In retrospect, I should have thrown the eggs.

16

Marvin's collection was displayed in what appeared to have been intended as the master suite. It was undoubtedly the largest room in the house, taking up, as it did, half the second story. Immediately upon entering the room I could tell that the air was purified. There was something else about it that made me immediately wary.

"Less oxygen," Marvin said, reading what was left of my mind.

"I beg your pardon?"

"Take deep breaths, through your nose, and exhale through your mouth. There is twelve percent less oxygen in this air."

Wynnell inhaled. "Why?" she said on the exhale.

"The idea came to me on a camping trip. I had some vacuum-packed meat with me, and I started wondering why it was it didn't spoil. Then it occurred to me that bacteria — that's what causes food to spoil — need oxygen to survive. But you see, bacteria aren't just in food; they're everywhere, in everything. I did some calculations of my own and came up with the perfect formula that still allowed me to breathe and dramatically slowed down decomposition in those canes that possessed biodegradable parts. Which was just about all of them except for one aluminum cane and one that is carved from soapstone."

I didn't know whether to be astounded at his brilliance or skeptical. After all, he was a proven liar.

"Have you run your theory past any accredited scientists?"

He laughed, which was a waste of precious oxygen if you ask me. "I'm an intelligent man, Abby. I don't need some narrow-minded Ph.D. to tell me I'm right. Just look around you. Everything is in tip-top condition."

I looked around. He really did have an impressive collection. It might have taken my breath away if the room hadn't done that first. In addition to having canes displayed in racks along the walls, as well as in glass-topped tables in the center of the room, Marvin had done a very thorough job of labeling each cane, along with its complete history.

"There's a man out on Wadmalaw Island who has a similar setup," I said.

Marvin laughed again. "Mac? Ha, I don't

think so. All Mac does is lower the humidity. Anyone can do that, using dehumidifiers from a home improvement store. But that isn't going to slow decomposition as markedly as using a dehumidifying system *plus* reducing oxygen levels. I'll swear by this. Ha, if I stashed a corpse in this room, I bet if you were to come back six months from now, you'd still be able to recognize him."

I saw Wynnell shiver and rub her arms. "I'm glad you said 'him' and not 'her.' "

It was definitely time to change the subject. "Which cane is your favorite?" I asked, having heaped as many compliments on him as my overtaxed brain would allow.

He led me to the center of the room, where a single cane occupied its own tabletop. The stick was nothing special to look at, just one continuous smooth piece of wood that didn't even have a handle, and there were random blotches of color on it, like spattered paint.

"This belonged to Michelangelo. It's olive wood. He used it to fight off dogs — roving, hungry dogs were always a problem back in the days before leash laws and commercial kibble. He took it with him everywhere. Those spots are drops of paint that fell from the ceiling of the Sistine Chapel."

"Where did you get it?"

Marvin, gym owner and all-around regular guy, switched into collector mode. "One doesn't 'get' a specimen like that. One acquires it."

"I beg your pardon. From whom did you acquire it?" Just to be on the safe side I affected a bit of an English accent.

My sarcasm was not wasted on him. "Scoff all you want, Abby. But it's that very attitude that separates you from the real players like Hermione Wou-ki."

"Ouch."

"But to answer your question, I acquired this piece from Count Giovanni D'Arroganti." Even the way he trilled his r's was impressive.

"I know this is a rude question, Marvin, but do you mind if I ask you how much this cost?"

"Not at all. We collectors live for just that question. Because of this piece's impeccable provenance, it's utterly priceless. But I'm willing to sell it for sixty-five grand. Table not included, of course."

"Of course." If sixty-five grand was priceless, then what was my house worth?

"It's funny," Wynnell said, "that Michelangelo would carry around such a simple stick. You'd expect it to be intricately carved. What if Count Whatever-his-name-was was making the story up?"

Marvin's nostrils flared. "It says right here that he acquired it from Cardinal Giuseppe DiGropa, who —"

"I feel faint," I said. "It must be the lack of oxygen." I headed for the door.

"Not so fast," Marvin said sharply.

"Excuse me?"

"Slow down or you'll get the bends."

I moved even faster. Once outside, after gulping air a few times, I began to feel better. Still, I didn't waste a minute saying my good-byes. Wynnell, bless her horny heart, didn't put up any resistance.

"Where to next?" she said, before we even got down the front steps.

"Back to the source of all my troubles."

Safe-Keepers Storage was just as ugly the second time around, but at least I was better able to appreciate its technical merits. Even from the parking lot I could see the giant air-conditioning unit, and a web of wires that undoubtedly had to do with other aspects of climate control.

Although Wynnell complained about having to walk on gravel, she kept up with me, and was looming behind me when I rang the doorbell. Darren Cotter answered immediately, as if he'd been waiting with his hand on the knob.

"Hey," I said.

His eyes twinkled. "It's you — the woman who is half an orphan."

"At least as of eight o'clock this morning. Depending on what Mama does the rest of the day — well, I could be a full-fledged orphan by bedtime."

"Abby," Wynnell said, clearly aghast, "never joke about your mama that way. Think how awful you'd feel if something did happen to her."

I know for a fact that Wynnell lost her mother when she was just sixteen. They'd had a fight that morning, over the length of Wynnell's skirt. My buddy had slammed the door on her way to school, yelling over her shoulder that she hated her mother and wished her dead. About an hour later or so, the police reckoned, a door-to-door salesman talked his way into the house. Wynnell found her mother in the upstairs bathtub when she got home from school. Her throat had been cut.

I tried to push the grizzly image out of my mind. "Mr. Cotter, this is my friend Wynnell Crawford. Do you have a few minutes to talk?"

The twinkle disappeared from his eyes

and I could almost hear him debating with himself. He sucked air through his teeth before speaking.

"I'd ask you ladies in, but I have a cat."

"Oh we don't mind cats," I said. "I have a big marmalade tomcat named Dmitri. And my friend, here, gets along very nicely with cats. Don't you, Wynnell?"

"Absolutely."

His blue eyes darted from me to her, and back again to me. "Yes, but this is a very large cat."

"Like a lion? Or a tiger?"

He smiled. "Not quite that big. She's a Chausie."

"Excuse me?"

"It's a new breed, a hybrid actually, between a domestic cat and the wild jungle cat. The jungle cat's scientific name is *Felis chaus,* so that's why this new breed is called a Chausie."

"Is it like a Bengal cat?" I asked. "I've heard of those."

"Same idea, but a different wild cat species was used in the founding of this breed."

"Why on earth would anyone want to have a wild cat in their house?" Apparently Wynnell's love of cats was limited to the domestic. "Isn't that cruel? And what about conservation of these species?"

"A lot of people are in love with the idea of owning an exotic cat," Darren Cotter said calmly. "So they manage to buy a leopard cub or lion cub off the Internet, and when it stops being cute and starts eyeing them for dinner, then they give it to a zoo, or just let the poor thing loose. The idea behind these hybrid breeds is to have an exotic-looking cat that has all the qualities of a domestic cat. Plus, it helps to raise the public's consciousness about the plight of wild cats, hundreds of thousands of which are killed every year for their fur, whereas only a handful are used to establish these new exotic breeds."

"Well," I said, "I'd love to see your cat. Does she, like you said, behave just like a domestic cat?"

He bit his lip before answering. "I may have stretched the truth just a bit. You see, it takes four generations for the inter-breeding to create a domestic breed. In this case, the Chausie. The one I have is only a first generation cross. That is to say, her father was a full-blooded jungle cat."

"But her mother was a regular cat, right?"

"Well — to be truthful, her mother was half domestic and half jungle cat. So she's kind of on the big side. That's why her name is Catrina the Great."

227

Math has never been my strong point, but even I could solve this story problem. "What you're saying is that she's three-quarters jungle cat, right?"

He nodded.

"Too much wild cat for me," Wynnell said definitively.

I could never pass up the opportunity to see such an exotic creature. "How big is she?"

"Sixteen inches high at the shoulder, but two feet high along the back when she arches. Weighs just over twenty-five pounds, although the males can weigh thirty-five. Come in and see her."

"I'll wait in the car," Wynnell said. The positioning of her eyebrows told me she was not a happy camper.

The first thing I noticed about the inside of Darren Cotter's house was that it did not smell of cat. Of course he read my mind.

"She pees in the sink. Bathtub too. In the wild they like to pee in streams, to move their odor away from them." He nodded at a red leather couch. "Please have a seat."

"Where is she? She's not going to leap at me from behind, is she?"

"No. She's probably sleeping on top of the refrigerator. I'll go look for her — but hey, would you like something to drink?"

"Diet soda?"

"Sure thing. Be right back."

No sooner did he leave the room than this monstrous creature came ambling in from the opposite direction.

17

Had I not been warned, I would have thought she was a cougar — well, maybe just a cougar cub. At any rate, she dwarfed Dmitri.

"Hey there, kitty," I managed to squeak.

Catrina the Great did not appear happy to see me. She arched her back to at least two feet and growled, a deep rumbling growl that seemed to come from her belly.

"Nice pussy. Nice puddy-tat."

She hissed at me, displaying two rather alarming pairs of fangs.

"Hey, that's not nice," I said, and hissed at her in return.

The next sound she made was more of an explosion than a hiss. Saliva drooled as she resumed growling.

"You really need to learn some manners, dear, if you intend to be a domestic cat."

The beast was not amused and advanced regally in my direction. Not knowing what else to do, I obligingly held out my hand for her to sniff. Her Majesty must have interpreted this as an aggressive move, because out flashed a paw. I jerked back, but not before she made contact.

The fact that I shrieked is completely understandable, I'm sure. At least it brought Darren Cotter back into the room.

"What happened?"

"She lunged at me. Swatted at me, too."

"Don't worry, she's declawed."

"Are you sure?"

"Positive. I had it done when I had her spayed. She was a kitten then so she recovered pretty fast. I wouldn't do it again, though."

"Don't worry, I won't get that close again."

"No, I meant the declawing. I used to think it was just a matter of removing the claws, but it's much more than that. They actually have to remove all her toes up to the first knuckle. And since cats walk on the tips of their toes, and not the balls of their feet, like we do, they are forced to walk on bloody stubs until they heal. They have to scratch in their litter with those stubs as well. Then for the rest of their lives they walk on scar tissue. Can you imagine having your fingers chopped off at the first knuckle?"

I shuddered as a wave of guilt washed over me. Dmitri was declawed, but back then I had no idea what it entailed. All I knew was that I didn't want my drapes and furniture shredded.

"Sorry," Darren Cotter said, "I didn't mean to lay a guilt trip on you. Most folks don't realize what it really entails. But please, keep it in mind for the future."

"Do you tell fortunes as well?"

"What?"

"You just said what I was thinking. Is it printed on my forehead?"

He laughed. "No, but you have a very expressive face. I like that, by the way. I can't stand the masks people wear."

"I hear you. But most of the time, those people are just trying to protect themselves, aren't they? Take your giant pussycat here, Catrina the Great. If she got sick, she'd do everything she could to not let on she was ailing, like hiding under the bed. If animals show that they are weak or vulnerable, they will be attacked by others. People are like that too, I think."

"You're right. I hadn't thought of it that way. So, Miss — uh — sorry, I've forgotten your name."

"Call me Abby."

"Then you call me Darren." He paused, regarding me for a moment with those blue Siamese eyes. "So, Abby, aren't you afraid of showing your vulnerability?"

"To be honest, I don't give it much

thought. But I hate public speaking. I wonder if that's the same thing?"

"It's the number one fear in America. Did you know that some people actually fear that more than death?"

"Wow. Well, I certainly wouldn't choose death over —"

I'd let my guard down for a moment, and now the cat was back. But instead of swatting and spitting, she was rubbing her head against my knee. Cats have scent glands in their cheeks, and by rubbing their cheeks against someone, or something, they are claiming that object as theirs. Marking their property, if you will. Now the monster, having given up on the idea of consuming me for brunch, was pacing back and forth, rubbing her cheeks hard against both knees, and purring louder than Greg can snore. Heck, this was even louder than Buford, my chubby ex, could snore.

Darren laughed. "She loves you!"

"I think she'd love to eat me if you weren't here."

"Seriously, Abby, she's never warmed up to anyone that fast."

"I'll take that as a compliment. Darren, I'd like to ask you a few questions, if you don't mind. Business related questions."

"Shoot."

"I'll start with the easy ones. First, why would someone, the person who rented shed fifty-three, for example, just walk away from their possessions?"

He shrugged. "That's not an easy one, because there are so many answers. Financial reasons, of course. Sometimes it's death, sometimes divorce. Believe it or not, some people just have so much stuff they forget where everything's stashed, or they just don't care anymore. But rest assured; if they haven't claimed their stuff within a year, I do everything I can to locate them, before putting it up for auction. But shed fifty-three was an exception."

"How so?"

"Because he'd been renting that space over thirty years, yet to my knowledge he never showed up."

"I don't understand."

Darren looked deep into my eyes, as if trying to get a fix on my character. "I normally don't discuss my business with strangers, Abby, but I feel that I can trust you."

"You can. Please go on."

"Well, Safe-Keepers Storage is a family business. My father ran it until he died almost ten years ago. When I took over — I was a lazy son who hadn't paid squat to the business — I found out that I'd inherited a bundle of headaches. Poor record-keeping was one of those headaches. And some things just didn't make sense from a business standpoint. Shed fifty-three, for instance, was listed as being paid up until the year 2000. After that, there was no record of monthly or even yearly payments.

"I managed to locate the original lease, but immediately discovered that the address and phone number listed were fake — no, I take that back. But I had to call the number a zillion times and finally got an answer; it was a pizza supply company."

"Do you remember the name on the lease?"

"Yes. It was Ken Yaco. One would think that would be an easy name to trace, but there aren't any Ken Yacos on any search engines that I know of."

I fished in my purse and found a pen and a grocery receipt to write on. "Do you mind if I take notes?"

"Not at all. I don't have anything to hide. Abby, if you don't mind my asking, why are you trying to trace him?"

"I'm just curious. I thought I might write a book about the antiques business. Of course then I would want to include some of

the more interesting things that I've encountered."

"I see."

But it was clear from his expression that
he didn't. It was time to gather my thoughts
and vamoose.

"May I ask you just one more question?" I
said, pushing my luck.

"Sure."

"Marvin Leeburg said you sent him an e-
mail hinting that there might be canes in
shed fifty-three. Did you do that?"

Meanwhile Catrina the Great was giving
her scent glands a real workout. When I got
home, Dmitri was going to be furious with
me, maybe even to the point of leaving a de-
posit in one of my shoes.

"Marvin," Darren said, "is one hell of a
nice guy. He's terrific at business, but still
manages to keep it real. As you probably
know, he's something of an expert on canes.
Anyway, yes, I did send him an e-mail telling
him I thought there might be some canes in
this lot. Sent the same e-mail to a few others
as well, including Colonel Humphrey. You
see, my daddy tried to keep a record when he
could of what folks were storing. Just to
cover his — uh, butt, so to speak."

"But that's unethical!"

"How so?"

"Isn't that like insider trading?"

"Abby, I'm one person trying to sell a bunch of junk that some jerk didn't care enough about to keep his payments up. I haven't committed a crime."

"Maybe, but still, it doesn't seem right somehow."

"Would you feel any better if I bought everything back from you?"

"No! I mean, what good would that do?"

He smiled. "Just checking. Abby, I can tell by your accent that you're from off —"

"You can?" That was disappointing. "From off" is anywhere other than Charleston, and particularly the peninsula part. Even though I am a South Carolinian born and bred, I will always be "from off." But ever since moving here I have made a concerted effort to exchange my charming Upstate accent for the flatter sounds of the Lowcountry. Proper Charlestonese, spoken by native Charlestonians, bears little resemblance to the pseudo-Southern accents of Hollywood. To my tin ear it is closer to the Tidewater sounds of Virginia, and yes, for some words, even Canada. That is to say, the word "house" is pronounced "hoose," and rhymes better with "goose" than any other word in the American lexicon.

"Abby, I didn't mean to hurt your feelings. What I was getting to is that some years ago, before you moved here, my daddy had a renter who fell in arrears for some years. Ha, guess I'm a poet. Anyway, Daddy knew he had some good quality paintings in there. Really large ones. Impressionist stuff. He knew that for a fact because he helped store the paintings — although I suppose the renter could have removed the paintings at night, or when Daddy was gone. Like I said, I was too lazy to pay attention to anything, or anyone, but myself. At any rate, when the time was right Daddy contacted dealers from around the area whom he knew handled Impressionist paintings and asked them for bids. Over 160 responded."

"And was there anything of value in the shed?"

"Absolutely, but it wasn't a painting. The police removed just under a ton of marijuana."

"Holy smokes! Or brownies, or whatever. You'd think who'd ever rented that shed in the first place would have kept up on his rent."

"He tried, but he was on death row in Texas."

"A very crowded place, I hear. So what happened to the pot — I mean, marijuana?"

"Whatever it is that the Charleston police

do with it. I heard once that they burn it someplace. I'd love to find that location and stand downwind."

It was time for me to go before the jungle cat wore my kneecaps to useless nubs. "Thanks for your time, Darren. It's been interesting."

A Southern gentleman — it matters not if he hails from the uplands or lowlands — always rises when a lady does, as well as when she enters a room. Darren did not let our region's reputation down.

"Abby, before you go, I'd like to ask you a somewhat delicate question."

"How to back out of your date with my mother?"

"What? No! I'm looking forward to it. But since I know what you paid for the shed's contents, do you mind telling me what was in there?"

Darren had not been present when I opened the shed. He'd handed me the key and then wandered off, presumably to give me privacy. Since I'd waited to open the gym bag, it was possible he had no idea what was in it. If that was the case, Charleston's finest had yet to interview him.

"Pornography," I whispered.

"Excuse me?"

I said it louder.

"That's what I thought you said. And by the way, Her Majesty, Catrina the Great, does not speak English. Look, Abby, I had no idea there was porn in there. It's time to fess up, though. Not all my units are rented by antiques dealers. I rent a fair number to anonymous people. Because the units are climate-controlled, a few of these people spend a suspicious amount of time in their sheds — if you know what I mean."

"I'm afraid I do. But Darren, don't you think it could be dangerous?"

"You mean blindness and hairy palms?"

I tried not to smile. "No, I mean terrorists. We are a port city, after all. The third largest in the nation. Terrorists could be assembling parts of a nuclear weapon they smuggled in on a cargo ship."

He fought back a smile as well. "No, I don't see it. If terrorists wanted to assemble, or even just to stockpile weapons of mass destruction, they'd rent a cheap apartment, or a house out in the country. They wouldn't risk a run-in with my security team."

Call me a fool, but he was going to find out anyway. I knew I might as well have the benefit of seeing his reaction.

"It wasn't pornography," I said.

"No?"

"It was canes."

"Well, so at least part of my memory works."

"But it wasn't just canes."

Darren rolled his eyes. "Fiddlesticks and damnation," he said.

"Excuse me?"

"I was brought up not to swear in front of ladies. Abby, you found the skull, didn't you?"

18

If I didn't close my mouth soon the cat was going to get my tongue. Literally. But it would be only a snack for a feline that large.

"Uh —"

"You seem at a loss for words."

"Uh — you're darn right! You know about the skull? You must, since you brought it up."

"Abby, relax. It's no big deal."

"Are you nuts? I mean — well, that's exactly what I mean. I might be in a lot of trouble because of that skull."

His hands were raised as in self-defense. "Whoa! I'd forgotten about Hortense, I swear."

"You knew her name?"

"No. I never even saw the skull, but Daddy did. He told me about it, but it was never written on the file, like the canes were. It's been years, and I forgot about it, Abby. I swear on a bag of cat litter."

Darren Cotter was driving me crazy. I wanted to leap up, grab him by the lapels and shake him. However, he wasn't wearing lapels; just a navy blue pocket T-shirt that accentuated a rather buff physique for a man his age. Besides, if I did shake him, Catrina the Great was bound to make mince-meat of me. Cats are not the most reliable of allies.

"There's no need to get your knickers in a knot, Abby," he said, which, of course, did not improve my mood. "Mr. Yaco was a sculptor. He bought the skull from a medical supply company. Well, at least that's what my daddy said. He told me about Mr. Yaco and the skull because Mr. Yaco had named it Hortense. That was the name of my daddy's sister. It isn't a very common name, is it?"

"That depends. In Dorset County, England, there are thirty-five Hortenses per square mile."

He smiled broadly. "You're sure of that?"

"Pretty sure. But it is a statistic, and sixty-five point three percent of all statistics are made up." I stood. "Thank you for your time. I'll tell Mama to be expecting you."

Much to my astonishment he reached down, grabbed the jungle cat, and hoisted her up unto his shoulders. "As long as she's up here she won't be making a mad dash for the door. If she ever got out, she'd be shot in a heartbeat. Some yokel would have his picture in the paper with her, claiming he'd shot a cougar. There have been rumors of cougars in the Francis Marion National Forest for years. No evidence, though. But it wouldn't surprise me. You can buy a cougar cub online. If you ask me, they should shoot the jerks who get rid of their so-called problem cats after a year when the cuteness wears off. A lot of people think they can just turn their cats loose into the wild and they'll be fine. After all, there are plenty of squirrels and rabbits in the woods to eat, right? And cats are great hunters. The truth is, the cats usually starve to death. A cat of any species has to grow up watching its mother hunt. No, I say shooting is too good for the jerks. Turn them loose in the woods without a gun, and see how long it takes them to starve."

"Amen and glory hallelujah," I said. I wasn't the least bit sarcastic.

"Wynnell. Wynnell!"

My shaggy-browed buddy was not in the car, nor was she anywhere in sight. Frantically, calling her name, I raced along the side of the parking lot that fronted the rows of buildings that comprised Safe-Keepers Storage. My only response was a shrill mockingbird.

I dashed back to my car. It was still devoid of a passenger. My heart in my throat, I began driving slowly back up River Road, in the direction from which we'd come. There was no sign of Wynnell. My pal has a reputation for being geographically challenged, so after about five miles I reversed my course for ten miles. At that point I'd not seen a living being along the highway with the exception of a limping armadillo. In desperation I called Greg.

"Yes," he said, picking up after the fourth ring.

"Sweetheart, I can't find Wynnell anywhere. Has she called you?"

"Abby, what kind of an apology is this?"

"Apology? For what?"

"Try the fact that you barged out of here in a snit and for the last two hours I've called your cell phone a million times and all I get is your voice mail."

Oops. I always turn it off at night for a bit of peace, and in the unpleasantness of the morning, I'd forgotten to turn it back on.

"I had it turned off, dear. And about that so-called snit —"

"Abby, I know your mother goes too far when it comes to Toy. But that doesn't mean I have to be your whipping boy."

245

"Greg! You are not my whipping boy. And I'm sorry, I really am. Will you forgive me?"

I meant it. But even if I hadn't, I probably would have apologized anyway at that point. I have found that a sudden, and complete, apology will disarm just about anybody. And once they are disarmed, and no longer gunning for you, it makes it easier to apologize for real. Therefore, putting the cart in front of the horse can be the wisest course of action.

"I'm sorry, too, hon. Dang, but I hate fighting with you. Are you okay?"

"I'm fine. Wynnell was coming up the steps when I *barged* out, as you put it. I had a breakfast meeting with a cane collector on the Isle of Palms and she came with. Then I went back to see Darren Cotter, the guy who held the locked trunk sale, but Wynnell wouldn't go in on account of a silly old cat. When I came out, she was gone. I couldn't find her anywhere."

"Hmm. I heard that silly old cat stands sixteen inches at the shoulder and weighs twenty-five pounds. I can't say as I blame her, Abby."

"Yes, but she's really a sweetheart — Greg! Is Wynnell *there?*"

"No, but she called. She said that she's

pissed at you for making her wait so long. She hitched a ride with a friend from church, and that when you apologize you should bring a dozen Krispy Kremes, still warm from the bakery."

"Then I'll have to buy two dozen." Krispy Kreme doughnuts on Savannah Highway displays a sign when there are fresh warm doughnuts to be had. While normally I can stop after just one or two doughnuts, if they are warm, I can eat to the point of bursting. "Death by Doughnuts" might well be my epitaph.

"Hon, just after you left I got a call from one of my contacts in the department. Tweedledee and Tweedledum have been given a two week suspension without pay. He also said he's going to keep an eye on Detective Gaspar. The guy is a rookie who's in a hurry to make a name for himself. He doesn't even want to stay in the area. Once he's made it, he's going to apply to the L.A. Police Department. Of course all this is on the QT. If you're ever asked, you don't know anything about this, right?"

"Right."

"Oh, and another thing. C.J. was right: the skull you found in the gym bag *is* the skull of a female mountain gorilla."

"Get out of town!" Having this confirmed

didn't bring the relief I'd expected. In fact, it opened up a very large can of worms. What other of my future sister-in-law's fantastic stories were true after all? Well, no matter what, I refused to believe that she caught Granny Ledbetter kissing Santa Claus under the stairs one Christmas Eve.

Greg, bless his heart, tries to give everyone a fair shake. "Due to a comparable size with a human skull," he said, "an amateur — I mean, someone without forensic, or anthropological, training — might temporarily mistake a female gorilla skull for human. But these yokels, Tweedledupe and Tweedledope, should have known better."

"I guess I should have left it alone," I said. "If my impetuousness was in any way responsible for Roberta Stanley's death —"

"Stop it, Abby. Hold it right there. I'm not going to let you assume any guilt. Her murder had nothing to do with you. And just so you know, my contact in the department said that the gorilla skull was not an unimportant discovery."

"It's not?"

"These animals, which are among our nearest relatives, have been teetering on the brink of extinction for a long time. Nobody knows how many there are. Maybe less than four hundred, which is barely a sustainable population. In my opinion, anyone who possesses a gorilla skull has some explaining to do."

"What if they worked for a zoo?"

"Then that would be an explanation. Abby, I'm not trying to argue. I'm just trying to be supportive."

"Thanks."

"So you're coming home now?"

"Well — uh, I thought I might stop at the mall and see if there are some good sales."

"And I think I'll paint the house green with purple polka dots."

"I'd prefer a yellow base color."

"Sarcasm doesn't become you."

"Greg, darling, love of my life, you know how I am."

"Stubborn as a blue-nosed mule?"

"Guilty. I wish I could promise to be right — H-Holy guacamole!"

"What is it, hon?"

"It's C.J."

"Our C.J.?"

"Do you know another Calamity Jane?"

"Where is she? Where are *you?*"

"I'm on River Road. Actually, I'm pulled over to the side. She pulled up right behind me and is getting out of her car. Can I call you later, dear? You know how she is. This may take a while."

"Take care," Greg said, and then hung up.

As they say, a word to the wise is sufficient.

19

I can't think of a single soul who would call me wise. It's not that I court danger; casual dating is more like it. I lowered my window, willing myself to be patient.

"Hey, C.J. What's up? Why aren't you minding the shop?"

"Up is a relative term, Abby. Up here would be down in Bangkok."

"Yes, but in both places you'd be side-stepping my question."

"Good one, Abby. I'm here to help you sleuth."

"Who says I'm sleuthing?"

"Abby, you can't fool me. You're like the sister I never had, but would have had if the pet store hadn't tried to charge Granny Ledbetter so much. I know you're trying to clear your name of Roberta Stanley's murder."

"C.J., I haven't been charged with anything, and even if I was, I wouldn't ask you to help me. I need you to run the shop."

"Don't be silly, Abby. Mozella said she'd love to look after things at the Den of Antiquity. You've got a really great mother, Abby."

The big galoot means well. If there really is such a thing as a heart of gold, I'm betting it's hers.

"Thanks. I'd be happy to have your help. And like they say, two heads are better than one."

"That is so true, Abby. But three heads can be a real headache."

I groaned. "Good one."

"I'm not joking, Abby. Cousin Tricia Ledbetter, back in Shelby, had three heads, and it was awful. They never could agree on anything. One time two of the heads decided to go to the mall, but the third one didn't want to go. Well, the two heads that were in agreement won the argument, of course, but all through the mall the third head kept shouting, 'Help, I've been kidnapped.' "

"C.J., bless your heart, gold or not, you're never boring."

"Thank you, Abby."

"But it's time to be honest. The last time you talked about your three-headed cousin, you said it was a he, and that his name was Merckle. So what's the truth, C.J.?"

She fixed her enormous gray peepers on me. "Abby, it really hurts me when you think I'm lying. Cousin Tricia and Cousin Merckle were sister and brother. The times when they got along they sang Gospel hymns in a two-person sextet."

"Sorry I accused you of lying."

"That's okay, Abby." She hung her own leonine, but very singular, head. "But before you start sleuthing, I have a confession to make."

I sighed softly. "Shoot."

"Well, uh — I didn't come out here to help; I came to talk about my wedding."

"I thought you had it all under control. And if not you, then Mama did."

"Ooh, Abby, it's not really the wedding so much as it's what comes after."

"You mean the bills?"

"No, the other thing."

"What other thing?"

Her large face reddened. "The warblers and wasps. That thing."

It took me a second. "You mean the birds and the bees?"

"Granny wouldn't tell me anything, except that I was found under a cabbage. I tried asking your mother, but she said all I needed to know is that a lady is supposed to grin and bear it, and that planning menus was a good way to pass the time."

How my mother had changed. Just a

decade ago, if pressed about her sex life, she would have claimed to be the world's first serial virgin. But now she was giving wedding night advice to my friend — wait a minute! That could mean just one thing.

"C.J., does that mean you and Toy — well, you know. I mean, did nothing go on between you two at my house last night?"

The massive head recoiled in genuine shock. "Abby, how could you even think such a thing? You don't think we'd eat supper and say grace later, do you?"

Much to my surprise, I knew what she meant. "No. But didn't you share a bedroom at my house last night?"

"Ooh, Abby, that would be wrong."

"But I saw you and Toy come out of the guest room together."

"Yes, but I didn't sleep in there. I slept in Mozella's bed. Really, Abby, you should get her tested for sleep apnea. She snores even louder than Uncle Ernst Ledbetter."

"So what were you doing in his room, and why were you wearing his T-shirt?"

"We stayed up real late playing Scrabble, and were both kind of sleepy, so your mama asked us to stay over. I tried wearing one of her nightgowns, Abby, but you know how tiny she is."

"Yes, three inches taller than I am."

"So Toy loaned me his shirt." She sniffed under each arm. "Frankly, Abby, your brother doesn't shower as much as he should. But after we're married I'll work on him. Maybe someday he'll shower once a week, like a man is supposed to."

"Once a *week?*"

"I know, that sounds like a lot. But I think men should shower more frequently than women, given the fact that they sweat more."

That certainly explained some things. Oh, well. While she trained Toy, I'd do my best to train her. That was an older sister's prerogative, wasn't it?

I smiled sweetly. "You still haven't said what you were both doing in the guest room."

"Ooh, Abby, you're always so impatient. I was just getting there. You see, I'd gone in there to ask Toy what he wanted for breakfast. He had a hard time making up his mind, on account of I said he could have anything he wanted, except haggis. Then the doorbell rang, and as they say, the rest is hysterics."

"I believe the proper word is 'history.' The rest is history."

"Not with you, Abby."

"Touché." It was time to change the subject. "So, C.J., are you ready to rock?"

"Lead the way," she said.

Fortunately, it wasn't far to Miss Sugar Tit's house.

Claudette Aikenberg was not in a sugary mood. Her eyes narrowed when she saw me. They became absolute slits when C.J. lumbered into view.

"So, it's you," she said.

"Don't worry, Mrs. Aikenberg," I hastened to explain. "I'm not here to give you a hard time."

"Whatever it is, you'll have to state your business out here on the porch."

"Mrs. Aikenberg — I mean, Miss Sugar Tit, your Royal Highness, do you know a woman by the name of Roberta Stanley?"

"Maybe. Gracious me, it is you, isn't it?"

"Yes, ma'am. Last time I checked."

She wasn't even looking at me, but at C.J. "Mutton Chops, please tell me I'm not dreaming."

"Why if that don't take the rag off the bush," C.J. said, affecting an accent I'd never before heard. "Tater Tot, is that you?"

"It is!"

Someone pushed me out of the way, and the two women flew at each other like a pair of highly charged magnets. It was the most embarrassing display of emotion I'd ever seen, bar none. It made Jimmy Swaggert seem like a stone carving.

I waited patiently. Eventually I had to put a little foot down.

"Enough. Isn't someone going to tell me what's going on?"

My protégé grinned so wide it nearly split her head in two, thereby giving her three-headed cousin's tale some credence. "Abby, this is my cousin Claudette Ledbetter Aikenberg, only back home everyone called her Tater Tot on account of — oh well, Abby, you really don't want to know. And Claudette, this is my very best friend in the entire world, Abigail Louise Wiggins Washburn. She was Abigail Timberlake for a spell, but I won't go into that."

"Lord have mercy!" I cried. I needed to sit down, preferably somewhere far away. C.J. was a pistol in her own right. Her cousin, I already knew, also had a mind of her own. Putting the two of them together must be the equivalent of drinking an ephedrine milk shake — not that I've ever done that, mind you.

"What's the matter, Abby? You look faint."

"Yes, maybe I should sit down. Excuse

me, ladies, while I go back to the car for a few minutes."

"Ooh, Abby, you're so silly. My cousin and I have a lot of catching up to do, and we don't want you to miss a single minute of it. Do we, Tater Tot?"

Miss Sugar Tit Tater Tot, or whatever she was now, did not appear to be as taken with the idea. "Mutton Chops, I know this woman is a friend of yours, but she's more annoying than a jigger bite where the sun don't shine. You heard her, she's here to interrogate me about the death of that old battle-ax, Roberta Stanley."

Any thoughts I had about sitting this one out vanished. "Who told you she was dead?"

The woman didn't even have the decency to appear cornered. "You're not the police, Mrs. Washburn. I don't have to answer anything."

"I may not be the police, Miss Tater Tits, but my husband is an ex-detective, and he has more connections than a box full of Tinker Toys. You can bet I'm passing this little bit of info on to him."

Pushing her cousin aside, she waggled her man-made bosoms at me like they were a pair of padded jousting poles. "Oh yeah? Well, my Granny Ledbetter wrote and told me that Mutton Chops has solved oodles of murder mysteries, and is thicker with the police than congealed gravy."

C.J. flushed. "Actually, Tater Tot, it was Abby who solved those murders. And how come Granny wrote you that stuff, when all this time she's been telling me that she doesn't know where you are?"

Miss Sugar Tit blushed, a deep pink that clashed with her red hair, but provided some much needed contrast for her diamond chandelier earrings. "Uh — maybe it wasn't Granny Ledbetter who wrote. Maybe it was my other granny."

The big galoot spread her legs and crossed her arms. "No, I don't think so. Your other granny was killed by a toilet seat when Ida Mae Rupert's house exploded due to a gas leak."

That took some of the wind out of her cousin's sails. "Yeah. Granny often warned Ida Mae not to serve her husband raw peppers. If I knew then what I know now, I would have sued that woman."

C.J., bless her heart, was not about to be distracted by flying toilet seats and hard to digest produce. "So why didn't Granny Ledbetter tell me where you were?"

"Because I asked her not to, that's why."

"But you're my favorite cousin."

"Mutton Chops, let's face it: you're a mite hard to take at times."

I could see the blood drain from my dear friend's face. "What do you mean?"

"It's not just you, Mutton Chops; it's the entire clan. It's Granny Ledbetter too. Y'all are so weird."

"Weird? In what way?"

"Don't you think it's weird that we have a goat for a cousin?"

"Cousin Zelda may not be much to look at, but she's as sweet as a piece of brown sugar pie. I'm getting married, you know — of course, Granny probably already told you that. Anyway, Cousin Zelda's going to be a bridesmaid. Abby, here, is going to help me trim her goatee."

"I *am?*"

Miss Sugar Tit snorted derisively. "You just proved my point. Heck, the only reason Granny Ledbetter knows where I am is because my mama tells her."

C.J. glowered at the woman whose empty beauty had won her trophies. "Come on, Abby, let's get out of here."

"No, wait," I said. "I still want to hear how she heard about Roberta Stanley's death."

"Yeah," C.J. said. "Tell us that."

20

The former beauty queen responded by backing up through the front door. "Get off my porch! Now! The both of you."

"You haven't seen the last of us," I said.

"I'm calling the cops!" She slammed the door.

By the time we got to the car, tears as big as wading pools rolled down my friend's cheeks. When a heart the size of C.J.'s breaks, it takes Hoover Dam with it.

"C.J., never mind her trash talk. She's Miss Sugar Tit, for goodness sake."

"Abby, you don't understand. When we were kids, we were closer than cats and dogs."

"Well there you go. I bet you hardly knew each other."

When she shook her head, I was drenched in a shower of salt spray. "Abby, honestly, sometimes I think you must be a little slow. Cats and dogs get along wonderfully when raised from little on. Trust me, because we had plenty of those. And that's practically how we were raised. On account of I had no parents, Granny Ledbetter always invited Tater Tot over to spend the summers. Sometimes even over the winter break. It was Tater Tot who taught me right from wrong. If it hadn't been for her, I would have grown up to be a hooligan."

"Somehow I doubt that."

"Abby, it's true. I was tearing tags off mattresses when I was only six. Once when I was twelve I lathered and rinsed, but I didn't repeat. Tater Tot made me do it over again."

"And it shows. I've always admired your hair. But C.J., I'm afraid it's possible your cousin, as much as you love her, might be a murderess."

"Ooh, Abby, don't be so silly. Tater Tot wouldn't hurt a flea."

"I think that's supposed to be 'fly.' "

"We had lots of cats and dogs, remember?"

"There are some who think she murdered her husband and dumped his body into the Wadmalaw River."

C.J. wiped her cheeks while she giggled. "You always were good at cheering me up."

"How does me suggesting that your cousin is a killer cheer you up?"

Giggles turned into snorting guffaws. With my pal momentarily distracted I backed out of Miss Sugar Tit's driveway and drove up Major Moolah Road a piece. But not as far as Mac Murray's tree house. If the ex-beauty really did call the police, at least I couldn't be written up for trespassing on anyone's property.

After a while C.J.'s snorts ebbed, as did her spirits. "Abby, you weren't joking, were you?"

"I'm afraid not. I have a witness who claims to have seen her dumping —"

"Abby, I mean you weren't joking about her being *married*."

"Of that I'm almost certain. She told me herself he was a big-shot lawyer. That's why she can afford such an expensive house."

"But we made a pact!"

"You what?"

"We were thirteen. In Granny Ledbetter's barn. We made a pinkie swear that we would be at each other's wedding. We even did a double Dutch toss."

"What's a double Dutch toss?"

"There were these two neighbor kids who were originally from Amsterdam. We threw them off the hayloft. Abby, that kind of promise has to be kept."

"But wait a minute. Until now you had no idea your cousin was living in the Charleston area. That means you were

263

going to break your oath as well."

When C.J. extends her lower lip she is the envy of four-year-olds and teenagers around the globe. "Okay, so maybe I wasn't going to invite her. You know something, Abby?"

"I know a lot. But apparently not as much as you."

"I think Granny Ledbetter was lying to protect me when she said that she didn't know where Tater Tot was. Just like when she told me Cousin Ordelphia died of pancakitis, instead of coming right out and saying that she got stepped on by a circus elephant. Because to tell you the truth, Abby, I haven't really liked Tater Tot since the day she was crowned Miss Sugar Tit."

"Do tell."

"The second the judge set that crown on her head, Tater Tot proceeded to put on airs. She didn't even want to associate with her kinfolk anymore. Especially the Shelby side of the family. Granny said that if Saint Peter gave Tater Tot a tour of Heaven, she'd ask to see the upstairs."

"I can believe it."

"And do you really believe she might have killed this Roberta Stanley? And this man they found in the Wadmalaw River?"

"Actually, the police never found a man in the river. Not this time, at least. They were called out to investigate, but decided they didn't have enough evidence upon which to base a search."

"Ooh, Abby, but they do have Roberta Stanley's body, and Tater Tot knew she was dead."

"I know. And that got me going for a minute, too. But the longer I think about it, the less important I think it is. A wealthy woman like your cousin has got to be plugged into a zillion gossip connections. And let's face it, you two have a lot in common."

C.J. gasped. "How did you know she has six toes on each foot? She wasn't wearing sandals."

"*You* have six toes?" Come to think of it, I'd never seen her in sandals, and I for sure hadn't seen her barefoot. Even this morning, dressed in my brother's T-shirt, she was wearing shoes.

She nodded, a wistful smile spreading across her massive face. "I was on the swim team in college. We made the national swim team finals."

"That's impressive."

"Those were the good old days. Abby, do you ever miss your college days?"

"Sort of, but not really. I met Buford in college; that colors things a bit. Anyway, the point I was trying to make is that you and your cousin are both very bright. I don't think she'd let that information drop accidentally if she had anything to hide."

"So what do we do now, Abby?"

"We — I mean, I — swallow my pride and solicit help from a real detective."

Greg could tell by the caller ID that it was me calling, but he still got points for picking up after the first ring. He sounded breathless, which probably meant I caught him on his treadmill.

"Abby!"

"Greg, I know I'm stubborn and have no business playing Sherlock Holmes. You are absolutely right not to want me —"

"Can we cut to the chase, hon?"

"I need a favor, dear."

"Abby, you're going to have to work things out with your mother by yourself."

"You're right. But that isn't the favor. What I'd like is for you to look in the phone book and see if you can find a listing for a James Aikenberg in Charleston. There might not be a residence number, so also please look in the yellow pages. He's an attorney."

"With which firm?"

"He works by himself, I think."

"Gotcha. What's this about, Abby?" Before I could answer he spoke again. "I know, it's a long story and you don't have time to go into it now and yadda."

"You need at least one more yadda, dear, and you're right, it is a long story. And I would really appreciate it if we could talk about this later. But in the meantime, did I ever tell you that you are the most wonderful husband in the world?"

"Every time you need a favor, hon."

"Right. I love you, Greg."

"Back at you, hon. Hey, before I forget, you got a message from a Ms. Wou-ki. That's spelled W—"

"That's all right; I know who she is. What did she want?"

"Something about you coming over to see her this morning."

"Was I supposed to?"

"Beats me. She didn't say."

"Shoot. I'm all the way out on Wadmalaw Island and —"

"She's on Kiawah Island, at her house. That's not too far out of the way, is it?"

"Her house? Why didn't you say so?"

"I just did, hon."

" 'Bye, dear." I hung up before either of us had a chance to further irritate the other. I knew I hadn't made an appointment to see

Hermione Wou-ki. If I had agreed to meet her at home, you can bet I would have been thinking about it all morning. I love seeing other folks' houses, the way they decorate, and the way they live. I think I was born that way. Mama said that when I was a little girl I'd go up and down the block asking to use the neighbors' bathrooms. It wasn't that I had a bladder problem, either; I was just curious.

Driving down to Kiawah Island would not be a problem, except for the fact that the barrier island community is gated. One can't even get on the island just to drive around without a pass code. This meant I had to swallow some pride and call Greg back in hopes he'd been given the code.

They say that it is natural to gain a few pounds every year as one grows older. Believe it or not, I've been very careful about counting my calories to prevent this, but have added a few pounds anyway. Therefore I must conclude that this unwanted weight comes from swallowing so much pride in recent years. I called Greg.

"It's 9857," he said, without even saying hello or waiting for me to ask. "Of course it's temporary; just for today."

"Thanks!"

"You're welcome," he said, and hung up.

Being justifiably annoyed is a luxury that must be savored. I had only a few seconds of this before the phone rang.

"Hello?"

"Hon, I forgot. You had another message."

"Oh?"

"It's your mom. She said she smells big trouble ahead."

"She always smells trouble."

"Yes, but she told me to tell you that this time she means it literally."

"Like how? I'm going to get hit by a Mack truck? Or maybe a grand piano's going to fall on me from a ten-story building?"

"Beats me. I'm just doing my part in passing it on."

"Thanks, Greg."

"Hon?"

"Yes?"

"This is going to sound weird, but I have a bad feeling this time too."

All of a sudden I also had an impending feeling of dread. It was the proverbial goose walking over my grave. A two thousand pound goose wearing army boots.

21

"Abby. Abby. Abby!"

I started. *"What?"*

"Are you all right?" C.J.'s look of concern was touching.

"No — I mean, yes. Sure I'm fine. Why do you ask?"

"You look as pale as my Uncle Fester."

"I thought he was an Addams."

"No, silly. That's just a TV and movie character. But come to think of it, my Uncle Fester was bald."

"Did he wear a robe?"

"Only in the courtroom."

"Your uncle was a judge?"

"Yes. Judge Knott. Have you heard of him, Abby?"

"I'm afraid not. C.J., I have to drive down to Kiawah Island. Would you like me to drop you back at your car?"

"No, Abby. I'm yours for the rest of the day."

I was afraid of that. Well, at least I wasn't going to be lonely.

"Oh crap," I said, thinking aloud. "I

forgot to ask Greg for Hermione Wou-ki's address."

"No problemo, Abby. I've been to her house oodles of times."

"You have?"

"Ooh, Abby, she gives the best parties. Do you know Tara Lipinski?"

"No." There was no use disguising the hurt I was feeling. And there is no denying that feeling hurt was really stupid of me, because I hadn't even met Hermione Wou-ki until yesterday, so I couldn't very well have been on her A list, now could I?

C.J., bless her heart, picked up on my feelings. "Don't worry, Abby, I'm sure that from now on she'll invite you to all her parties. And anyway, a party is just a party, unless of course Oprah throws it. Then it's more like a cruise — oops, did I say the wrong thing?"

"Absolutely not, dear. But at the moment I'm too busy recalling my fabulous weekend with Tom Cruise to pay attention. But when we get to Kiawah Island, and I need directions, I'll be all ears."

"Ooh, Abby, isn't spending time with Tom wonderful?"

"The best," I said, through gritted teeth.

The guard at the gate was very pleasant, if

a bit irritating. "Good to see you, C.J.," she cooed. "Where's that boy toy of yours?"

"Toy is invited to those parties as well?"

C.J. chose to answer the guard first. "He's interviewing for a position at Grace Episcopal Church."

"Wow," the guard said, "that would be so cool if he gets it. My aunt goes there, and I visit sometimes."

You can bet your bippy that as soon as we were granted permission to enter the stomping grounds of the rich and famous, albeit most were not as famous as Tara Lipinski and Tom Cruise, I was on C.J. like a hen on a June bug.

"What do you mean Toy is interviewing for rector of Grace Church? He hasn't even graduated from seminary yet. And do you *really* know Tom?"

"Ooh, Abby, don't be silly. Toy isn't applying to be rector. But eventually when he is ordained as a deacon, he will need a church to spend his apprenticeship in, and he wants it to be Grace. Then who knows? Maybe he *will* be rector of Grace Episcopal Church someday. Wouldn't that be wonderful?"

"Weird is more like it," I said. "Then my mother will have to call her son Father."

C.J. giggled. "Maybe I should call him

father too. And so should you."

It was time to change the subject. "So what about Tom? Do you party at his house a lot? Can you show it to me?"

"Abby, Tom doesn't live on Kiawah Island. Toy and I see him — oops, turn here."

"But you said —"

"Now turn left."

I did as C.J. directed, and after going through a second gate, soon found myself on a part of Kiawah Island that I never knew existed. The part of the island I was familiar with was home to the merely "comfortable." That this new enclave was the playground of the fabulously wealthy was driven home when I passed a new Mercedes with the Merry Maids logo on the side.

"Abby, you better put your tongue back in before it gets caught in the steering wheel. That happened to Cousin Cornelius Culpepper once —"

"Where do these folks get their money?" I moaned.

C.J. shrugged. "Abby, you really wouldn't want to live this way, would you?"

"Try me."

"But just think. They've probably never been to Wal-Mart, or Arby's, or to a garage sale. Think of all the fun they've missed."

I stopped thinking about this fun when C.J. directed me to turn onto a property that looked like the movie set of Tara — and not the Lipinski variety — before the Yankees burned it down. Of course Scarlett's family didn't have their own helicopter pad.

I gave C.J. the honor of ringing the doorbell. Just as I had reached the conclusion no one was home, despite the plethora of cars, the door was opened by a butler in full livery who looked like he chewed nails as a hobby. But one glance at C.J. and his dour features rearranged themselves into an almost handsome visage.

"Good morning, miss." He caught sight of me. "Deliveries around to the back door, please."

"Ooh, you're so silly, Rufus. This is my best friend, Abby. We're hear to see Hermione."

"Ah, yes. You must be Mrs. Timbersnake," he said.

"Actually, it's — close enough. But now it's Washburn. I save Timbersnake for my business dealings."

"I believe that's why you're here, madam."

"Yes, of course." If it wasn't for the fact that I was a lady, I might well have kicked him in the ankles.

Lurch — or Rufus — or whoever he was, led the way through cavernous rooms kept cool by thick velvet drapery and furnished in early Victorian style in the English mode. If I caught a glimpse of the stout monarch herself, it would take a few seconds for me to register surprise.

Noticeably absent was anything Oriental. There was not even the occasional Chinese vase, something that would have been quite at home in the rather eclectic collections of that period. Since my mind was obviously getting easier to read as the day progressed, the dimness of these great rooms did not pose a challenge to C.J.

"Her mother was English," she whispered, "and so was Mr. Wou-ki's grandmother. Trust me, Abby, their California home is very Chinese."

"Keep reading, dear, you're not done."

"Of course she doesn't have to work, silly. She works because she enjoys it. Wouldn't you want to keep busy even if you didn't have to?"

"Charities, or fun busy?"

"Hermione does lots of stuff for charity, Abby. But just like you might want to go bowling for fun, Hermione likes running her shop. That's what makes it so successful. Antiques are her passion, not just her business."

"Bowling? I haven't been bowling in thirty years."

"Granny and I used to bowl with cabbages," C.J. said wistfully. "Then one day Cousin Cole Ledbetter came to visit, and while Granny and I were off to church, he shot up all the cabbages with his double gauge shotgun. Splintered them all over the place. Granny was very practical, and when she saw all those shredded cabbages, she mixed what she could with mayonnaise and served it for Sunday dinner. 'Cole's Slaughter,' she called her recipe. Well, the pastor and his family were eating with us that day, and before you know it everyone in Shelby was wanting to try this new dish. Soon everyone with a shotgun, and even a couple of people with axes, were busting up their cabbages. Over the years the name got changed to Cole's Slaught and then finally coleslaw. You can bet Granny about hit the roof when she learned that someone had sent her recipe into lots of different cookbooks and not given her credit."

Rufus stopped abruptly, causing C.J. to plow into him, and me into her. Fortunately we all remained standing, so no real damage was done.

He cleared his throat. "Miss Cox and Mrs. Timbersnake to see you, madam."

I peered around two sets of elbows. What I saw made me gasp.

22

Hermione Wou-ki sat resplendent on a green and gold sofa on the far side of a palatial room. Perhaps it was a ballroom. She was wearing a shimmering, pink silk pantsuit, and her thick, dark hair cascaded free over her shoulders. Her porcelain face and hands gave the impression that one was looking at a doll. A very large and expertly crafted doll. At this great distance that might well have been what I was looking at.

"Ah yes," she said, "please come in."

Rufus, who was as powerfully built as a Neanderthal, managed to slip around us and disappear, all in the blink of an eye. As C.J. and I crossed the polished hardwood floor, my nervousness escalated. I felt like I was approaching the queen.

C.J. did not share my state of mind. "Hey Hermione," she said, her loud voice echoing in the sparsely furnished room, "did you get the invitation yet?"

"To your wedding? Yes, how lovely. Unfortunately, C.J., I'll be in England then. Prince Harry has a significant birthday coming up, and after all, I am his god-mother."

C.J. squealed with excitement. "Give him hugs and kisses from his Auntie C.J."

Auntie C.J. indeed! It's one thing to have a trolley that skips the tracks every now and then, but to have one capable of getting airborne for bizarre flights of fancy is downright admirable. I was going to have to get a list of the big gal's meds and see if my doc would prescribe me the same. If that didn't work, I would try and steal her address book.

"I sure will," Hermione said with a straight face. She turned to face me. "And how are you today?"

"Would you like to hear the polite, Southern version, or the wicked unvarnished truth?"

She patted the sofa beside her as she laughed. "Come, sit with me. C.J., be a darling and pull up a chair for yourself."

My buddy had to walk practically the length of a football field to get a chair, but she did so without complaining. Hermione made good use of that time.

"I expected you to come alone," she whispered.

"But I thought you liked C.J."

"I do. However, this is a very delicate matter. Can she be trusted?"

"Absolutely. I'd trust her with my life."

"What about *my* life? Can she be counted on not to gossip?"

"Sure. But you'll have to tell her it's not for anyone else's ears. No, be more direct than that. C.J. is very literal."

That was an understatement. Once, I sent my assistant to an estate sale to buy a particular French commode I'd seen listed in the inventory list that was published in the *Post and Courier*. My instructions were that she buy the piece at all cost.

She did just that, paying three times what the commode was worth for resale. This shocked me because normally the big galoot is a savvy businesswoman. But instructions are instructions, and I was counting on her to bring the piece home. I might have remained annoyed at her for a long time had it not been for that fact that as I was cleaning the commode I discovered a "secret" drawer that contained a bundle of letters, tied up with a rose-colored ribbon.

The letters, written in 1848, were to a prominent Charleston housewife from her lover, an escaped slave who managed to find his way north to Pennsylvania. I offered this treasure trove to the housewife's descendants, who currently live in Charleston. They wanted nothing to do with the letters, and threatened to sue if I even implied to anyone that they might be descended from this escaped slave. So vehemently did they deny any connection that I concluded they were, indeed, the product of this unorthodox union.

Eventually I put the letters up for sale at an auction house, with an international reputation, in New York City. There the letters fetched three times what I had to pay for the commode. Thanks to C.J. It was literally found money.

When my big-spending employee returned with a chair, Hermione Wou-ki wasted no time in getting down to business. "I assume you've both heard that Roberta Stanley was murdered."

"Yes, ma'am," we said in unison.

"Abby — I believe you gave me leave to call you by your first name?" Her voice rose at the end, forming a question out of what sounded like a statement. Perhaps Hermione was secretly a Canadian. I've heard there are a great number of Canadians living in stealth in this country. Someone even suggested to me that these hidden Canadians are planning to take over the U.S. and turn it into their country's eleventh province.

"By all means," I said.

"I understand that you are a sleuth, as well as a collector who is held in high esteem by her colleagues." Again the rising inflection.

"I am? I mean, they really say that?" I was turning into a Canadian as well. A couple of *"eh's"* and I would be totally assimilated.

"Abby, in this business tongues wag all the time. Fortunately for you, they wag in admiration."

"Wow. Who would have thought?" Wisely, I took a moment to bask in the good news. Good news, like a really tasty fortune cookie, is a rarity in my experience.

"Cousin Dewlap changed his skin every year," C.J. said, apropos of nothing.

"That was your Cousin Monty Python," I said, and gave her the Timberlake glare. That glare, and my two beautiful children, were all I got out of my twenty year marriage to Buford.

Hermione knew just as well as I did that having C.J. in the room would prolong any conversation. "C.J., would you be a dear and see if you could help Rufus bring us a spot of tea? Oh, and bring those shortbread biscuits Abby is so fond of."

"Sure thing," C.J. said, and clomped out of the room just as cheerfully as if she'd been invited on a picnic.

"Gotta love her," I said. I meant it.

"Yes, she is very special. Abby, I wish you'd come here by yourself — but never mind. It's too late now. You see, dear, I have reason to believe that I'm next."

"Next to what?"

Her eyes flickered impatiently, but her voice remained cultured, under control. "The next to die, Abby."

I leaned toward her, so as not to miss a word. "You mean like Roberta?"

She nodded. "Hopefully not *just* like Roberta. That is too gruesome to contemplate. I've never been a fan of violent death Twenty-three lifetimes ago — or was it just twenty-two — I was thrust into the Roman coliseum, my hands tied behind my back. There were a bunch of us; all Christian, all women and children. And five hungry lions. That, I remember clearly." A faraway look glazed her eyes. I waited patiently, long enough for the lions to satiate their hunger, before she shook her head, returning to planet Earth. "Sleeping pills in my tea would be much preferred," she said, without a trace of embarrassment.

"So you know who the killer is?"

"I haven't a clue. I was hoping you could help me with that. All I have is a possible motive, and I daresay it's not a very good one."

"And that would be?"

"Because of my connection to Beauregard."

Beauregard? Did I detect familiarity that went beyond the usual shopkeeper/client relationship?

"Could you please elaborate," I said.

"Colonel Humphrey — except that he wasn't a Kentucky colonel back then — was a world-class big game hunter. Some people think it takes guts to hunt a tiger, but I think all it takes is tiny nuts, if you'll pardon me being so crass. Yes, the animals are dangerous — there's no denying that — but in the end the hunter has a gun, something a tiger never has. In my opinion people who hunt large animals that they won't be eating themselves are trying to compensate for feeling powerless in other areas of their lives.

"Anyway, before he took up hunting in Africa, Colonel Humphrey hunted tigers in India and Burma, and rhinos in Sumatra. My father was a broker for traditional Chinese pharmacists, and hunters from all the world would come to his office and sell various animal body parts that were, and still are, in demand. Bear feet, rhino horns, tiger bones, even tiger penises." She paused to catch her breath. "Do you know how much a tiger penis can go for to the right buyer?"

I shook my head. I'd done my share of dozing off during college, but I doubt that this subject had been touched on in any of my courses. I'm almost positive I would have woken up for that.

"At least three thousand dollars. In Taiwan there are restaurants that sell tiger penis soup. Wealthy old men eat this soup believing that it will cure their impotence. The tigers they prefer are from northern China, from the Amur River region. There are about only three hundred of these tigers left. It frustrates me to no end that these adult men can't see beyond their immediate desires. When the last of these tigers is slaughtered, then what will they do?"

"Buy Viagra?"

Her laughter contained no mirth. "Conservationists have been trying to pound that lesson home to them, but without much success. The traditionalists say that this is how it has been done for thousands of years, and that the West simply doesn't understand. But understand what? Annihilation of a species? I span two cultures, Abby. Unfortunately, I can see both sides."

"Why is that unfortunate?"

"Isn't it easier to see everything in black and white? I have just as much faith in Chinese medicine as I do Western, or so-called modern, medicine. I know of so many cases in which patients did not respond to modern medicine but were cured by Eastern practitioners."

"Yes," I said, "but things are changing. I think both traditions are becoming open to examining what the other has to offer. Take acupuncture as one example: many pain management clinics in the West now have acupuncturists on staff."

"That's good. But I think it's easier to accept new ways than to disregard old ways. Wild tigers, I think, are doomed. My father is dead now, but I like to think he would have seen the handwriting on the wall and gone into a less destructive occupation. Which brings me back to Beauregard."

"It does?"

"Abby, Beauregard claims to have repented from his wholesale slaughter ways. My, that is a mouthful. Anyway, I think it's possible he may possess knowledge of some black-marketing in endangered species, and that's why his lover was killed."

"So Roberta was telling the truth. They really are — were — lovers!"

"My dear, surely this does not come as a

surprise. Everyone in Charleston knows this."

"Not everyone. I bet the man who cleans the restrooms at the bus station doesn't know."

She looked perplexed, rather than annoyed. For women like Hermione Wou-ki, "everyone" does not mean *everyone*. Instead, it pertains to all the folks who are at her social-economic level. To be brutally honest, my "everyone" doesn't include the Trailways janitor either.

"I'm sorry," I said. "I was nitpicking. At any rate, I don't understand how it is that your father's business connection with the Colonel has anything to do with Roberta Stanley's death, or you being 'next', as you put it."

Before she had time to explain the obvious to my dim-witted self, we both heard a rather lively conversation between C.J. and Rufus as they approached from the hallway. Hermione leaned so close that her lips almost touched my ear.

"Abby, if anything happens to me, then you'll be next."

"I beg your pardon?"

"These people — the smugglers — have a lot of power. More than you can imagine."

23

A second later C.J. entered the room bearing a silver tray loaded with tea things. Rufus was nowhere to be seen.

"Oh, don't stop on my account," the big galoot said. "Who am I to judge? But Abby, don't you think you should ask Greg if it's all right with him if Hermione kisses you?"

I can't always think fast on my feet, so it was a good thing I was sitting on the sofa. "You're absolutely right, C.J. Hermione, we're going to have to put our affair on hold until I've had a chance to tell Greg."

Worldly woman that she was, Hermione smiled. "Abby, I believe you take cream, and C.J., if memory serves me right, you take both. Something about your granny having invented cottage cheese that way while having tea with the Queen at Buckingham Palace."

"Yes, ma'am," C.J. said, "but back then it was called palace cheese. It wasn't until Granny Ledbetter took the idea back to Shelby that folks started calling it cottage cheese."

I'd heard this story so many times I was beginning to think it was true. "Hermione, do me a favor, and don't ask C.J. how farmer's cheese got its name. Swiss cheese either."

She nodded, her eyes twinkling. "Please, ladies. Help yourselves to the pastries. These are savory — miniature quiche — and these, I believe, are sweet. Let's see, this looks like almond paste, and here we have various Danish, and, oh, look at these strawberry tarts. I have never tasted strawberries as delicious as the ones grown locally. They have got to be the best in the world."

Hermione was right. Lowcountry strawberries are unparalleled, not only in my opinion, but in the minds of the thousands of people who can be seen bent at the waist in "you pick 'em" fields every spring. Perhaps it has something to do with the warm sunny days and cool nights that accompany strawberry season in this climate.

At any rate, just the sight of the strawberry tarts made me salivate, and they were the first thing I reached for. Ditto for C.J. and Hermione. C.J. and I practically inhaled our tarts, but Hermione popped one in her mouth and chewed twice before turning the color of that luscious fruit.

"C.J.," I said, "I think she might be choking."

Hermione nodded vigorously, all the while slapping her chest.

"I'm calling 911," I said, and reached for my cell.

In the meantime the big galoot had gotten out of her chair, picked Hermione off the sofa, and put her arms around the woman's diaphragm. The next thing I knew a strawberry flew across the room with the force of a speeding bullet. Hermione grunted, then moaned loudly.

"I think you might have broken one of her ribs," I said, and punched 911 even though the crisis had passed.

"Yeah," C.J. said, "that does tend to happen with me."

"What do you mean? Is this a regular occurrence?"

"I can't help it, Abby. Granny always said I didn't know my own strength. Which is why I got banned from the Annual Shelby Car Toss."

"The what toss?" I asked, only half paying attention. Hermione's face was returning to its normal color, and I was beginning to wonder if the emergency folks were going to be cross with me for having issued a false alarm.

"Abby," C.J. said, no longer the least bit concerned about our hostess, "Shelby isn't nearly as big as Charleston, but to tell you the truth, Shelby is a whole lot more exciting. Y'all have Spoleto, but we have the Annual Car Toss. And even then, the toss isn't an official event, but just something we locals do for fun.

"Anyway, the first time Granny took me to the toss, I registered as a contestant. Of course folks teased me because I was the only girl to do so. And of course they insisted that I, being the only girl registered, had to go first. So I got down there on the field — we use the high school football field — grabbed the front of the car with my right hand, and tossed it over my left shoulder. It wasn't hard at all, because that silly old car didn't even have an engine in it.

"At any rate, you should have heard all the hollering and complaining, folks saying that I cheated, on account of I used only one hand, and was ten, instead of twelve, which is the official minimum age for contestants. But I knew what was really going on."

"What?" Hermione asked. She seemed to have totally recovered.

"They were embarrassed, that's what. You see, most men can't lift the front of the car but a few inches off the ground, and here

I was actually tossing it. But y'all, they shouldn't have the word 'toss' as part of the name if they don't want you to actually do it. And as for that other little thing — well, if you ask me, Coach Shafor should have known to duck."

"Yes, he should have," Hermione said with a laugh. "That reminds me of the time I went kayaking in northern India. It was just me, the Dalai Lama, Prince Philip, and — Shhh! I hear something. It must be Rufus. Ladies, forgive me if I must again appear as a pompous ass."

Wailing sirens was all anyone heard for the next few minutes.

C.J. and I slipped out while the paramedics rushed in. That's how I would like to remember our exit. The truth is, I had to drag C.J. out by a bra strap, and every few steps I had to kick her gently in the shins. I felt like I was riding a burro up the north side of the Grand Canyon.

"But Abby, why can't I —"

"Not now, dear."

"Abby, do you think Rufus is up to something? I mean, something no good?"

I waited until I got her in my car. "It's clear she doesn't trust him. While you were in the kitchen helping him with the tea, she as much as told me that Roberta Stanley's death was connected to the fact that Colonel Humphrey used to supply a broker in Hong Kong with contraband animal parts. Her father was that broker. She seems to think that because of that she'll be the next to go."

"Abby, you're not making a lick of sense. Who would want to buy animal parts?"

"Unfortunately, a lot of people. Even though these animals are endangered, there are still people who want to buy ivory, snow leopard skins, sun bear paws, you name it. Think, C.J. Use that oversized noggin of yours — oops, I'm sorry. That was ugly of me. I didn't mean to say that."

"Yes, you did, but that's okay, Abby. I have to bite my tongue lots of times."

"You do?"

" 'Abby, you mental midget,' I think to myself. 'Just because you're tiny doesn't mean you have to have a small mind. Good things come in small packages? Ha! So do bee stings and fire ant bites. If there was room inside that teensy-weensy head of yours for a brain, you'd be dangerous.' That kind of thing."

"Touché." I burst out laughing. "Do you really think those things?"

She nodded gravely. "Ooh, Abby, sometimes I think things that are much worse. I know people think I'm as loony as a Warner Bros. cartoon, but I constantly have to deal with folks whose IQs are half what mine is. Can you imagine how stressful that is?"

"Not by half. C.J., buckle up your seat belt and let's get ready to rumble."

When she giggled, I knew I had my friend back. She giggled again when my cell phone rang. It is programmed to sound like a kitten's meow, but quite frankly it sounds more like a queen in heat. Even Dmitri, who is neutered, has shown an unnatural interest in this electronic device.

"Wassup, dog?" I said, mimicking Randy Jackson from *American Idol*. By the way, I knew it was Greg on the other end.

"I'd like to speak to Miss Abdul, please."

"Sorry, dude. Will Mrs. Washburn do?"

"In a pinch. Hey Abby, I did the checking you asked me to do. Not only does this Aikenberg guy still practice in Charleston, but he is *the* number one ambulance chaser in the county."

"I thought that dubious honor went to — uh — you know. I can't think of his name at the moment, but he's got beady eyes and breath that could kill a dragon."

"Aikenberg doesn't need to advertise. It's all word of mouth for him. You know how I feel about ambulance chasers, Abby, but I'm keeping this guy's name on file."

I thanked Greg for the info and pressed the pedal to the metal. My Mercedes purred.

Rubberneckers love a grizzly death, but will settle for murder by gunshot. The crowd milling in front of Colonel Beauregard Humphrey's mansion was even larger than the previous day's crowd. A massive black taffeta bow had been affixed to the double front doors, but the wrought-iron gates were padlocked and there was no docent masquerading as the Colonel.

"Alley, here we come," I said. But stupid me. The grand homes that line the Battery have no alley behind them. Instead, they are backed by other grand homes that face Atlantic Street. Between them are high brick garden walls that delineate property lines. In order to sneak in through the kitchen door, one of us would have to divert the crowd's attention.

"Ooh, ooh, let me do it."

"Not by the hair on my chinny chin chin."

"Abby, I've been meaning to speak to you about that."

What?" I felt my chin, which, I am relieved to report, was still as smooth as a baby's bottom.

"Gotcha." The big galoot giggled.

It was time to take the matter into my own minute hands. What was good enough for Marvin was good enough for the minions.

Cupping my hands to my mouth, I called upon every decibel that lurked in the depths of my diaphragm. "Look over there beyond the seawall. A whale just spouted!"

The mob turned and moved as one person. In the meantime, C.J. and I made a mad, unobserved dash for the side garden and the kitchen door. Much to my relief, the door was unlocked. At worst we could be charged with entering, but not breaking. To cover my tiny, and C.J.'s rather large, tracks, we'd stopped at the Harris Teeter supermarket and picked up a prepackaged fruit basket. Sympathetic neighbors bearing gifts couldn't be prosecuted, could they?

"Yoo-hoo," I called softly. My intent was not to make our presence known as much as it was to determine whether we were alone — at least in that part of the house. When Daddy died we were besieged by helpful friends and family. But the Colonel had no family in town, and hadn't really lived here long enough to make close friends. That as-sessment went hand in hand with his penchant for engaging tourists in the little dramas he staged out front. The man was lonely.

Perhaps Roberta Stanley had been his only real friend. If that was the case, he would most probably have to make the arrangements for her funeral, which meant that the Colonel was probably spending the day looking at caskets, hooking up with clergy, and the like. No doubt there were also visits to the police station, the morgue, and his attorney.

"Ooh, Abby, look," C.J. whispered, stirring me from my reverie, "the poor man is so heartbroken he couldn't even finish his cereal this morning."

There are few sights sadder than a bowl of soggy flakes left uneaten by a grieving lover. One of them is a crossword puzzle worked in ink with as many wrong guesses as there were right ones.

"Come on," I said. "There doesn't seem to be anyone here. Now's our chance to look around."

"That's so wrong," C.J. said.

"I know. But C.J., if I left it all up to the police, your buddy, Hermione, could end up dancing with the fishes."

"Not that, silly. I mean the crossword puzzle. Sixteen down should be *im*plode, not *ex*plode."

I grabbed one of C.J.'s oversized mitts and pulled her along behind me. Whatever lay ahead in the dark labyrinth of rooms, we would face together. Perhaps even, with a bit of coaxing, I could get C.J. to lead the way.

24

The rear rooms of the house exhibited none of the bravado so evident in the rest of the mansion. The floors were covered with either cheap linoleum or carpeting so threadbare it was no longer possible to distinguish woof from warp. The faded wallpaper hung in flaps, as if the house was shedding its skin from the inside out.

I needn't have worried. The good folks of Shelby, North Carolina, are famous for their inquisitive minds, and C.J. was no exception. Soon she was pulling me along, delivering a running commentary on the various rooms.

"And this must have been the maid's quarters, because it's the room nearest the kitchen with a bed. But either she was the world's worst housekeeper or someone's been rummaging through her stuff."

She was right. The covers looked like they had been torn from the bed, not just thrown back, and clothes were hanging out of drawers, and dangling from hangers in an open armoire. It reminded me of my children's rooms when they were teenagers.

"But Abby, see how her shoes are lined up neatly inside the armoire? What's with that?"

"Maybe she —"

"Ooh, now look at this; see how the carpet doesn't match here? This used to be two rooms. Look, the wallpaper doesn't line up either. Having the armoire here is supposed to help disguise that — ooh, ooh, look behind it, Abby! That's some kind of secret door."

"It looks more like a big hole. Maybe a wall safe went there."

My buddy has muscles that would be the envy of many a metrosexual. She pulled the heavy piece of furniture away from the wall, raising a cloud of dust motes from the mismatched carpet.

"Abby, it's not just a hole in the wall. Look, it's a tunnel of some kind."

"So *that's* where the tunnel starts."

"Abby, have you been here before?" She sounded crestfallen.

"No —"

We heard the voices at the same time, and C.J., bless her younger heart, was the first to react. I didn't mind being pushed into the tunnel, but I did mind having the door slammed in my face. And with C.J. outside.

I held my breath. It was a habit formed some forty years ago. A precursor to hide and seek. If you held your breath and closed your eyes, you were invisible. If you were already invisible, like I was now, then you were doubly safe.

The voices grew louder, and I could pick out C.J.'s, but individual words were hard to catch. ". . . because, you see . . . with three eyes . . . wrong to marry a goat?" C.J., bless her oversized brain, was trotting out her Shelby stories. Whomever she was addressing was either mesmerized by the tall gal's tall tales or fleeing the room in order to protect their sanity. The voices grew dim, and then I couldn't hear anything except for the pounding of my heart.

My hands searched the door in the darkness, finding only splinters. I pushed, first with my hands, then my back. Finally my feet. Not an ounce of give.

I rapped softly on the door with my knuckles. My heart rapped back, but no C.J.

"C.J.?"

Nothing.

"C.J.! Can't you hear me?"

By now the dead over in Mount Pleasant could hear me, but apparently C.J. could not. Unless — my heart skipped a noisy beat — my dear friend, and soon-to-be sister-in-law, was no longer capable of answering.

They say that when the going gets tough, the tough get going. What they don't say is that it is darn hard living up to a proverb in utter darkness. I started by crawling away from the door, but soon discovered that the flooring beneath me was littered with nails and rough scraps of wood, even some broken glass. Safer, and much quicker, progress could be made by moving upright, scraping my lead foot sideways, pushing aside the debris as I went.

The air was stale and hot, reminding me of what it was like in the great pyramids of Giza that Greg and I visited on our delayed honeymoon. There, at least, there were overhead lights to illuminate the steps and a rope to hang on to. Here there were overhead cobwebs to drag through my hair, and the business end of nails and staples whenever I reached out to catch my balance. Funny how one's sense of balance, like one's hearing, dissipates in the dark. Or was that while nude? Was balance affected by nudity as well? Did darkness affect sanity? If I hadn't already been stark raving mad upon climbing into Alice's wooden wonderland, surely I was by now.

Ahoy there! What was that on the horizon. Light? Perhaps another door? I moved faster, buoyed by hope that soon faded. The light was coming from a hole only the size of a quarter. And to get to it, one had to first squeeze into a leathery cone — no, not a cone, the warthog head! This was the same warthog head I'd caught Roberta Stanley peering through. I wiggled into place, until my left eye was lined up with the socket made empty during the Colonel's move to Charleston.

The boar's head reeked of preservatives and animal essence. It was like pulling a dirty sock over one's head, an activity in which I engage in only sparingly. But I could see down into the room. And I could see C.J.! And the Colonel. They appeared to be alone, except for the menagerie of mangy beasts mounted on the paneled walls.

Their voices were muffled by the thick skin of the warthog, but as long as I separated the thudding of my heart from the sound mix, I could hear most of what they said.

"Be sure and tell Miss Timberlake how much I appreciate the fruit basket. That woman is top drawer all the way. A real looker, if you ask me."

"Ooh, Abby looks okay if you squint."

If you squint?

"And a good sport too. Don't get me wrong, Miss Cox. Roberta Stanley was the love of my life, but that boss of yours could really get my heart racing."

"Only if it was attached to a Nascar entry."

"Hey!"

C.J. whirled. "What was that?"

The Colonel was clearly confused as well. "Perhaps an echo. These rooms are much too large to suit me. Now with Roberta gone — Miss Cox, are you seeing anyone?"

My future sister-in-law patted her dishwater blond hair with a hand the size of Rhode Island. "Shame on you, Colonel Humphrey."

"I think you misunderstand me, ma'am. I merely wish to employ you."

"You do? As what?"

"As my housekeeper. I know you sell antiques, but look around. Everything here is antique, including myself — har har. Who better to look after them? And if the title housekeeper bothers you, I'd be happy to change it to whatever you'd like. Domestic engineer? Har har."

"How about curator? No, make that head curator."

"Perfect. So it's a deal?"

"What would you pay me?"

"I'll double whatever you're making now, and medical coverage."

"Dental too?"

"Okay, but not vision care. The so-called designer frames they sell these days are ridiculously priced. Designer this, designer that, what's the point of all this designer stuff? And you know what really takes the cake? Designer paper towels. How can something you use to wipe up spills and then toss in the garbage possibly be called designer?"

"Ooh, but I just love the ones with the blue ducks and tulips on the borders."

"You're a hard sell, Miss Cox. Okay, I capitulate, you can get designer glasses. But only one pair a year. I'll have my lawyer review your benefits package with you. So then, we're all set?"

The big gal cocked her head. "Hmm. I'll have to give the little one a chance to top this offer. Can I get back to you in a couple of days?"

"Take your time. Worthwhile things are worth waiting for, my mama used to say."

That did it. "She's taken," I yelled, a half octave lower than normal in an attempt to disguise my voice.

The Colonel, bless his geriatric heart, looked like he'd seen a ghost. And C.J., the ungrateful turncoat, looked as confused as a hen that had been put to work incubating duck eggs and soon discovered that her faux progeny loved to swim. You could have knocked her over with a steel feather.

"That's right," I bellowed, "this is your conscience speaking."

C.J. was looking wildly around the room. "My conscience, or the Colonel's?"

"Wait just one cotton-picking minute," the Colonel said. He raised his cane and headed straight for the warthog head.

In my haste to exit the warthog, I caught my hair on a snatch of metal webbing used by the taxidermist to retain the head's peculiar shape. I struggled to disentangle my hair, but in so doing thrust myself even farther into the head. With a loud groan the unlucky beast pitched forward, before ripping off the wall altogether. I felt a hard jolt, then a lesser bump, and then retreated back into darkness.

25

"She's coming to," I heard C.J. say. "Look, her beady little eyes are beginning to flicker."

I purposely flickered my beady little eyes for a moment or two longer than necessary, before even attempting to sit. The foul-smelling warthog had apparently landed square across C.J.'s broad shoulders, and being a rather ancient specimen — the hoofed creature, not my employee — split in two, eventually depositing yours truly on the hardwood floor.

"How many fingers can you see?" the Colonel asked, and held up three digits so crooked that, to my beady eyes, they at first looked braided.

"Twenty-four," I said, just to be obstreperous.

C.J. pulled back one of my eyelids, as if that would tell her something. "Guess again, you silly goose. No one has twenty-four fingers. Not even Granny Ledbetter."

"What is your name?" The Colonel was clearly concerned that I might sic a personal injuries lawyer on him.

"Wighelmania Ledbetter," I said weakly.

C.J.'s eyes nearly popped out of their sockets. "Auntie Wighelmania Ledbetter?" I'd learned early on in our friendship that the big galoot had an aunt with an even weirder name than Mozella, my minimadre's moniker.

"I'm one and the same," I croaked.

"But you don't look a day over sixty, and my Auntie Wighelmania will be ninety in September."

I sat up. "Thanks a lot, C.J. It's me, Abby, and I'm not even fifty."

She grinned. "I knew it was you, Abby. Did you hurt yourself?"

"Nope. Thanks for breaking my fall."

Now that he knew I was okay, the Colonel was not amused. "You've destroyed my warthog, Miss Timberlake. Do you know how much it will cost to replace it?"

"No, but I'd be happy to look for one on eBay."

"I see. Will the one purchased on eBay have been shot by me — a single shot, mind you — while on safari to Tanzania with my first wife, Esmeralda?"

"Hmm, probably not."

"Most assuredly not. Miss Timberlake, at the very least you can refrain from being a smart-aleck."

"Yes, sir."

"Now tell me what you are doing in my house, and in that stuffed animal in particular."

"Well, we brought you a fruit basket —"

"Abby, he knows."

"He does?"

"I told him everything. But I made him promise not to tell anyone that I work for the CIA, and that you're my flunky."

"I *am?*"

"Which still doesn't explain what y'all were doing in my house. Surely Roberta's murder is not of national interest."

"With all due respect, sir, she was found on your property, which lies near the harbor. The entire coastline is of national interest." Of course I felt terrible alluding to the dead in my boldfaced lie, but frankly, I am far too cute to spend time in the slammer.

"Abby," C.J. whined, "you're supposed to let me do the talking."

"Sorry, sir. Sometimes I get carried away."

The Colonel, whose shoulders had been sagging in grief, stiffened. *"Sir?"*

"Oops, did I say that?"

"Indeed, you did."

"Apparently Agent Coccyx didn't tell you *everything*."

C.J. laughed. "Ooh, Abby, you're so silly. That was Cousin Mortimer Ledbetter from Middlesex —"

"Ladies!" The Colonel's voice boomed like a cannon, rattling the windows. "Enough of this nonsense. You have until the count of three to explain your presence. One, two —"

"I found a skull in a gym bag that was in the storage shed I bid on Saturday and the two stupidest policemen who ever lived had me arrested but my husband got me out and then I learned the skull belonged to a female gorilla but before that your maid and maybe lover chased after me to the seawall and tried to tell me something very important but that night she was murdered and the police came to ask me questions again so I start thinking this must be connected somehow and asked more questions of my own and learned that you were a big game hunter who sold endangered animal parts to a broker in Hong Kong and then this very same broker's daughter has her life threatened so then I come back here to look for some answers and that's when C.J. bless her oversized heart finds a secret passageway which I get trapped in and the next

I know I land on top of her —" I started to black out.

"Bravo, Miss Timberlake. I do believe you hold the world's record for the longest sentence."

I could tell C.J. was shaking her head just by the breeze it created. "Nuh-unh. You should read Joseph Conrad."

The Colonel chuckled. "Actually, I have. It was reading *Heart of Darkness* that inspired me to visit Africa. It was also my cure for chronic insomnia."

"Hey," C.J. said, "you don't sound mad anymore."

"Sir," I said, "I mean you, sir, Colonel, not her sir, because she isn't one, does this mean you won't call the police?"

"Let's just say I'm willing to put that on hold for a moment while I consider the situation at hand." He rubbed his chin, his eyes half closed, as if his movements had been scripted for community theater. "Well, Miss Timberlake, I must say, you certainly have a problem. But before I address it, and what I think your options might be, I would like to make a few things perfectly clear.

"First, I stopped hunting over forty years ago when I realized that certain species were headed for extinction. I resent any implica-

tion by Ms. Wou-ki that I might still be involved in illegal animal trade. And the
second is, well — I think I know who killed
Roberta."

26

I leaned forward on my chair. "Who?"

"I can't say."

"You mean you won't."

"Don't you be telling me what I mean, Miss Timberlake."

"Ooh, but Colonel, Abby is one of the smartest people I know. And so wise. Even Granny Ledbetter said I should listen to Abby, on account she was ten times wiser than a barn full of owls."

A fleeting smile caused his mustache to jiggle. "As wise as all that?"

"C.J.," I said, somewhat annoyed, "I read somewhere that owls are actually pretty ordinary when it comes to matters of the intellect. Are you calling me a birdbrain?"

"Shhh, Abby, I'm trying to help."

"Thanks, dear. So Colonel," I said, "you did at least tell the police who this person is, right?"

His features hardened, his wrinkles turning to stone. "Why should I? So he can have a trial by his so-called peers, then sponge off the state for the rest of his life?

The answer is an emphatic no! This weasel is going to beg for mercy, and I'll show him the same mercy he showed Roberta."

"But sir," I said, "you're just one person. The police have an entire department at their disposal. They even have dogs. Wouldn't the job get done quicker with lots of people working on it?"

"Ooh, not necessarily."

"C.J., please. This is no time for a Shelby story."

"This isn't a Shelby story. It's about Russians."

"I'd like to hear it," the colonel said.

C.J. tossed her mane victoriously. "The Russians got this idea to breed domestic dogs, huskies, with jackals to produce search dogs with exceptional smelling abilities. But they discovered that hybrids, with fifty percent wild blood, were not as trainable as their husky parents. So the Russians bred the hybrids back to huskies and then got exactly what they wanted: small dogs with exceptional smelling abilities that could creep into small spaces to search for drugs, and that were easily trained."

"I get it," I said excitedly. "What you mean is that the dogs represent the police, and the Colonel represents the jackals, which means the hybrids must be Greg. Right?"

C.J. clapped her hands with glee. "You got it, Abby!"

The poor man looked like he wanted to check himself into the nearest old age home just to escape the likes of us. "I think you're both nuts," he said.

"Wait and hear me out," I said. "What she means is that my husband, Greg, while not the expert tracker you undoubtedly are, was a private detective. You could tell him what it is you don't want to tell us. I'm sure he could help."

No sooner did I close my mouth than I regretted what I'd said. One of the blessings of Greg's career change is that now I don't find myself worrying every day that he might not come home alive. Taking a boat out to sea does have its risks, but at least Mother Nature is impartial. It's the thought of my darling having to deal with human children, drug-crazed and armed with semi-automatic weapons, that makes my blood run cold. By offering my beloved's services to the honorary colonel from Kentucky, I was agreeing to put Greg right back in harm's way.

Colonel Humphrey stared intently at me. Whereas for the last couple of days folks had done a pretty darn good job of reading my mind through my exceptionally thick skull, the Colonel seemed bent on getting at my gray matter through the portals that were my eyes. He was taking so darn long I considered offering him the reading glasses I always carry in my purse.

Finally he spoke. "Well, I must be nuts to even consider this, Miss Timberlake, but I'd just as soon we kept it between the three of us and not involve your husband."

"Are you saying you're going to trust us with your secret?"

"It's not *my* secret, Miss Timberlake; it's merely the truth. So, do I have your word that you will keep this information to yourselves?"

C.J. nodded vigorously. "Cross my chest and hope to choke, tell a soul and I will croak."

"She means yes," I said.

The Colonel leaned forward conspiratorially. "In that case, ladies, hang onto your seats."

27

"I shall begin by telling you how I met Roberta Stanley." His voice cracked and he paused for a few seconds, blinking rapidly, but no tears appeared. "I was on safari in the Kivu —"

"That's in the Congo," I interjected for C.J.'s benefit.

"Ooh, Abby, I know all about the Congo. One of my seventeen languages is Tshiluba, and of course I speak Swahili."

The Colonel had the temerity to glare at me, not her. "Actually, it was the Belgian Congo then. The first Mrs. Beauregard Humphrey and I were relaxing after a day's shooting around a roaring fire in the common area of Kushefa Lodge. Lake Kivu lies at a considerable elevation, you know, and the nights can be quite cool. At any rate, in walks this couple, also from America, and they are arguing vociferously. I cannot remember what the topic was, but at one point she tells him to shut up, and he hauls back and hits her. She immediately hits him right back, and with a closed fist.

There were other guests in the room as well, and some of the them applauded. I might well have remained a bystander, but the bully hits her again, and this time she falls. Virtually into my lap.

" 'I'm awfully sorry,' she said, 'but it seems that whenever I try to stand on my own two feet, life knocks me right down again.' I sized up the twerp who'd punched her. Even Miss Timberlake could have laid him out.

" 'I beg your pardon, ma'am,' " I said, 'but that wasn't life who knocked you down. That was your pint-sized husband with the Napoleon complex.'

"Well, as you can imagine, that didn't sit well with the little cockerel. 'You want to make something out of it?' he said.

" 'Don't mind if I do,' I said, and gave the twerp the thrashing of his life.

"That night, after my wife went to bed, I was standing out on the verandah, enjoying the cold night air while observing the ghostly shapes of the volcanoes in the moonlight, and the woman whose husband I'd beaten comes out of the shadows to thank me for what I'd done. By now I'm sure you've guessed who that mystery woman was."

"Roberta Stanley," C.J. and I said together.

"Close, but no cigar."

C.J. raised her arm like a schoolgirl with the correct answer. "Was it Audrey Hepburn?"

"C.J.," I chided her, "the Colonel doesn't have time for this."

"Let me decide that," the coot in question growled. "As a matter of fact, Miss Cox, you aren't so far off the mark. Miss Hepburn was in the Congo at the time filming *The Nun's Story.* She wasn't, however, up in Kivu Province."

I feigned a yawn. "Colonel, with all due respect, do you mind getting to the point? I need to do some Christmas shopping."

His eyes flashed, then twinkled. "Perhaps I am getting a tad long-winded, but I like to think that it's a prerogative that comes with age. The correct answer, ladies, is Aida Murray."

I gasped in surprise. "It is?"

"Ooh, I used to love her books," C.J. cooed. "*Tonem Sklat* was brilliant. She really outdid herself on that one. Did you read it, Abby?"

"I tried to, dear," I said, "but I could barely get past the weird title. That was years ago, and I haven't picked up any of her books since."

"*Tonem Sklat* is the name of the protagonist. But Abby, you did know, didn't you, that in order to really understand the book you have to read it backward?"

"Say what?"

The Colonel nodded. "Aida Murray was always an intellectual snob. She picked up the backward trick after listening to *Abbey Road*, by the Beatles, played backward. Supposedly there are hidden messages in that album about Paul McCartney being dead — which, of course, he wasn't."

"*Abbey Road*! Now that's a good title," I said. "Colonel, are you serious about having to read the book backward?"

"Oh definitely. When read the conventional way, Aida's novels are merely witty, relying far too heavily on humor and wordplay. When read backward, one discovers layer upon layer of literary depth. The woman is a genius — but trust me, she's also a witch. Or perhaps I should say *was;* she's been dead now for almost twenty years."

"Colonel," I said, "I regret to inform you that you've been singing 'Ding-dong the witch is dead' for naught lo these many years. The witch, as you called her, is alive and well, and living in an oak tree on Johns Island."

"That is stuff and nonsense," he said

gruffly. "Aida died while on safari, about ten years after we met. In those days big game hunters were like a loose-knit society; our paths crisscrossed like a cat's cradle. By chance one night my hunting party and hers bivouacked adjacent to each other on the shores of Lake Victoria. She was high as a kite, having just received the news that *Tonem Sklat* had hit the number one spot on the *New York Times* best-seller list. She had too much to drink that night, and at some point must have wandered away from camp. After an extensive search over the next several days, she was officially listed as having drowned. Of course drowning was a euphemism for getting eaten by crocodiles. The lake is teeming with them, unlike Lake Kivu. Mac, her husband, was supposedly so distraught he didn't leave his tent until a private plane came to fetch him back to America. Ha. Distraught, my ass."

He stared at the spot just to the left of me, as if watching the tragic incident play out on a TV screen. "There were no witnesses to Aida's death, so of course there were rumors. I can't recall them all, but the worst is that Mac was seen taking a small boat out into the lake and pushing something — possibly a rolled-up carpet — over the edge and into the water. If that something was —"

I jumped up and grabbed one of C.J.'s hands in both of mine. "Come on, dear, we've got miles to go before we sleep."

"Ooh, Abby, don't be so silly. It's not even suppertime yet."

"Miss Timberlake," the Colonel said, disappointment creeping into his voice, "don't you want to hear the rest of the story?"

"I've already heard it, sir."

I tried to sneak through the back door of my storeroom at the Den of Antiquity without Mama noticing. With C.J. along, that was like leading a dozen dancing elephants in pink tutus undetected through the floor of the Democratic National Convention. Just when I thought we'd made it, Mama burst into the storeroom from the shop entrance wielding a brass lamp.

"Eeeee-yahhhhh!" she shrieked, and assumed a pseudojujitsu pose.

If my heart had been free to jump out of my chest, it might have won me a spot on the Olympic broad jump team.

"Hey, Mozella," C.J. said placidly. Apparently in Shelby it was common for little old ladies to shriek in foreign tongues and threaten one's person with lighting fixtures.

"Abby," Mama said, lowering the lamp base, "are you trying to give your poor mama a heart attack?"

"*Excuse* me? C.J., check and see if I have any gray hairs?"

"Ooh, Abby, don't be silly. You dye your hair."

"I most certainly do not!" I turned my attention back to the world's biggest attention grabber. "Mama, what on earth were you doing? What if I had been a real intruder?"

"Abby, I took judo, or did you forget? I can defend myself."

So it wasn't jujitsu. It is so hard to keep track of the petite progenitress and her myriad interests. Thank heavens she'd finally come to the conclusion that coal-walking was hard on her pedicures.

"Nonetheless, next time call 911."

"Speaking of phones, dear, why didn't *you* call *me* to let me know you were coming?"

"Well — because — well, you know."

Mama turned to C.J. "What is my daughter not telling me this time?"

C.J. shrugged. "The little one is hard to figure out sometimes, Mozella. But she did say she wanted us to sneak in because you tend to make everything about you, and that if you knew we were back here, we'd never be able to leave."

"No offense taken, dear," Mama said to her best friend. "But you, Abby, you can think again. All about me, is it? Was it all about me that I endured thirty-six hours of excruciating labor? Was it all about me that I cashed in a saving's bond to pay for your wedding to that unspeakable man up in Charlotte — oh, speaking of Charlotte, you'll never guess who I saw today. She walked right into this shop."

"Queen Elizabeth?" For the record, my answer was only partially sarcastic. Somehow Mama does manage to meet some very important people.

"No, but you're close. Guess again."

"Camilla?" C.J. said, getting into the spirit of the game. "What a beautiful woman."

"It was Rob's mother."

"Our Rob?"

"Now *there's* a beautiful woman. Slender, well-dressed — she was even wearing those roach-killer shoes. Abby, this woman buys her purses at Moo-Roo."

"That's nice," I said.

"Dear, you don't seem surprised."

"Bob told me she was coming. I helped him come up with a game plan to make sure she doesn't overstay her welcome."

"Why, Abby, how you talk! Does that mean you and Greg have a game plan to get rid of me?"

"What?"

"Am I just a nuisance? Just an old lady that gets in the way so much you have to sneak into your own shop?"

"Oh, Mama, you're much more than that! You cook, you clean, you drop fresh bleach tabs into the toilet tanks — but most of all, I love your company."

"You do?"

The cow bells strapped to the door jangled. If there wasn't already a customer out front, there was now.

"I do. Now please make yourself even more indispensable and man the fort, will you?"

"Aye aye, sir," Mama said happily, and skipped from the room, slowing to squish her crinolines through the door.

"Abby, you are so lucky," C.J. said.

"I know." I walked over to a Balinese armoire with delicately carved drawers. The scene depicted was that of Lord Rama's kidnapped fiancée being rescued by the Garuda, a winged creature that is half bird and half man. I'd been deliberating the wisdom of keeping this exceptional piece for my own use rather than selling it. This dilemma, I've learned, is one that many antiques dealers face on a regular basis. Until I made up my mind, this handsome piece of furniture was going to be enjoyed fully by no one. In the meantime, it was a good place to store the bundle of canes I had decided not to sell to the Colonel.

I withdrew the bundle, which was wrapped in brown butcher paper, and spread the canes across a Federal period sofa. Sadly, my opinion of the pieces hadn't changed since the last time I'd laid eyes on them.

"They're not very attractive, are they, C.J.?"

"If they were children, Abby, I'd say 'bless their hearts.' "

"That bad, huh?" I picked up one at random. "I think the Colonel got the only good one; the cane with the jade handle. Look at this. It's hardly even an antique. This staff was machine-turned."

"Why are we doing this, Abby?"

"Because of this." I tapped the handle. "What does this look like to you, Miss Cox?"

"A very ugly carving of an herbivore of some kind. Thompson's gazelle, I think, but in that case, the side stripes —"

"I mean, what do you think this is made of?"

"Some kind of horn?"

"C.J., you're only guessing."

"Forgive me, Abby, but I don't want to be

wrong. It feels horrible to be wrong. I was wrong on June thirtieth, 1987; April tenth, 1993; September —"

"My point is that you, who knows just about everything, can't identify this material. That can only mean that you haven't seen it before. C.J., have you ever seen a rhino horn?"

"Rhinos don't really have horns, Abby. What people call —"

"Could this be it?"

"Ooh, Abby, how do I know if I've never seen it?"

"Touché. But I bet dollars to doughnuts — just not Krispy Kremes — that these canes are worth a whole lot more on the black market than they are here on King Street. And I'll wager my thirdborn that I know who wants these canes bad enough to kill for them."

"But Abby, you don't have a thirdborn."

"Then I've got nothing to lose."

Going off half-cocked seems to be a specialty of mine. I suppose, though, it is somewhat fitting, given that most of my ideas are half-baked. In my defense, I try not to be half-assed in my execution of these schemes.

Preoccupied as I was, I was grateful that

my car knew the way to Mac Murray's house. More precisely, my global-positioning device did. At any rate, on the way over C.J. asked a zillion questions, some of which I answered.

"Abby, you didn't even listen to the end of the Colonel's story. We didn't know for sure what was in that rolled-up rug."

"I do."

"Ooh, Abby, don't be silly. You've never been to Africa, except for Egypt, and even if you had, you're barely old enough to remember something that happened in the late 1960s."

Being petite, I'm invariably pegged as younger than I am. "I'll take that as a compliment. But you see, C.J., I heard another version of this story from the horse's mouth; from Mac Murray himself. But in that version it was Miss Sugar Tit who took a small boat out into the middle of the Wadmalaw River and dumped a rolled-up carpet over the edge. If my hunch was right, he was using one of his own real life stories as a basis for his lie. Folks do that all the time, it's a natural thing."

I could feel C.J.'s big gray eyes boring into me. "I don't get it. What does Tater Tot have to do with Mr. Murray?"

"Nothing. But when Mama and I came

snooping around, a red flag must have gone up, and his immediate reaction was to deflect our interest in him by casting suspicion on a neighbor, by weaving a tantalizing, juicy story. C.J., do me a favor and call the Barnes & Noble in Mount Pleasant and ask Patti — she's the CRP — if Aida Murray has ever signed in their store."

C.J. can be very professional when the situation calls for it. Within three minutes she had an answer for me, and since C.J. has a phenomenal memory, she was able to quote Patti verbatim.

"Aida Murray did a signing there last October for *Diputs Snup*, a derivative novel of a Lowcountry plantation and the generations that lived and loved there. Apparently since no one could pronounce the title, sales were abysmal. It wasn't until Sarah Snup, the matriarch of the clan, threatened to sue, that the book garnered any interest. In the end neither the book nor the lawsuit went anywhere."

"Well, isn't that interesting."

"But Abby, that means Aida wasn't eaten by a crocodile."

"No, but her husband was."

C.J. clapped and hooted. "Ooh, ooh, I think you're on to something."

"According to the Colonel, Mac was a

small man, and after his wife went missing, he retreated into his tent. But in reality it wasn't he who retreated —"

"It was Aida, wasn't it, Abby?"

"That would be my guess. Aida Murray has been presenting herself as two people ever since 1969. She's Aida whenever she has a book coming out, but the rest of the time she's Mac."

"Why would she do that?"

"For business reasons. C.J., it costs a bundle to live on Major Moolah Road. Aida could never afford to live there on just the sales of her pseudoliterary novels. Heck, I bet even a best-selling mystery writer couldn't afford the taxes on a place like hers. And that manuscript collection she owns — priceless."

"Maybe she inherited the money. Great Uncle McPherson Ledbetter found a pot of gold at the end of a —"

"Rainbow? Please, C.J., this is not the time to wax sentimental about your leprechaun ancestors, none of whom, by the way, you resemble in the least. The point I was trying to make is that Aida must have another source of income — apart from writing — and I think I know what it is."

"Isn't she a little old for that, Abby?"

Someday, time, finances, schedule, and

mood permitting, I'd have to take C.J. to the Golden Girls Ranch in Nevada. Don't ask me how I know about this place, but it does give hope to the wrinkled, and those of us festooned with patches of cellulite.

"Rhinoceros horns," I said.

"Ooh, Abby, that sounds painful."

"For the rhino, most certainly. They have to kill it first — although strictly speaking they don't, but that's another story. The thing is, C.J., that rhino horns are still very much coveted in parts of the world. In recent years there have been steps taken to prevent the trafficking of rhino horns, particularly between Africa and Asia, but smart smugglers always seem to find a way around the system."

"And anyone who can write a book backward, Abby, has got to be smart."

"Perhaps. It's the authors of silly humorous mysteries that are as dumb as posts. Anyone can alliterate, for heaven's sake. Now where was I?"

"You were talking about smart smugglers, Abby."

"Yes. C.J., what do all those canes I got at the locked trunk sale have in common?"

"They're ugly as sin, Abby."

"Go on."

"Well, the staffs are okay, but the heads

are very crudely carved from some hideous material — ooh, Abby, they're rhinoceros horns, aren't they?"

"That would be my guess. And to whom did the canes originally belong? Well, I'll tell you. A very elusive man by the name of Ken Yaco — perhaps otherwise known as Aida, or Mac, Murray."

"Abby, how do you spell Yaco?"

I fished in my pocketbook, keeping my left hand on the wheel, and dug out the notes I'd made. "It's in there somewhere."

C.J. is one of the kindest people I know. No doubt that's why it took her so long to formulate a response.

"Abby," she said some mercifully silent five miles, or four minutes, later, "please don't be mad, but I think you're mistaken."

"I beg your pardon?"

"That's a company name, not a man's."

"Excuse me?"

"Kenya Company. That's what it says. Not Ken Yaco."

I found a landing spot for my Mercedes along Maybank Highway on an unusually wide strip of shoulder. "Give me that paper."

She relinquished the note page, but insisted on pointing at it with a sausagelike forefinger. "See what happens when you run 'Ken' and 'Yaco' together, except that you didn't run them together intentionally. Face it, Abby, you write like a drunken chicken."

"I'm sure you've led a great many chickens to drink, C.J."

"Yesiree. Granny always said there were two ways to make coq au vin; the French way, and her way."

"Spare me the recipe, dear." I stared at the squiggles. "Well, I'll be dippity-doodled."

"Granny has a recipe for that too."

I glanced over my shoulder, and seeing no one on the road, executed a launching that would have made NASA proud.

28

So Aida Murray was indeed alive and involved in the trafficking of rhinoceros horns that had been smuggled into this country as antiques. But then, strictly speaking, so was I. Ignorance of the law is no excuse, a maxim Greg had pounded into my head ad nauseam. Come to think of it, what proof did I have that Aida, a.k.a. Mac, had broken any endangered species laws? I, on the other hand, had a barrel of antique canes, each of which could probably bring me twenty years in the slammer. Never mind that I could never live long enough to even see parole, the fact remains that I am just too pretty for prison life.

Well, I would just have to see to it that Aida sang like a canary. To do that, I would need evidence of her participation in a smuggling ring, and to procure that I would need the element of surprise. Fortunately, the world's biggest bundle of surprises was sitting right next to me.

"C.J., do you feel like having an adventure?"

"Ooh, Abby, you know I love adventures!"

I put on the brakes just around the bend from Aida's treetop mansion. "Good, because this is where the adventure begins."

"Abby, I don't see anything but trees and the river."

"That's because Aida Murray lives around the bend in a tree house. My plan calls for you to walk up there and ring the doorbell. To do that you'll either have to climb the stairs or take the elevator. When she comes to the door, tell her your car broke down and you need to use the telephone. Then call me. I'll tell you what to do next."

"But I have a cell phone, Abby."

"Leave it in the car. Tell her you lost it."

"Ooh, but Abby, you know I can't lie."

"C.J., let me see your phone."

She handed me a phone so small it wasn't hard to imagine a child swallowing it. That's all the world needed, children ringing in church. I lowered my window and lobbed the mini gizmo as far as I could. It disappeared amidst the leaf clutter on the ground. It might even have landed in the river and not made a noticeable splash.

"There," I said, "you've lost your phone."

C.J., ever the good sport, remained as placid as the sphinx. "But Abby, this isn't my car, and it isn't broken down."

"Then tell her the car you were riding in broke down, for heaven's sake. Just don't mention my name. Omitting facts is not the same as lying."

By the look on C.J.'s face, it was.

"Look, dear, which is worse, omitting my name or having something horrible, and quite likely fatal, happen to your dear friend, Hermione Wou-ki?"

My buddy lit out of there like a grouse after a grasshopper.

I'm more afraid of snakes than I am of wacko authors with chain saws, so I kept my eyes peeled for water moccasins and cottonmouths. When I grabbed a branch in order to steady myself, two "somethings" plopped into the water just a few feet away. At least they didn't plop on me.

That grand Wadmalaw Island oak that served as the foundation for Aida Murray's tree house spread out over the water for at least a hundred feet. The limbs dipped down as they spread, and at the high water point (the Wadmalaw is a tidal river) they practically skimmed the surface. Inside this canopy a secret floating dock had been built. Tied to it was a surprisingly large boat; one surely capable of being taken out into the ocean.

A ladder led from the dock down into the water, which was a welcome sight because the dock itself perched well above both ground and water levels. This meant, however, that in order to reach the ladder I had to swim and/or wade through the same dark water into which several potentially dangerous "somethings" had plopped.

Whether it be the Wadmalaw River or the local community pool when it first opens for the summer, the trick is to jump in all at once. I'm sure I made more sound than the snakes, but the sound I made, while it might have drawn Aida's attention, no doubt scared the snakes away. Thank heavens for that; my pale tasty flesh moving slowly through the water would have been like waving a buffet in front of these reptilian monsters.

The dock was rough, but dry, and I could tell by the relative paucity of dead leaves covering it that it was used regularly. This was also an indication that the door leading out to the dock might be unlocked. Charleston, particularly the outlying areas, is still a city in which folks don't bother to lock frequently used doors during the daylight hours, if at all.

Sure enough, the door, which by the way led to a mudroom of sorts, was not only unlocked, it was slightly ajar. Could it be a trap? I poked my head in.

"Hello," I said softly. And stupidly.

I thought I heard footsteps approaching through the house, and was about to turn tail and race back along the dock when I heard the doorbell. The sound was faint but unmistakable. A few seconds later I heard the distant booming of the big galoot's voice.

Wasting no time, I opened the inner door and slipped into Aida's kitchen. Perhaps writers, even cheesy novelists, are too busy to cook, because the room bore no resemblance to my kitchen. The appliances gleamed, the countertops were clear, and most astonishing of all, the floor looked literally clean enough to eat off. I'd heard that tired cliché a million times in my life, but this was the first time I'd actually seen a floor that I'd consider using as a plate. Maybe a nice fillet, cooked medium rare, or perhaps something lighter as a main dish, such as meat-filled pasta — my ravioli reverie was cut short by the sound of approaching voices. I slipped back into the mudroom.

"No, water would be fine." C.J., bless her anatomically enlarged heart, was practically shouting for my benefit.

"Would you like ice with that?"

"No, just water. If you don't mind, I'd like to drink it in the foyer."

"Of course. But I assure you, ma'am, that I am a gentleman. You have nothing to fear from me."

"It isn't just that," C.J. said. "It's because my Granny Ledbetter always says that water is for horses and front door guests. Sweet tea is for family and back door guests."

"Did you say your Granny Ledbetter?"

I could imagine the big head nodding. "Yes, ma'am — I mean, sir. Granny is full of wise sayings. Would you like to hear some of them?"

There followed an excruciating silence. "Did you say Ledbetter?"

"Yes, sir. Granny is the wisest thing on two legs."

"Are you by chance related to my neighbor, Claudette Aikenberg? I believe she is otherwise known as Miss Sugar Tit."

C.J. squealed with delight. "How did you know?"

"You have the same accent — and, dare I say, the same eyes."

"Large and gray?"

"Small and piggish would have been my words."

How dare the woman! C.J.'s eyes are her best feature, aside from her dishwater-blond hair. What had she ever done to Aida to illicit such rudeness?

"Oh, no," C.J. said, without the least bit of malice, "it's Cousin Myopia who has the tiny eyes. But she has the sweetest personality you could ever ask for."

"Pray tell," the word-wielding fiend said, "why it is that you came knocking on my door for a drink of water when your cousin lives within walking distance?"

"Because I really didn't need to use your phone, and Abby's car really isn't broken, but I *am* thirsty."

I groaned aloud. I couldn't help it. Having agreed to take the big galoot with me was as smart a move as taking the *Titanic* out for its maiden voyage in an ocean full of icebergs. I glanced around the mudroom for a possible weapon. A fishing rod, old shoes, a rack of baseball caps, a can of wasp spray — that, at least, had possibilities. I tiptoed over to the can and hefted it. Hmm, almost full. I tucked it under my blouse, in the hollow of my back. The waistband of my slacks held it firmly in place.

"You're an idiot, Miss — Miss whatever your name is."

"C.J. Although my given name is Jane Cox. You see, my friends nicknamed me Calamity Jane on account of I'm sort of a walking disaster, but they shortened that to C.J., which could stand for a lot of things, and maybe it does because Jane Cox isn't my real name; Granny just picked it out of the phone book when she found me under the cabbage. Lots of folks ask me why Ledbetter isn't my last name, and I did too, but Granny said there already were enough Ledbetters to suit this world, and not enough Coxes."

"Miss Cox, I assure you that your name is now indelibly imprinted on my mind, and will forever be associated with the image of the world's biggest —" Aida stopped to consider the implications of C.J.'s visit. "Why are you here, Miss Cox?"

I could almost hear C.J. squirm. "I already told you, sir."

"But what does Miss Timberlake want with me?"

"Why don't you ask her yourself?" I said, appearing in the kitchen door. I was careful to have my empty hands in front of me.

Aida Murray didn't even have the decency to pretend surprise. "Yes, let me hear it directly from the pony's mouth."

"Good one," I said. "Cruel, but good. Although you aren't exactly vertically blessed yourself. It is hard to visualize a woman your size rolling her husband up in a rug and then dragging him down to a boat. I should imagine getting him in, and out, of the boat were especially hard."

"Woman, did you say?"

"Aida Murray, I presume. Killed her own husband and dumped his body into Lake Victoria, after which she assumed his identity — oh heck, you already know all that."

"You have no proof." Her voice quavered as it shifted into a lower gear. "I saw the crocs go after him. There is no way you can pin that one on me. Besides, the statute of limitations has run out."

"I'm sure it has. But your smuggling history — that's current."

She stared at me, her mouth opening and closing like that of a baby bird begging to be fed, but without making a sound.

"Be careful," I said, "or you might swallow a fly."

C.J. snickered. "Ooh, Abby, that's not the right expression. It's swallow a swallow, not swallow a fly. Cousin Ignacious Ledbetter —"

"Not now, C.J."

"I'd like to hear the story," Aida said.

C.J., lacking even one wicked bone in her body, brightened. "You would?"

"Absolutely. I'm fascinated."

I stared back at Aida Murray. Mesmerized as I'd been by her gaping mouth, and distracted by C.J., I hadn't noticed her right hand reaching behind her, into a counter drawer, and withdrawing a pistol. But that's what must have happened. What kind of person kept a gun in the kitchen, for goodness sake? Under the pillow, I could see — but that was only for the week immediately following some nasty threats from my ex — but the kitchen? What for? To shoot the soufflé if it didn't rise properly? To order the steak back under the broiler until all the pink was gone?

No, it was undoubtedly intended to kill uninvited houseguests like me.

29

It was obvious that C.J., oblivious to wickedness, didn't see the gun. "Well, you see," she said, "Cousin Ignacious had a bad habit of letting his mouth hang open, and it bothered Granny something fierce. She warned him that if he kept it up, a swallow might fly in. And sure enough, he was out watching the sunset one evening when a swallow swooped down from the sky —"

"How much does a good size rhino horn go for these days?"

"Silly, Abby." C.J. noticed the gun and wisely closed her mouth, just like Cousin Ignacious ought to have done.

"That depends, Miss Timberlake, are you in the market for one?"

"Let's say that I was."

"Twenty grand. Guaranteed to be the real thing."

"That's ridiculous. My source said he charged a thousand."

"When was that?"

"Back in the 1970s."

Mac and Aida took turns laughing.

"That's ancient history. Cost is related to supply and demand, and while supply has shrunk to practically nothing, demand is as high as ever."

"Don't you care that these animals are already so close to extinction that they probably won't survive past our lifetime?"

"Then what's the problem? Since they're doomed anyway, somebody may as well benefit from their demise."

"You're despicable."

"I take it then that you're not interested in making a purchase?"

"Until now I've been against the death penalty. But now I might consider purchasing a ticket to your execution."

"You're very harsh, Miss Timberlake. I like that in a woman. Under other circumstances we might have been friends."

"Somehow I don't think so."

"Although I'm still trying to figure out why you got involved in my business affairs."

"You tell me! I was minding my own business, trying to make a living while dealing with all the crap life throws at one on a daily basis, when all of a sudden — boom, everything starts to unravel."

"You should not have been the one to win the bid."

"Excuse me?"

"I bid as high as I could without drawing attention to myself. I didn't expect some idiot to keep bidding on some storage room junk."

Mine is not the brightest mind, therefore when the proverbial lightbulb clicks on, I am generally quite startled. "Uh — ah —"

"Ooh, ooh!" C.J. waved her arm aloft. "I know what you're thinking."

"Not now, dear. Aida, that shed had been rented by your alter ego, and erstwhile husband, Mac, am I correct?"

She grunted.

"But you hadn't been able to gain access to the contents for decades; ever since you killed your husband. Am I right?"

"Wrong. Mac didn't trust me with everything. I didn't even know he had a rental over there until last month when I was going over some old files. One had Safe-Keepers Storage handwritten across the top, and several columns of payments, but there was no unit number listed. Then the ad appears in the paper for the auction, and lists three sheds that were in arrears. How the heck was I supposed to know which, if any of them, was Mac's?"

"Oh the woes of being a con woman."

"You're a smartmouth, Miss Timberlake. I don't like smartmouths. I'm surprised you have any friends, including her." She flicked the gun at C.J., and then back at me.

"At least I have friends. Now that I know you're really Aida, you don't make a very convincing Mac. I'm surprised your friends and family haven't blown your cover. Or are they all hardened killers like you?"

Her laugh sliced the air like a butcher knife. "I have plenty of friends, Miss Timberlake. Mac and I had just moved to Charleston when we took that — uh — fatal trip to Kenya. As for family, who needs them when you've a passion, such as I have."

"She loves rare books," I said for C.J.'s edification.

"Ooh, I just love rare books!"

"Would you like to see my collection?"

C.J. nodded vigorously. "Have you seen the Dead Sea scrolls? They came to Charlotte last year. At the Discovery Center."

"Seen them? I own a fragment."

"Cool beaners! Abby didn't let me have time off to go, because she really isn't into old books."

"Nuh-unh," I said.

Aida had the audacity to glower at me. "Well, in that case, Miss Cox, would you like to see the fragment I own?"

"Yes, ma'am. Very much."

She swung her gun arm around and pointed the darn thing right at C.J.'s chest. "Miss Timberlake, before we proceed, I'd like you to place both hands above your head."

"What about my feet? I used to take yoga."

C.J. giggled.

"Shut up! Both of you." She turned, forcing C.J. to turn with her. "Now come this way. Miss Timberlake, if you even think of causing any trouble, I'll blow this woman's brains out. Not that the world would notice, ha ha."

"Why you conceited witch," I said. "Just because you write books doesn't mean you're smart. Miss Cox might not have mayonnaise on her sandwich, but she can think circles around you. Did you know she belongs to Mensa?"

"Then you must belong to Densa, Miss Timberlake. I wasn't kidding when I said shut up. The next word you say will be your last."

I followed helplessly, just not wordlessly. I do believe I am genetically incapable of long-term silence. Greg says my mouth is like a dripping faucet; it can't be stopped short of drastic measures. That's because my darling is mechanically challenged and has never had to fix a dripping faucet. If he'd been a single mom, like me, he'd know that a washer isn't only a big machine that swishes clothes and belongs in the laundry room. A washer is also a flat ring of metal, or rubber, that is placed between two larger components to make them fit snugly. At any rate, my tongue will only stop wagging when I die. Or when I decide to pierce it — which will be the fifth of Never.

"So tell me, Mrs. Murray — or do you prefer Aida? — why was it that poor, lovestruck Roberta Stanley had to give her life in the pursuit of your happiness? What did she ever do to you?"

"Because she recognized me at the auction, you twit. That's why. After all these years!"

"Let me guess. You were afraid she'd ID you. And it wasn't that you were afraid of being arrested for your husband's murder; there were no witnesses to that. You were afraid that the unexpected appearance of some of your husband's business inventory — a business you took over — might rear its ugly head and bite you in the behind."

"So aptly, but vulgarly, said. I'm the one who put it in the Colonel's mind to retire to Charleston someday. Of course that was years ago. But still, stupid me. Kentucky colonels should remain in Kentucky, if you ask me. You could have knocked me over with a feather when I learned he'd moved to Charleston. As for Roberta, well, she had no business aspiring to a position she was not born to."

"Don't speak ill of the dead," I growled. Unfortunately an Abby growl is not all that intimidating — or so I've been told. "But just out of curiosity, which position would that be?"

"She was my maid, for crying out loud. After Mac's death —"

"Mac's murder!"

"Anyway, she quit, and before long I'd heard that she'd been hired by the Humphreys. I supposed she returned with them to Kentucky, where she became the bane of all his future wives. Well, enough of this silly chitchat. Let's go show Miss Cox the Dead Sea scroll fragment I own. I have a translation with it, but I must warn you — you might not like what it says. It's rather controversial."

"I love controversy," I said. "Lead the way!"

She led us through a multilevel maze of rooms and to the now familiar manuscript room. After ushering us in with the gun, she motioned us to a far corner, one that I hadn't inspected when I was there the first time.

"Just so you know," she said. "I'm not turning soft on y'all. As soon as we're through with time travel, the two of you will be dinner buffet for the fishes. Sort of like Mac" — she cackled wickedly — "except that in his case the fishes didn't even have time for hors d'oeuvres."

"Heh-heh," I said under my breath.

"What was that?" she snapped.

"I said 'Hear, hear.' I always toast my own death."

30

She clicked off the safety. "Shut up. I don't like you." She pointed with her chin to a nearby glass case. "Miss Cox, it's in there, if you wish to take a look."

"Ooh, ooh, can Abby see it too? Please? Pretty please with vinegar on top? She didn't have time to see the exhibit in Charlotte, either."

Because it was probably the last minute of the last day of my life, I felt my heart flooding with love for C.J. Were I, by some miracle, given a second chance at life, I would try to live mine like she did hers; honestly, and without guile. I doubt if a mean thought ever crossed her prodigious mind. When God was through making her, he threw his extra-large mold away. I now think some of C.J.'s generosity must have become airborne and the particles were breathed in by Aida Murray.

"Okay," she grunted at me, "you can see it too." She backed away as I moved closer to C.J., the better to fix us both in her sights.

Frankly, I was disappointed by what I saw; the case was about the size of a card table, whereas the manuscript fragment was only the size of a playing card. C.J., however, was so excited she was practically jumping in place.

"Abby, just imagine, this was written two thousand years ago."

I stared at the fragment, trying mightily to be somehow affected by its presence, but to no avail. The squiggly lines written on a tiny scrap of animal skin were not in the least inspiring. I felt absolutely no connection to the past.

"Can you read it?" I asked.

"This particular scroll was written in Hebrew, so I can read most of it. But the words are run together, so it's hard to understand without the general context."

Beneath the fragment was a printed page in English with the translation. . . . *thou has forsaken me. The light from thy face has ebbed, like the sun setting behind the purple hills of Judea . . .*

"Does it match with that?" I asked.

Bent over the case as she was, J.C. swatted me in the face with her hair. "No," she whispered, "this says 'stupid uneducated foreigners, we have tricked you again with our forgery . . .' Abby, does that make any sense to you?"

"Plenty."

Aida cleared her throat. "What are you two mumbling about?"

"We were talking about how stupid and uneducated you are."

Her face turned white with rage. "*What* did you say?"

"I said, how much did you pay for this Dead Sea scroll fragment?"

"That's not what you said, and how much I paid for it is none of your business." But she hesitated only a few seconds, as I knew she would. Ostentatious consumers, by their very nature, must have their purchases validated by the envious looks of others. "Fifty grand. It is two thousand years old, after all."

"Wow, you did good. I would have guessed at least seventy-five thousand. Unfortunately, the glass in this case has some glare. May we open the case so that Miss Cox can take a closer look? Without touching, of course."

Again, her hesitation was brief. "I guess. But no touching. And try not to breathe on it."

"Deal. C.J., you open it. Little ol' me might drop the lid, but you, bless your heart, are as strong as an ox."

As my good-natured and unsuspecting pal opened the lid, I whipped the can of wasp spray out of my waistband.

Aida turned an impossible shade of pale. "What was that? What do you have in your hands?"

"My secret weapon. I'm afraid, Mrs. Murray, that the ball is now in our court. Please be so kind as to toss your weapon on the floor. Try to get it as close to our feet as possible."

She hesitated once more. "That's only a can of wasp spray! What do you expect to do with that?"

While still facing her, I pointed the aerosol can in the general direction of the exposed document. "I expect to obliterate your Dead Sea scroll fragment if you don't comply. If I'm going to die, I may as well extract my revenge. Right?"

"Miss Cox," our hostess-with-the-leastest shouted, "you're not going to let her do that, are you? You're an educated woman. You can appreciate how important this fragment is."

C.J. said nothing.

"Miss Timberlake, I beseech you. No, I'm begging you. Please don't harm that antique scroll. You, of all people, should understand that its value is not strictly monetary."

"What about the value of majestic animals, such as the rhinoceros, or the tiger, still roaming this world in the wild? How many rhino horns, or tiger penises, did you broker to pay for this scrap of the past?"

"But they're only animals. God put us in charge of them to do with them what we like. It says so right in the Bible."

"Buzz! You're wrong. We're to be stewards of these creatures, not their decimators. Now do something right for a change and toss me your gun."

"No."

"Then say sayonara to your scroll fragment."

"You wouldn't dare!"

"Try me."

"Okay, I'll call your bluff."

Never dare a four-feet-nine-inch woman. We've had to fight just to be noticed. Not physically, of course — well, maybe sometimes. But at recess no one ever called, "Red rover, red rover, we dare Abby over." I wasn't even chosen during gym class, but assigned at the start to the team unlucky enough to choose last. I was, in fact, the booby prize. One can be sure, therefore, that given the opportunity to strike terror in Aida's murderous bosom, without actually doing any real harm, I needed no further urging.

The wasp spray not only stank, but hissed like a dragon when released. For Aida, there was no mistaking that the deed had been done. Shocked to the core, she dropped the pistol. C.J., who can move fast for a woman of substance, threw herself on the floor and snatched up the weapon before Aida quite knew what was happening.

I almost pitied Aida. Her howl of anguish almost struck a chord in my heart. Almost. While C.J. held the contraband smuggler at bay, I called 911 on my cell phone and then called Greg.

"Abby," he said, before I had a chance to say anything, "are you watching a nature show?"

"No — well, sort of."

"It's about rhinos, isn't it? I saw this episode recently on *Animal Planet*. Some poachers had just killed a female rhino, and her calf was bawling in terror. Isn't that the one you're watching?"

"Not even close, dear."

Aida Murray stood trial in Charleston for the murder of Roberta Stanley. Animal rights activists, conservationists of all stripes, Miss Sugar Tit fans, and the entire state of Kentucky flooded the city for the duration. C.J. and I both had to testify, as did Darren Cotter and Hermione Wou-ki. The guilty verdict came as no surprise. What did surprise me — in fact it shocked and disgusted me — was the fact that Aida Murray's career took off like never before. *Tonem Sklat* jumped to the number one position on the *New York Times* best-seller list and stayed there for seven sickening weeks.

In the course of the trial it was revealed that Aida Murray was the brains behind an international ring of poachers and contraband animal product distributors. She also smuggled stolen antiquities into the country, specializing in rare manuscripts. Aida eventually admitted to these charges in hopes of lightening her sentence. She even admitted to having created the cane mutiny in my shop in the course of two separate, hasty searches for the rhino-topped canes she believed had been stored in shed 53. She said she hadn't bothered making off with the jade-topped stick because, like me, she didn't recognize its value. The whack job performed her mutinous mayhem at night disguised as a ghostly pirate. I am pleased to say that the judge showed no lenience with her sentence.

Much to the media's delight, it was revealed that Aida did not read Greek,

Hebrew, or Aramaic. Purchasing the faux Dead Sea scroll was not the only time she'd been duped. While helping the authorities take inventory of her possessions, C.J. identified six full-length manuscripts that were forgeries. Aida's receipts indicated that she'd paid over a million dollars for the privilege of owning these worthless piles of paper.

I had the distinct privilege of writing the wicked woman a letter, informing her of just how duped she'd been. When the story broke, Aida became the laughingstock of America. In Charleston, to this day, she is referred to as "that stupid author."

31

C.J. has no father, and rather than choose among her myriad Shelby cousins, she asked the Rob-Bobs to give her away. They were, of course, happy to oblige.

It was at C.J.'s rehearsal dinner at Blossom's that I first met Rob's mother. I was standing in the line for the ladies' room when she suddenly appeared behind me.

"Are you the famous Abby?" she said.

"Excuse me?" Then instantly it dawned on me that this was yet another Charlestonian who'd seen my picture in the paper, thanks to Aida. PINT-SIZE HERO SAVES THE DAY, the headlines in the *Post and Courier* screamed. That alone made me mad, as C.J. deserved equal billing. At any rate, I was trying very hard to put that trying experience behind me, but there were still folks who just had to express their admiration or, inexplicably, wanted a celebrity to acknowledge their existence. "If a celebrity knows my name," one woman confessed, "then I know I'm someone too."

"Guilty as charged," I told Rob's mother,

then added quickly, "of being Abby, that is. Is there something you'd like autographed?"

She seemed startled by that. "Should there be?"

"Ma'am, I don't supply the paper, and I'm not even sure I have a pen with me. And just so you know, I don't sign on either skin or undergarments."

"I don't want your signature!"

I forced a smile. "Well, if you'll excuse me, then . . ."

"I'm Rob's mother. Mrs. Goldburg."

Of course she was. She looked just like him, except that she was beautiful, whereas he was handsome. But the same features served them both well.

"It's nice to meet you," I said with enthusiasm born of embarrassment.

"Abby, could we talk?"

"Sure. Are you at the dinner? I mean, I didn't see you. If you are, maybe right after —"

"Now, please."

I felt like I'd been given a royal command. Since Blossom's boasts a lovely courtyard, replete with splashing fountain, I led her outside. She launched into her agenda immediately.

"You know that my son is gay." Her voice

rose barely enough to make it a question. Could she be another secret Canadian?

"Yes."

"And, of course, you are aware that he lives with a young man from Cleveland."

"Yes." Bob hails from Toledo, but there was no point in correcting her.

"Abby, you know my son well. What does he see in this man?"

"Well — uh — I think they complement each other. Bob is a bit uptight, perhaps a bit obsessive-compulsive, and Rob is — well, you know — almost perfect."

"But Abby, Rob told me that his roommate had been married once. What if that means he's not really gay? My son could be hurt if that young fellow decided to go straight again." She sounded hopeful that it would happen.

I'd kept my promise to Bob, by the way, and had been there when he broke the news of his failed union with a woman to the real love of his life. Rob was understandably hurt that his partner had withheld such an important detail of his past, but soon forgave him. One thing I knew for sure: Bob would "turn" straight the same day Tom Cruise turned gay.

"People are born either straight or gay," I said. "It's not something one chooses. Who would choose to be discriminated against, and hated, their entire life? Yes, Bob was married. Like a lot of gay people, he got married in a desperate attempt to conform to society's expectations."

"Maybe. But still, this Bob character" — she shuddered — "Abby, he cooks things I never even heard of. Last night he made alligator aspic followed by kudu croquettes. What the heck is kudu? I was afraid to ask."

"I think it's a type of antelope. They raise them on game ranches in Texas these days. But strictly speaking, ground antelope meat would be a burger, not a croquette. Bob doesn't like to use the B word. Sounds too plebian for him. Besides, he likes his food to alliterate. What did you have for dessert?"

"Quail egg custard. Bob said it took a dozen eggs per serving. I think I ate about an egg's worth." She shuddered again. "Well, on the bright side, I won't have to work hard to keep weight off."

"I hear you. But you're going to be here only a couple of weeks anyway, right?"

"You're quite wrong, my dear. I plan to make Charleston my home."

Any thoughts of having to use the powder room went poof from my mind. *"What?"*

"You like it here, don't you?"

"Yes. But I have a career to keep me

busy, and my own home — I mean — are you thinking of buying your own home here?"

"*Me?* Buy a home? Darling, why on earth would I do that?"

"Oh, so you plan to rent a condo. I see. Well, I suppose that does have its advantages. Upkeep on a house and yard are time-consuming. There is no denying that."

Her perfectly applied lips parted in a brief smile. "Now I see why my Robby finds you so amusing. Darling, I plan to live with the boys, of course."

"You do?"

"Don't sound so shocked, dear. Rob is my son, after all. And this Bob fellow — well, I'll just have to make do with him, won't I?"

As fate would have it, the object of her disdain passed the window that looked out into Blossom's charming courtyard. Mrs. Goldburg's back was to the glass, and she couldn't see Bob grimace and shrug.

I risked a wink, which thankfully appeared to go unnoticed. Little did the woman know that I had just declared war on her. What fun it would be to join forces with my buddy from Toledo to drive her crazy — or, at the least, out of the Rob-Bobs' nest. Yes sir, saving Bob's sanity was going to be my next big project.

"Well then, Abby, I guess we're in agreement."

"You'll never know just how much," I said. "Welcome to Charleston."

The gods and goddesses of Charleston smiled down on C.J.'s wedding; the day was sunny and clear and remarkably cool for late spring. It was Toy's day too, of course, but by the way she carried on, you would have thought it was Mama's.

"Are you sure it looks all right this time, dear?" she said, fussing with her corsage for the millionth time.

"Mama, if you don't stop, you won't have any flowers left, only ribbon. Everyone's going to think you stuck a Christmas bow on your dress."

"But Abby, these aren't flowers, they're dandelions. Who on earth chooses dandelions for their wedding?"

"Our beloved C.J., that's who. She claims it's an ancient Ledbetter custom, dating all the way back to Richard the Dandelionhearted — don't ask — and that breaking this custom would bring bad luck to the entire clan. But you have to admit, it was a cute idea to have the flower girl blow apart the puffy seed balls as she walks down the aisle, instead of dropping rose petals."

We were standing just outside the bridal room of Grace Episcopal Church, that beautiful Gothic-style church to which Mama belongs, and where she prays that someday I will be a member as well. I'd taken a peek into its awesome sanctuary, and had been stunned to see that not only was it full, but ushers were setting up chairs in the vestibule. It seemed like all of Shelby was there, and half of Charleston. I was pleased to see that my two much-loved children, Susan and Charlie, had already taken their seats and appeared to be anticipating the moment when C.J. would officially become their aunt.

"Mama, you need to go downstairs so the usher can walk you to your seat. It's time for the show to begin."

Mama nodded. Thank heavens her eyes were dry now. She'd cried so many tears since getting up that morning that I'd made her drink Gatorade to replace her electrolytes.

"Tell C.J. I love her," she said. "And remember to stay away from that goat, or she'll eat your bouquet."

"She's not a goat, Mama. Besides, I happen to think Zelda Ledbetter is very pretty."

"Well, I do like the ribbon in her beard."
Mama gave me a kiss. "Pass that on to C.J.,
dear. And tell her to crack a rib."

I did.

About the Author

Tamar Myers is the author of twelve previous Den of Antiquity mysteries: *Gilt by Association*; *Larceny and Old Lace*; *The Ming and I*; *So Faux, So Good*; *Baroque and Desperate*; *Estate of Mind*; *A Penny Urned*; *Nightmare in Shining Armor*; *Splendor in the Glass*; *Tiles and Tribulations*; *Statue of Limitations*; and *Monet Talks*. She is also the author of the Magdalena Yoder series, is an avid antiques collector, and lives in the Carolinas.